Families at Home

Reeti Gadekar was born and brought up in New Delhi. She studied German Literature and now lives in Berlin, Germany. *Families at Home* is her first novel.

Families at Home

Reeti Gadekar

HarperCollins *Publishers* India

First published in India by
HarperCollins *Publishers* in 2008

Building 10, Tower A, 4th Floor, DLF Cyber City, Phase II,
Gurugram Haryana – 122002, India
www.harpercollins.co.in

2 4 6 8 10 9 7 5 3

P-ISBN: 978-81-7223-754-7
E-ISBN: 978-93-5029-505-2

Typeset in 11/14 Elision
Jojy Philip New Delhi - 15

Printed and bound at
MicroPrints India, New Delhi

For Pascal

'Sir, this fellow, K. Joseph is, *in reality*, a novel character,' he said rather plaintively.

Delhi, June 1995. Many years have passed since then. Many years and with them their long summers and winters. Delhi, that city of pimps and princesses, Mughal emperors and handmaids, was undergoing yet another transformation. Two hundred years of subjugation replaced with sweet liberation only to be soured by the relentless onslaughts of corrupt socialist rule. And what did this new god of the media, this funny sounding word so reminiscent of Gandhi's dream, liberalization (or was it liberation?) really mean? What is it to gain freedom? Is it the right to vote for corrupt politicians? To die in sectarian violence? To be killed by your own police force? Is it for people to decide their way of death? Yes, but not this alone.

Freedom meant at that point in Delhi, the right to earn – by fair means for a change. So much money had changed hands in the License Raj, and the merciless, unceasing demands of the state to have triplicate copies of the birth certificate of your great grandmother (*certified by the Sarpanch and Lambardar of the village and in towns/ city by the Municipal Councillor and attested by either SDO (C)/Executive Magistrate/Tehsildar/Naib Tehsildar/ Programme Officer (ICDS/CDPO/BDPO/FU*) so that you had the right to stand in queue to buy sugar...were these days truly drawing to an end?

Thus mused Juneja in a structure typical of Indian government buildings, a murky shade of yellow with windows few and far between. These in turn were imbued with a depressed grey, brought about by long years of neglect and lack of ventilation and far too much smoke. In rooms to which the public had access, there were fans. The long-stemmed variety, which complete a single rotation per minute, doing little to relieve heat or humidity. However, in this most sacred office of the ACP there was a desert water cooler. It, too, did little to cool Juneja's rising irritation.

'Whaaa?'

'Sir, this fellow, K. Joseph is, *in reality*, a novel character,' said Sinha again. Rather sadly this time, shaking his head.

The very air quivered beneath the weight of the humidity it bore. The police chowki of Basantpur, South Delhi was in any case not the sort of place you'd associate with any kind of portentous utterances.

'What do you mean? Doesn't he do his work properly or is there another problem?' Juneja managed, in tones warning of an impending explosion.

'Sir, he does not *adjust*.'

Juneja looked down at his table, trying not to let Sinha notice him giggle. He coughed, instead.

'Water, sir?'

'No, bring me his file.'

This *sir* of Sinha's really got on his nerves. He had to learn to hear it for the sir it was.

ACP Nikhil Juneja was a harried man of forty. The career of a hardworking policeman is exacting and strenuous and Juneja's face showed more than its fair share of wrinkles. It was a hard face, the eyes permanently screwed up against cigarette smoke, a receding hairline, the rest liberally sprinkled with silver ('the remains of the pate' was Juneja's big party line, thinking, quite wrongly really, that the bald head made him look like a youthful Yul Brynner), thin lips, usually pursed, holding back untoward betrayals. Juneja had had a fairly smooth climb up and intended for it to go on that way. He'd worked hard for this success – the only problem was his unmarried status. Lack of spouse and children, which Juneja loathed with a passion, were bound to stand in his way in the long run. Currently he was obsessively looking for a suitable match and had seriously contemplated an advertisement in a matrimonial column, vociferously demanding a sterile bride.

This bloody fool Inspector Sinha was another irritant at the beginning of a day full of the usual problems and deceits.

Sinha reappeared looking dafter than usual, clutching a sweaty, much fingered thick file. Juneja took it gingerly, smelling the rancid hair oil of a past peruser.

'Who is this fellow, anyway?'

'Sir, he does not *adjust*. Not at all. All the others are complaining. All the time. Nobody wants to do shift with him, sir.'

The file was tantalizingly vague. K. Joseph was evidently much hated by all his colleagues. No one wanted to work with him. He, in turn, seemed to have complained about all the constables that he had ever been on a shift with. In fact, he'd even dared to complain against a superior officer. 'Bloody troublemaker,' muttered Juneja under his breath.

'Yes, sir, he is always in trouble.'

'No, a troublemaker,' Juneja said, enunciating clearly.

Sinha looked distinctly uncomfortable with this pronouncement.

'He is a very nice man, sir. Sober, very helpful. Always sharing his lunch. Very cooperative. Only, he cannot *adjust*. He is bringing delicious food. Please help, sir.'

Juneja leaned back in his chair, bemused by Sinha's outburst for a second time.

'Okay, you go now. I'll look at it and let you know what to do.'

Sinha waddled out of the office, looking distinctly uneasy with the trouble he may have wrought. Strange, mused Juneja. Sinha usually wallowed in Schadenfreude.

Complaining about one's colleagues was a strict no-no and permissible only on pain of death – mainly to save one's ass. Which was the case here. Sinha had a virtual mutiny on his hands.

This bloody fool K. Joseph had complained about all sorts of things, including corruption and harassment. His colleagues had apparently taken bribe money, harassed female members of the public, pocketed money from speeding tickets – the list was endless. In fact, all the sort of things any full-blooded Delhi cop considers the normal perks of the job had been attacked by K. Joseph.

Juneja looked at his personal details to glean any further details, which might explain this strange conduct. Kuriakose Joseph was a Syrian Christian – a devout believer. He was a hardworking member of the Convention of Mary Immaculate (CMI). Juneja sniggered at the thought of an immaculate Mary and also at the thought that this idiot had entered the CMI as his hobby in his official records. He was 37 and married to Mary Jennifer. Juneja sniggered some more. They had three daughters aged twelve, ten and five. So much for immaculate, thought Juneja. The last was adopted. Good grief, some people really couldn't have enough of a good thing.

Joseph had lived in Delhi for the past fifteen years in, wonder of wonders, Janakpuri. Juneja, a Punjabi by birth, felt quite sick. Janakpuri was light years away from the relative civilization of South Delhi, where Juneja maintained a swinging bachelor pad. Janakpuri was the heartland. Only Punjabi Bagh could be considered worse (Delhi is full of such distinctions – rich Mayfair Gardens of the Sindhis, Chittaranjan Park for the Bengalis, Neeti Bagh for the lawyers, the Diplomats in Diplomatic Enclave and endless slums for the slummy). No one spoke anything other than Punjabi in Janakpuri according to Juneja, every one was called Praji or Behna, any and every festival or occasion was celebrated with a fervour and heartiness, quite alien to Juneja's own English-speaking soul. What the hell was a devout Keralite Catholic doing in Janakpuri? In fact, how was he surviving?

He had done precious little to survive in the police force at any rate. He'd complained about so many officers, it was unlikely he'd ever get promoted. Juneja himself was viewing complacently the prospect of becoming DCP in the near to distantly near future. Why couldn't these bloody louts adjust?

The object of these vicious thoughts sat in front of the police chowki. K. Joseph did not look remotely near his

37 years. He was a short swarthy man given to large amiable grins of a profoundly stupid nature. Perhaps it was this air of bonhomie that made him look so youthful. He had large melting black eyes. Jet black hair, kept firmly in place with the help of copious amounts of coconut oil, ensured a neat and tidy appearance. (Meaner minded spirits in the constabulary had been known to comment on this particular aspect of Joseph's appearance. Remarks like, *coconut head, full of oil and little else* were not unknown.) Joseph prided himself on presenting a clean and respectable face of Delhi Police to the Delhi public. At the moment, though, he looked rather disconsolate. Although Mary had told him that by the Grace of Blessed Kuriakose Elias Chavara (who, Joseph believed, was on first-name basis with Jesus) all would be well, Joseph did not think that ACP Juneja, who was probably in direct contact with the Devil, would be kindly inclined.

Juneja had a vile reputation among the constables. He was a hard taskmaster, who had no compunctions about passing off his own mistakes as his juniors'. He was ruthless and ambitious.

Everyone knew that he came from a wealthy Punjabi business family. His father had wanted him to join the family business. All had been going well, till his father suggested a matrimonial match with another business dynasty. Juneja had rebelled, turned his back on the clan and joined the police. He was a driven man. He intended to be Commissioner, Delhi Police, before his father's death. And everyone knew his father was already 67 and had had two heart attacks.

Juneja was known to hate women and children. All respectable women. Some people said they had seen him in the fleshpots of the city or in strange dark bars with women who smoked and wore short skirts. And as for children, everyone knew that when the chowki-in-charge finally had a son after six daughters, Juneja had looked at him as if he were mad, instead of congratulating him or even helping himself to the proffered sweets!

Joseph thought fondly of his own darling girls. Jamuna Elizabeth, the oldest one, was doing well at school. The second girl, Kamla Doris, was also hardworking and obedient. But it was his third daughter who was the apple of his eyes.

Mary had been told by their local priest that charity began at home. An adage they had both taken very seriously. When an unwed mother (a prostitute really, but Joseph didn't like to think of the mother of his baby in such uncharitable terms) had decided to give up her baby, they had taken the little curly-headed bundle home. Gloria Godaveri was the sparkle in the eye of the Joseph household. She was named Gloria after Mary's mother and Godaveri in the river tradition that they had adopted for Jamuna. Also, Mary said that living as they did in Janakpuri, it was good to have an Indian name and not just Christian names.

Joseph had never quite come to terms with Delhi and after more than a decade, still felt quite lost in this huge city with its funny sounding names: Chandni Chowk – Moonlight Square – which was so filthy, and then a banal name like South Extension, which was so expensive. Vasant Vihar – Spring Abode; very luxurious, Vasant Lok, Spring Realm cheap and tawdry. But Mary knew everything. Sometimes, thought Joseph ruefully, he felt he had married a Punjabi!

Mary was a Delhi girl. She had come to his village in Kerala to attend a wedding. He fell in love with her at first sight. His friends had been appalled. Yes, she was a Catholic, but she spoke no Malayalam or hardly any. She cooked Punjabi food and spoke fluent Punjabi and preferred Govinda over Mammooty. But Joseph didn't care. He'd left Kerala without a second glance and thrown himself into the magnificent chaos of Delhi, all in the hope that Mary would accept him. She did. And life had never been the same again.

Joseph thought of those early days in Delhi with nostalgia. He'd been so lost. All their neighbours, who now seemed so familiar and dear, had at the time seemed so foreign. The Kapoors, the Bhatias, the Chhabras and of course, Mrs Gupta. They had all looked at him with so much curiosity. He'd felt like a newly wedded bride. He'd been unable to talk to them without stuttering and stammering. He'd hardly understood any Hindi then, he still spoke very little Hindi – in any case, they all actually spoke Punjabi. The Hindi had been only for his benefit, not that it had helped. They didn't speak any English and Mary had laughed and laughed. Mrs Gupta had said he was a sweet boy. He'd felt terribly shy and had almost wept when they gave him mustard leaves to eat. They tasted foul and he'd wanted to spit them out. None of them ate fish and when he produced some fish moilee from home they'd looked disgusted. He had thrown it away – no one wanted to eat it with him.

Jamuna Elizabeth and Kamla Doris – he was always careful to use both names – also disliked fish. But Gloria Godaveri, or Glorious as he always thought of her, loved fish. Father and daughter would go together to eat fish. In fact, she was his companion in everything. More than Mary. Not that he didn't love Mary – she was still the goddess he worshipped. But she had managed to retain her exotic aura even after all these years. The way she wore salwar kameezes – no sari for her. She sang Hindi songs, even went to a church where the service was in Hindi. With Glorious he could relive his childhood: she had learned Malayalam much faster than the other two. In fact, he'd much rather be with her right now than have to sit around waiting for Juneja to deal with him.

He sighed despondently. There was in any case no chance that he would be dealt with justly. All his colleagues always talked about dirty things. At first he'd not been able to understand what they were talking about. But as his Hindi improved he started understanding – they were always talking about whoring around. He shuddered – even using such words in his head was bad – what would Blessed Kuriakose Elias Chavara say? He could see into his head. Joseph began to mutter fervently,

Lord God,
you raised up Blessed Kuriakose Elias your priest
to strengthen the unity of the Church.
Grant that through his intercession
we may be enlightened by the Holy Spirit
to read the signs of the times with wisdom
and

...

'JOSEPH, JOSEPH, JO–'

He started at the bellow. It was Sinha, looking rather embarrassed. 'Juneja sir is calling you.'

Joseph heaved himself to his feet and started towards

the building. Sinha shook his head sadly. It was probably the end. Juneja had been in a foul temper the entire day. He would show no mercy to poor Joseph.

Joseph looked sadly at Sinha. 'Thanks for all you have done, sir.'

'Mention not, Joseph. All okay. Juneja sir is waiting.'

Joseph entered the den with trepidation. Juneja was indeed waiting. He'd also been smoking endless cigarettes and the acrid smoke stung Joseph's eyes and throat, making him choke.

Juneja looked disgusted. 'C'mon, take it like a man. Now, Joseph,' the voice had hardened perceptibly, 'you have shown very little respect for your colleagues. Working in the police means teamwork and cooperation, doesn't it?'

Joseph was quite stunned by Juneja's English. He'd expected Juneja to spout the same peculiar Punjabi mix that his colleagues spoke. Joseph himself was quite unable to hide his pride in being a graduate in English Literature.

He cleared his throat. 'Sir, if you'd be patient enough to give me a second of your kind consideration?'

Juneja drew in breath to explode. This bastard actually had the gumption to give him lip, he dared interrupt and then mock him in English with his smarmy accent:

'How dare you –'

The telephone rang. THE telephone, the direct line.

Nasal tones breathed into the phone, 'Jt. CP Gupta would like to see you.'

'Now?'

'Umm.'

At that moment the door opened. 'Ahh, Juneja, here you are. That foolish secretary of mine must still be trying to call you. Bloody fool!'

Juneja had already shot to his feet, Joseph was trying to erectly crawl his way into the corner. The Joint Commissioner of Police (Crime) was everything Juneja was reputed not to be. Kind, jovial, a family man. Nonetheless, he was the Jt. CP and Juneja was trying hard to impress him and not succeeding.

Gupta knew Juneja's father and as such, Juneja operated under his particular aegis. No postings to Bihar or the North-East for Juneja. He stayed in Delhi or wherever his little heart desired. Nonetheless, Gupta was deeply suspicious of Juneja's single status. A junket to Europe had convinced him that Juneja was gay and rogering his juniors. Juneja had tried hard to convince him otherwise without giving utterance to the unspoken, but it was rapidly becoming a case of protesting overmuch.

'Sir, do take a seat. Joseph, water. Sir, would you like a cup of coffee, perhaps? Tea?'

'No, no, Juneja, no need for formalities. I have a small case for you. Arre, Joseph, how are the girls, hmm? Started saving for their dowry? Now, Juneja.'

'Yes, sir. No, sir.'

'Joseph, get out.'

That was Juneja, already suffering under tobacco withdrawal symptoms, thought Joseph meanly. He felt rather hurt by Juneja's brusque order. Gupta sir had been asking about Glorious.

'No, no, Juneja. Wait. Maybe Joseph should assist you?'

Juneja blanched. Coconut Greasepot, work with him? Gupta on the other hand was looking quite entranced with his inspired idea. A family man like Joseph would make Juneja long for a family and if that didn't work, maybe he really *was* a pervert.

'No, sir, Sinha has been quite capable –'

'No, Juneja, I think Joseph would be quite good for this case. It's just a matter of a few days. Very simple case.'

'Sir, actually, he is facing an inquiry. Disciplinary action needs to be taken against him. Insubordination...' Juneja was having a hard time keeping control over his temper. The other juniors vied for the honour to work with him and he should accept this overtly potent fool?

'Arre, Joseph, still trying to change the system, hmm? Juneja, meet one of the last crusaders, defending Gandhian principles to the end.' Then the death knell came.

'Juneja, work with Joseph. It'll give him a chance to work with you and learn how to get along with his superiors, hmm Joseph? Matter of maximum two, three days. Juneja, yaar, you can also learn from him, hain?' Loud guffaw. 'Arre Joseph, bring some sarson for Juneja saab. He should see why all men need women!'

Juneja smiled politely. He knew why he needed women and he'd show it to any immaculate Mary who crossed his path with mustard leaves. How local! His current craving was warm ciabatta with fresh ricotta and black olives.

Joseph laughed loudly. Relief mixed with dread. Gupta sir had been told by Blessed Kuriakose Elias Chavara that Joseph was his most loyal servant. Mary had been right!

He would buy tandoori chicken today. That would make her happy. Work two days with the devil's spawn, Juneja. Maybe Gupta sir was right. Joseph would bring him Mary's delicacies. That would soften him.

Gupta continued, 'Arre, it's really a simple thing.'

Juneja was beginning to hate this 'arre' of Gupta's. He'd forgotten how much Gupta's excessively avuncular bonhomie irritated him.

'You know the Talwar family? Talwar Esq.? Old Delhiwalas. Old money. Arre, the Talwar daughter has committed suicide. I spoke to Talwar myself. Very straightforward case. Very young girl. Unmarried.' Gupta paused meaningfully. 'Since it is a medico-legal case, you should go there and see that everything is done according to procedure. No questions need to be asked. It is a very simple case. Very tragic. Very tragic.'

Gupta seemed lost in the tragedy. He started when Juneja spoke up in a last-ditch effort.

'Why do we need to go together?'

'Arre Juneja! You don't want to take Joseph or what? He will learn from you. You should start teaching your juniors. They need to learn from you. Cooperation, teamwork, this is what a good policeman needs to learn.'

Gupta would have gone on but for his mobile buzzing.

'Arre, my Mrs is calling.'

'Please greet Bhabhiji.' This was obviously Joseph. Snivelling bumlicker.

Juneja refused to ingratiate himself in this slimy manner.

'Sir, should I have a look at the file? Just in case?' Everyone was someone in Delhi. You couldn't give an idiot a speeding ticket without checking out his genealogy first. And if this suicide was fishy, he knew there wasn't going to be much to do in any case. In other words, a case, which would require a certain amount of finesse. Even less reason to take Mr Honest Bumpkin with him.

'See, Joseph? Juneja is a true professional. Straight away, he says, give me the file. Wah! Arre, yes, yes, have a look. They found the body this morning. Day after tomorrow is the cremation. So have a quick look, talk to them before those idiot journalists come. Dekho, you go there and have a look. Address and number my PA has given Sinha.'

'Yes, sir. Coffee before you go?' Juneja was quite proud of this tactful touch.

'No, Juneja, very professional, hmm. Very impressive. Thinking of promotion, hmm? Arre, you will get it, you will get it!' Juneja could hear him cackling outside but he waited till the sound faded. He turned to look at Joseph, now looking at him with a tad of complacence, which faded rapidly as he faced the glittering malevolence in Juneja's eyes.

'Get out.'

The first deep draw on the cigarette almost choked him, but he managed to exhale in time. How could this have happened? He knew that a case like the Talwars would really help him.

They were an old family. Probably the first real estate developers of Delhi, maybe even of post-independence India. Now with the market opening and foreign firms coming in, their offices no longer looked so smart but the city was dotted with their creations. Strange ziggurat type of structures, supposedly state-of-the-art fittings at the time, usually government offices, which meant that in due course, they all looked shabby and cheap. But a real estate developer had little to do with the maintenance.

R.K. Talwar, the youngest son, or Rags as the press called him, was in the news quite often. Married to a rather sexy young thing, Devyani, whom Juneja knew personally. He hadn't met her for some time. Rags was in the news more as a playboy, not as a businessman. Maybe the older son was the businessman? Rags certainly wasn't. He and Devi were part of the new emerging jet set and seemed to spend their time watching cricket matches in Sharjah and holidaying in Australia. There were some more brothers as well but Juneja wasn't really sure.

The old man, Vishnu Som Talwar, had set up the entire business. He had retired a long time ago but Juneja remembered being irritated by the number of buildings named after him: Som Towers, V.S. Apartments, Vishnu Talwar Shopping Mall. The man may have done some decent work, but was that any reason to rename half the city after him?

'Sinha, bring me the Talwar file and the contact details that Gupta sir gave you.'

Juneja settled down at his desk. He'd cleaned it this morning. Sinha appeared clutching another decidedly slim and rather clean file.

'Sinha, clean out this ashtray and send that fool Joseph for two packets of Gold Flakes. Also one coffee.'

Juneja barely noticed Joseph when he entered with the cigarettes.

The file hadn't yielded much information. It was the result of his efforts that it existed at all. In an attempt to try and get these lazy bastards to do some work for a change, he'd made them cut out articles from newspapers to maintain some sort of an archive. A kind of Who's Who. It was quite useful really. One knew who was coming and going, inaugurating things. Juneja used it as an extension of his social calendar and made calls to congratulate and commiserate.

The information on the Talwars was an eccentric mix of banal notices ('V.S. Towers open to public today') and titillating gossip ('Rags Seen with Upcoming Starlet – Raging Affair??'). On the whole, it didn't help much, other than confirm his opinion that there were indeed a few more siblings in the Talwar clan – a Narendra Kumar and an R.K., Rajendra Kumar. They were responsible for the finance and construction sections of the company, said the article. Lo and behold, there was the daughter, smiling shyly at an inauguration, Saudamini, 23. Unmarried at that age...sterile?

Juneja heaved himself to his feet, unaware he had an audience. Time to get cracking. He stretched languorously, only to be taken aback by liquid eyes looking anxiously at him.

'What the hell are you doing here?'

'Sir, cigarettes, sir, waiting for orders.'

Juneja felt like screaming.

'Tell Sajjan Kumar to take out the jeep. Let's go.'

The Talwars were indeed one of Delhi's elite. Families like their's are the real old money, thought Juneja in the jeep.

Old Man Talwar had been a trusted man of the Brits in pre-independence India. He'd had plenty of time to salt away money and to lay the foundations of the Talwar empire. Due to his contacts in the government, Talwar had been able to take over seemingly endless property deeds in the walled city for a song, months before Independence. Today each was worth a fortune. The grapevine had it that every time the Talwars needed money, they could liquidate one of these endless properties. For the marriage of Rags, one such property had been sold. Orchids from Thailand, musicians from Pakistan, dancers from Egypt – the media had had a field day. Juneja himself had been present at one of the endless cocktail parties surrounding the affair and had fairly pleasant, if somewhat blurred, memories of a certain Egyptian dancer. As one of the important businessmen of post-independent India Talwar had been quick to hide the dubitable origins of his empire – he was a servant of the people, embodiment of the Gandhian spirit. Juneja snorted.

The Talwar abode was in Vasant Vihar. Strange, they must have shifted. Juneja remembered the large house in Golf Links. Vasant Vihar must be a new acquisition. It was a massive house on the main road. The usual Dholpur stone façade, a huge garden, dwarfed by the even bigger mansion behind it. Juneja smiled, it was what he'd always called pastry houses...they looked like large pieces of a strawberry cake, creamy trellis on the top, air conditioners from every window in place of silver balls...

Juneja put on his subdued, sombre funeral look. He was greeted by a servant, who told him that the sahibs were sitting upstairs.

'Joseph, you go with him to the kitchen.'

'Give him a cup of tea,' he told the servant. The driver, Sajjan Kumar, was to receive his tea in the garden.

The house was the usual mix of strangely opulent and shabby. Velvet sashed curtains from the last century, heavy with dust, and white marble flooring. The air was already redolent with incense. Somewhere, Juneja could hear a woman snivelling in an ostentatious way, making sure everyone could hear her suppressed sorrow.

The stairs ended in an open area, which was probably the TV room. Five men in spotless white kurta-pyjamas – designer cremation garb – were sitting there. Juneja recognized Rags, who got up to greet him.

'ACP Juneja, Basantpur police chowki. Please allow me to offer my condolences.'

'Yes, yes,' said Rags, who obviously had no clue who Juneja was. 'So, when can we have the body back?'

'I've come to see the body,' said Juneja, bewildered by this question.

'Your fellows picked up the body this morning for autopsy. Bhaiya, the police don't know what they are doing. What is this, yaar?'

'No, no,' said Juneja trying hard to cover up. 'I had given orders that the body be returned and thought it must be here by now.'

'N.K. Talwar,' said a man in his forties, standing up to lead Juneja to the sofa.

'My brother Raghav is very impetuous. Let me introduce you. Raj, R.K. Talwar, my younger brother, and this is my youngest brother, Raghav. We are all very upset. She was the baby of the family, only 27. We were planning her marriage at the end of the year.'

So it was a gathering of the menfolk sans Papaji. The three scions. The resemblance among the brothers was striking. Fair, Punjabi good looks, the kind that Bollywood embodies, thought Juneja with a pang. Pinkly fair, thick black hair, probably a dandruff problem, thought Juneja kindly.

'Sir, what happened? I know this is hard for you but we must ask.'

N.K. exchanged a quick look with R.K. before graciously smiling. 'Of course, what name did you say? Ah Juneja...my sister had been depressed for some time. You know my father's condition has been serious for some time. He's been in the hospital for the past several weeks. Pulmonary emphysema, you know. All these smokers, it catches up after a while.

'My sister was always very close to my father. The youngest child. After the death of my mother...'

'Ma has been gone twenty years and when was Saudamini going to get married?' interrupted Raghav rather rudely.

'Raghav,' spoke up senior R.K., 'this is not the time to be discussing these things. The wedding date had been confirmed last week. That you don't know this is because you never visit our home. He lives in Golf Links. But even there, he is never home.' He smiled deprecatingly at Juneja. 'Always at some party or the other.'

'So,' continued N.K., 'Saudamini, Pinky we called her, was the baby of the house. I fear my father spoilt her. She must have felt very insecure in the face of my father's illness. Our family doctor, Dr Sahni, had recommended tablets for her, but I fear it did not help and we didn't realize how serious the problem was.'

'I see, sir,' said Juneja, seeing that there was a lot more going on here. 'Sir, if I may use the telephone, I'll ask what progress the lab is making.'

'Of course. Raghav, take him to the side bedroom, there is a telephone there.'

The bedroom into which Rags led him was large but sparsely furnished. The single bed looked dusty and the room had an unkempt look. 'My ex-room,' said Rags smiling wryly, 'I'll let you phone in peace.'

Juneja sat down gingerly on the bed, fearing he'd get dust on his trousers. The telephone at least was new – he'd half expected one of those old phones, where you really had to dial.

He called the lab, wondering whose ass was going to fry for this fuck up.

'ACP Juneja, Dr Khurana, please.'

Dr Khurana was the Chief Pathologist. Even if he wasn't handling the case, he'd know who the hell was.

Suddenly Juneja heard a slight hum on the connection.

'Khurana,' said a deep voice on the other end.

'Juneja here. A body came in this morning. Saudamini Talwar, 27, female. Suicide. Who took the body?'

'Hmmm, Talwar, yes I did. Rather interesting.'

Juneja cut in before he could say any more. 'I'm at the Talwar's house, I'll be with you directly.'

'Today in the afternoon, before four?'

'Yes, that should be fine.'

He hung up and picked up the phone immediately. Click.

All three men were in the room. No one looked like they'd just rushed back in. He couldn't hear the female sobbing, though. He addressed N.K., the eldest. 'Sir, I'm very sorry but I was unable to get the Chief Pathologist on the phone. He must still be in the theatre. I'll go over there immediately. Perhaps I could come back today in the evening?'

'Arre, we don't want you back – we want the body. There's a cremation to organize, in case you haven't realized.'

'Raghav!' cut in N.K., 'What is wrong with you? Is this the way to talk to a guest? I am very sorry. Raghav is very upset. Raj, take him inside.'

Raghav looked more surprised than upset, thought Juneja, and grovelled. 'No, no. That's perfectly all right, sir. I can understand at a time like this.... I meant, I could come over in the evening with the body. My constable must be in the kitchen, I'd sent him with the servant. If you could just call him, I'll be on my way.'

Joseph pottered around Ram Singh, who it turned out, was the chief servant. Joseph had never seen such a huge house. The air was cool and fresh. Although Joseph knew what air conditioning was, he'd never been to a house where even the kitchen was AC-d!

Ram Singh told him that Pinky Baby was the youngest, the baby of the family and the favourite of Papaji – Old Man Talwar. In fact, Ram Singh was trying not to smirk at Joseph's reaction. The constable was having a hard time listening to him. The huge kitchen, the big machines, the massive pot on the stove, smelling rather divinely of chicken, even this small alcove for the servants, it was all rather overwhelming.

'Chicken?' asked Joseph, rather tentatively.

'Of course. Every day we eat meat. For food only we spend at least Rs 15,000 in a month. Sometimes chicken, prawns, meat, crab, everything. I thought today we'd have to eat vegetarian but Raghav sahib told me to make chicken.'

Joseph nodded, suitably impressed.

'If you want, I can give you some.'

'No, no,' protested Joseph, 'just a cup of tea is fine.'

As Ram Singh got up to make tea, a tall gaunt man in khaki uniform entered.

'This is Om Prakash, the night chowkidar. You know, the Talwars are a very important family. Important people, MPs, top businessmen visiting every day.... Security is very important.'

Joseph smiled at Om Prakash, nodding understandingly. Such a big house, obviously these people were very important. Juneja was right to have sent him to the kitchen. Why, he wouldn't know how to talk to them. And here he could try and learn things. Maybe Juneja was a good man after all.

He turned to Om Prakash. 'Your job must be quite dangerous. Don't you feel scared at night?'

Om Prakash guffawed. 'You, a policeman, ask me if I am scared?'

Abashed, Joseph tried to cover up. 'No, no, I mean, such a big house, a lot of thieves must want to break in.'

Om Prakash preened – indeed, this was the case, 'Such a big house. Of course, people stop on the street and stare. It is the Talwar house. Thankfully Raghav sahib has moved out, otherwise always, people coming and going. He had a party every night.... Women wearing small skirts.... Even yesterday....'

'There was a party yesterday?' Joseph was surprised.

'No, no,' said Om Prakash, 'but till late at night there was noise. No peace. In the evening every one had gone to the hospital to visit Papaji. He has been in the hospital now since the last three weeks. He has severe problems in the heat – even this house is too hot. Raghav sahib wanted to take him to Switzerland but the doctor did not allow.

'But even after they came back, they were all anxious. You know, it is very upsetting for them to see Papaji so ill. Saudamini memsahib had been staying with him. But even then it was very hard for him. And now this. Who knew that Baby was so sad in her heart? Always smiling, such a nice girl.'

'Exactly,' piped in Ram Singh, handing out large cups of tea and biscuits. 'They are a very close family. I have been working here for twenty years.... Pinky Baby was so sweet. Today I have lost someone from my own family... What will I say to Papaji? I could not take care of his daughter?' And his eyes suddenly brimmed over.

Joseph felt quite choked himself. What a family! These were the very values he wanted his daughters to emulate! Had he not said just yesterday to Mary, that these days children did not take care of their parents – and here was a servant thinking of his employee as his father! Truly the *old values* gave meaning to life.

His stomach rumbled loudly – Joseph felt quite embarrassed. Om Prakash laughed. 'Ram Singh, maybe you better give him something to eat before I tell him my story!'

'No, no,' protested Joseph again. 'In any case, how can I eat chicken today?'

'I know,' sighed Ram Singh, now looking quite embarrassed himself. 'I told Raghav sahib we should not cook today. You know, when somebody dies, kitchen fires should not burn for one week. The neighbours came by in the morning and told me they would send food. In the morning I said okay, but then I didn't know that Raghav sahib would insist.... It is not respectful.'

Om Prakash, who had been getting quite impatient, broke in, 'You know these young chaps. They need chicken every day. Never mind, I must ask Policeman sahib something important. You know,' he said turning confidingly to Joseph, 'I have two daughters.'

Joseph thrilled to this information and nodded encouragingly.

'I have brought them up alone. My wife died during childbirth. Now, my older daughter has found a fellow whom she wants to marry. He is a clerk. Nice chap, but his parents say that my Shanti is not good enough for him, her father is only a watchman. I have educated my daughter. Thanks to Talwar sahib, she has even done evening college and now she works in the Christian Charitable Home for Illegitimate Children.'

'CCHIC, run by the Carmelites, CMI?' exclaimed Joseph. Why, they had found Glorious there!

'Yes, you know it? They work very hard.'

'They are angels!' said Joseph, crossing himself fervently.

'But his parents call her a witch! They say she is working with women of loose morals. How can they let their only son marry her? Now, after I have got them references from Mother Prudence, they are demanding a colour TV and a video. Tell me, is this not dowry? Can't you help me?'

Joseph was appalled. He looked at Om Prakash, horror writ large across his face. He could hardly believe his ears. The Sisters insulted, dowry demanded, this poor man harassed, what kind of people were these? Was there no limit to the depths they were willing to sink to?

'I will talk to Juneja sahib today itself. These people can't treat you like this. The Carmelite Sisters are angels. They are doing a great service to society. Where should these women go? They aren't having these children from free will.'

Ram Singh and Om Prakash looked at him admiringly. It was rare to see a policeman who took his job so seriously.

Joseph's voice swelled. He wanted to get on top of the table and tell his audience that he would help them: He was a *Policeman*.

'Where are the fathers of these children? Huh? Important, rich people, hmm? After all, rich people like these Talwars are the ones who have these illegitimate children!'

Joseph realized what he'd said but it was too late. Om Prakash looked stunned, Ram Singh enraged. 'You better leave.'

Another servant came into the kitchen. 'The big policeman is saying you should come to the jeep.'

Joseph left.

It was baking outside. Joseph felt sick, his head reeling from the difference in temperature.

Juneja, who had more experience with air conditioners, knew what to expect – but that didn't make it any better. The air was thick and humid. Within minutes his uniform started sticking to his body. God, if only one could hibernate in summer, spend the entire six months from April to September locked up in a cool room.

'So, what did you investigate? Hmm? Anything interesting?'

'Yes, sir,' said Joseph, manfully trying to quell the desire to go to sleep.

'They are very important people, sir. Very important. Every day they eat non-vegetarian food. Even today, but this is not good. Raghav sahib should show more respect. Also, he goes to too many parties, even yesterday was a party.' Joseph paused, no, he was making a mistake. How could this be important?

'Even yesterday was a party,' he repeated. 'The poor

nightwatchman has a very hard time, sir. Even yesterday, people coming and going. They are demanding dowry from him, sir.'

'What? The Talwars want dowry from the watchman? Have you gone mad?'

Joseph got hold of himself. 'No, sir. The watchman has a very hard life. He has two daughters. Now the older one wants to get married. Highly educated girl, sir. The father of the deceased (Joseph was proud of this word) himself had her educated. Now she is working with CCHC, sir, but the parents of the fellow want dowry. Colour TV, sir.'

Juneja looked at Joseph with ill-concealed dislike. The fellow was even more stupid than he looked. It was two in the middle of a particularly stressful afternoon. Was there no respite to be had?

The meeting with the Talwars had been little short of catastrophic. Juneja did not take kindly to being made to look silly in public – going to see a body which was already in the possession of the police got full marks for incompetence. Thank God this fool hadn't been with him!

He lit a cigarette, the acrid smoke making him feel slightly nauseous in the heat. The jeep rattled down the Ring Road. This journey to Connaught Place was going to be a killer. Juneja felt sinking into a sodden torpor. Africa Avenue, down to Hyatt Regency, and then straight till Ashoka Hotel. He would give anything for a cool beer now. Past the PM's house and onto the broad shady roads of Lutyens' New Delhi. Akbar Road, Man Singh Road and into the madness of the India Gate circle. The journey back would be even worse. The home going crowd here was a nightmare – all those government offices belching out hundreds of petty bureaucrats onto the hapless roads.

But Delhi wasn't the moloch people made it out to be. She was an old lady who refused to age gracefully, stubbornly wearing short skirts and crying indignantly about being goosed. Why didn't she just accept it as her lot? Like all women should? Delhi was the one thing he felt quite passionate about, besides himself, acknowledged Juneja ruefully to himself. His city. She didn't deserve these rich bastards getting away with murder, or the dirt and filth and disease that stalked her by-lanes.

Delhi could be so achingly beautiful. The balmy evenings, the magic and mystery of the old city, the charm and dignity of the original Dilliwallahs, and now she was raped day and night by these bloody politicians and their natural allies – a corrupt police force.

Juneja smiled benevolently at Sajjan Kumar, who triumphantly rammed the vehicle through the cars, turning left from the far right lane. No one protested, though a few brave souls honked, including a silly emancipated type, who stuck out her middle finger. If he'd felt like it, he could have jumped out and screamed at her. His cohorts would have laughed along, insulted her with the choicest titbits of their varied and pornographic vocabulary. Nothing like a policeman to wax eloquent on the orifices of the female body and what could best be deposited there. It made him quite sick to have to be part of this bunch of losers. He reached for another fag as they rolled into the hospital.

'How about a cup of tea, hmm?' Treating them to a cup of tea wasn't going to cost him much, plus this day would almost certainly go into overtime. They marched into the hospital canteen, where no one gave them a second glance. Policeman were du jour here. All accidents were 'police cases', which meant no citizen would stop at the sight of a bleeding, maimed body on the road. A police case meant endless harassment and questions, so kill and let die. Hospitals like this one, which specialized in *Accident/ Trauma*, had at any given time an equal number of patients and policemen.

Joseph was surprised at being treated to a cup of tea. On his beat it had been quite usual for everyone no pay their own way. No one was really in a position to pay for the rest. He felt better now. The jeep had been like a furnace, what with the hot air and Juneja's incessant smoking.

Juneja looked at them benevolently and told his favourite driver, Sajjan Kumar to get a round of samosas to go with the tea. He hated going to the morgue. Khurana got on his nerves with his antiseptic manner and the dead bodies disconcerted him. Better eat something now, before going in. After meeting Khurana no one could eat.

'Joseph, you go out to the neighbouring kotwali and get some forms. Fill out a report. We'll have to go back to the Talwar house from the hospital. I'll need an hour at least here. Can you finish the report by then?'

'Yes, sir. Hundred per cent sir.'

'Sajjan Kumar, you call up Basantpur and tell Sinha we'll be back in about three hours. Maybe we'll go to the Kotwali first and then to the Talwars.'

The samosas were fresh. Even though no one had acknowledged his arrival, the canteen fellows knew him. He'd thrown a magnificent fit over a cold cup of tea. One of his best really, if not one of the best of the entire Delhi Police. Now for him everything was fresh, tea hot, and if he so wanted, free. He'd threatened the bastards with a hygiene inspection. As if such a thing existed! He'd almost wet himself when he said it – hygiene inspectors had a hard time closing congealed, filth-ridden abattoirs, he'd have been hard pressed getting them to come here.

'All right you fellows, you wait here. No running off, okay? If there's a problem, Joseph, Sajjan Kumar knows where the morgue is.' He grinned – Joseph looked horror-struck at the prospect.

No rest for the wicked, he told himself as he plodded down the corridor. Khurana was a legend in police circles. He ran the morgue with an iron hand. One of those Punjabis who'd been forced to leave Lahore during Partition, he'd made it up his own kind of ladder. Public service instead of private practice. He could have left the morgue and started his own lab; God knows he'd have been successful. The man was efficient, courageous, and much to Juneja's own discomfort, conscientious. He'd have happily palmed off this job on a junior – Khurana could be quite tedious about going into details – but with the goodwill of the Talwars being at stake, he'd have to put up with Khurana himself. The biggest problem was that Khurana was a personal acquaintance of his own father. He was much too intelligent to actually say anything directly to Juneja, but he had a way of looking at him or of alluding to certain things which made Juneja quite uncomfortable.

Khurana was one of those doctors who embody cleanliness. Everything about him was white. A halo of white hair, white clipped moustache, and of course, he was always clad in white. Nothing took away the odour of death, though. Here in Khurana's realm, *Khurana* determined how death should look.

And how did she look? Clean, scrubbed, well...controlled

really. Controlled was the right word. Death was cut into pieces, labelled, described and understood. Khurana always spoke of 'the *body*'. 'The *body* will not accept it' or 'The *body* reacts to such an attack by...'. As if the *body* had an entity of its own! Khurana had great respect for the *body*. He refused to let anyone make fun of it. 'The *body* was the greatest machine ever designed.' Hmm. And what did Saudamini Talwar's *body* say?

Juneja took in his last gulp of fresh air and marched in. He never knocked in the hope of catching Khurana violating the *body*. It hadn't happened so far. Khurana didn't seem to care one way or the other. The orderlies never knocked either. Not because they had the same idea but because *their* hands were always full, carrying some, literally, strange bits.

'Nikhil, how are you?' Khurana looked unchanged. He was an emaciated, albino lion thought Juneja. Khurana's voice was a deep whisper.

'This must be an important case for you to come personally. I haven't seen you for a long time. I did visit your father, though. He's looking quite tired. But you must know that.'

Juneja let it pass, 'It is an important case. Saudamini Talwar is, *was*, the youngest daughter of Vishnu Som Talwar. You must know him, actually. Who sent the body here? It's a case of suicide, isn't it?'

'The builder? Hmm, yes, I have met him. But know? I

know only the *bodies* on the table. They tell me the real story. People never do. But I understand this must be important for you. After all, they're big people. The Joint Commissioner, Gupta, sent the body to me. He was quite certain...a suicide. I think not,' answered Khurana rather pompously.

He started walking towards the covered corpse, while Juneja tried to figure out what was going on.

'Come here Nikhil, don't be shy!' Khurana smiled. It was a lovely smile and it took Juneja back to his childhood. Khurana unveiled the corpse gently. He was always gentle with the *bodies,* which is what had given Juneja the idea that Khurana might be a closet necrophiliac in the first place.

'Cause of death? Suicide? No, I don't see how. She was hit on the back of the head and hanged. The blow wasn't hard enough to cause serious damage – just a light tap. Probably knocked her out for a bit. She might even have been conscious at the time of hanging. Quite inhuman really. She had been tranquillized, though.'

'Maybe she fell after hanging herself? She was apparently seriously depressed. Her mother's death, and now the father is seriously ill. And then she was prescribed tranquillizers by the doctor for her depression.' Juneja was appalled at the turn things were taking.

'She fell after hanging herself...no, I don't think so, Nikhil. There are clear signs to the contrary. Although the murderer was careful, there are light abrasions in the wrist area, showing she was restrained. The injury certainly happened before she was killed.'

'She was to get married in November, she was depressed!'

Khurana remained calm. The only sign that he was

surprised at Juneja's outburst was the slightly raised eyebrows. He uncovered the body.

Saudamini Talwar was surprisingly plain. Her features compared to her brothers', were coarse. More than slightly overweight. Thick lips, eyes far apart. She had been prone to pimples and the skin was blotched with faded acne marks. The same black hair, worn in a long braid. She didn't look very young either. Or, maybe it was just the look of death.

'I doubt it. And marriage? Hmm, November is a little late.'

Juneja desperately needed a cigarette. But he knew better than to antagonize Khurana. He opted for a deep breath instead and found himself choking on the fumes of formaldehyde from the jar Khurana was extending to him.

'This came in a few weeks ago. Cancerous lung tissue... you should really consider quitting.'

Bastard, thought Juneja.

'Ah Nikhil, I've known your family for such a long time. Don't look like that. I'll be retiring soon. You think I want to have you on the table before that, hmm? Now stop looking so grumpy and have a cup of tea with me, all right?'

Juneja pulled himself together. The man was right. This was no time to be going to pieces. It had already been a long day and more was to come.

'What else can you tell about her? Anything else I should know? And what's so late about November?'

Khurana had finished wrapping up the corpse and moved towards the door.

'Come on,' he urged.

They went into the adjacent office. Even the usual hospital look had been licked into shape by Khurana. Not for him the vomit green walls and tubelights so reminiscent of dead flies. The walls were a pristine white, the furniture scrubbed.

Khurana poured tea from a thermos flask into porcelain cups that sure as hell didn't belong to the hospital.

Neither did the light, fragrant tea for that matter.

'The murder...it couldn't have been a woman? I mean, would a woman be strong enough to move her? I mean, Miss Talwar seemed quite heavy.'

Khurana looked back at Juneja. 'I doubt it strongly. Definitely not without help. When she was conscious, it's unlikely she'd let herself be hanged without a struggle. And semiconscious, she'd still be a very heavy dead weight – even for the average man.'

'What else should I know?' persisted Juneja.

'Hmm, anything else you *should* know about the patient...now that is really the question. Should you know it? I don't know. You know, all of us have secrets. But in death, the body can't keep its secrets any more. The mind hides its thoughts and closes all doors. But the *body*, it can't. It's like a child. You can force it to tell you things the owner would never have wanted you to know. Things he'd never have told you. And that brings us to the question, should you know them?'

Juneja pursed his lips. 'I could catch the murderer, since you're so sure her death wasn't due to natural causes.'

'Based on what I tell you, you'll catch him? Really?'

'I might!' answered Juneja, grinning suddenly. The tea was good and this was the first time he felt Khurana was talking with him instead of looking down on him. If only he had an assistant who was this intelligent instead of that goofy Joseph.

Khurana smiled back. 'I doubt you'll catch the murderer.

Looks like an inside job. It's not going to be very pleasant. And as for what the *body* says, I doubt if Miss Talwar, as you call her, would have wanted you to know...but for what it's worth, she was pregnant. Getting married in November would have been too late. She would almost have been due then.'

'What does that mean? I mean, how can you tell?'

'My dear boy, surely I am capable of determining the presence of a foetus?'

Juneja started feeling sick again. This was worse than he had imagined; he was beginning to feel quite sorry for himself. He closed his eyes.

'But she was unmarried!'

'Come on, Nikhil! Surely one can have sex without marriage. Even you must know this!' Khurana was looking seriously worried.

'Yes, of course. But to have been raped...' Juneja shook his head, trying not to imagine the indignity.

'Oh, Nikhil!' Khurana looked at him with a great deal of tenderness and amusement, 'You people think you're so modern. You accuse our generation of being old-fashioned, but actually it's you. It's you who are conservative and close-minded, bigoted and judgmental... Did I say anything about this being rape? The woman could have been having consensual sex for some time. Quite some time. There were no open wounds or anything. No signs of sexual intercourse before death. Certainly no signs of any kind of forced activity or rape or anything. I can't tell you any more than that. The *body* doesn't give dates and time, you know!'

Juneja looked down. Pregnant. Unmarried. Dead. Saudamini Talwar.

Juneja told Sajjan Kumar and Joseph to take the jeep back to the police station after dropping him home. It was 7 p.m. The Talwars could wait. After they had allowed their silly sister to get knocked up, surely they couldn't be in a hurry to get her body. He would barely make it in time for dinner. Enough of murder, Khurana. Time for *life* to start.

The shower was a welcome cold embrace. Juneja was careful to soap himself twice. Remove every smelly trace of Khurana and that silly fat cow, Saudamini Talwar. Pregnant and unmarried *and* ugly. Despite being rich. He shrugged. Some people were just plain stupid. People would forgive you the one cardinal sin of being pregnant or unmarried or ugly, if you were rich. But all three? What had she been thinking of, to indulge in such wanton behaviour? Well, she wasn't thinking any more now.

He cast a quick look at the time. It was 7.40. He called up Geetu. Her parties were gastronomic delights and he had no intention of missing this one. Besides, she and her husband Rajiv lived around the corner so he could get plastered and then stroll back home.

Memsahib was in the shower, said the servant. After making sure that the servant had recognized him, Juneja told him he'd be half an hour late.

That gave him time for a cold gin on his terrace. Juneja loved his flat. With passion, with vengeance.

It was another reason to doubt the institution of matrimony. Why share paradise? He'd shifted several times from a mattress on a friend's floor to one barsati after another. Poky little hellholes. And then the silent money transfers started happening. Juneja had thought about it, whether this was a slur on his manhood or his pride or other integral parts of his being. And come to the conclusion that since the transfers were silent, he would respond in kind. His manhood and bank balance would thrive simultaneously.

This flat was his dream. A philistine colleague had been living here and had thankfully been transferred to some hellhole. He'd mentioned his flat casually to Juneja, who'd been moaning about his own current accommodation. An overpriced hole. Not that this one was cheap. It was silently expensive. But despite the price and the idiot who lived next door and his stupid progeny, despite the traffic jams that he had to endure everyday, the location and the flat were unique.

It was a three-bedroom flat. One was his, one was Diwan Singh's and the third, which was the only one with a potted plant, was for guests. These had been few and far between. Rajiv or another pal occasionally, too drunk to get home. Juneja's sleepovers tended to be of the female kind and he usually tried to persuade them to share his humble bed.

Diwan Singh's bedroom was towards the back and he had never entered it. One female visitor had asked why Diwan Singh didn't sleep in the servant's quarter next to the garage. Juneja had told her it was none of her business and shortly afterwards thrown her out of the house. She hadn't been very hot in any case.

Juneja hadn't bothered to decorate the flat much. Easy chairs on the balcony, a decent bed, a cupboard. A well equipped kitchen that allowed the current lady to cook when the fancy took her and allowed him to make a decent cup in the mornings. He didn't really need Diwan Singh, his servant, or so he chose to say in public.

Diwan Singh had been with the Juneja family since Nikhil's birth. He was the son of another family retainer. He had moved in when the split happened. The fact that he was old enough to be Juneja's older brother meant he often behaved like his father as well! But he was a terrific cook and thankfully, decidedly taciturn. Besides, why do your own laundry and clean when Diwan Singh could and would and quite frankly should? The massive refrigerator, on the other hand, was a luxury. It contained his entire bar. Fancy wines to impress the chicks, gin and vodka for him. Ice cubes are fine, but they melt less quickly when the gin is half frozen. Just a sprig of mint to make it perfect.

Opposite his house was the Chor Minar, the Tower of Thieves, the Tower of Beheadings. It wasn't the massive Red Fort or the splendid Jama Masjid. It was the simple Chor Minar, where the decapitated heads of thieves used to be displayed. It dated back to the thirteenth century.

Juneja carried his drink back to the balcony, and sat back to gaze at his favourite work of art. It was almost an embodiment of him. It made him reflect endlessly on justice.

Was law meaningful, when it horrified? Was punishment necessary? The kind of brutality the Chor Minar displayed was a part of India. A part of Indianness. And today the Chor Minar was a monument. To what? The brutality hadn't stopped. It lived on. On the other hand perhaps that was the true reason. Unlike the Taj Mahal, where lakhs were spent on its maintenance, the Chor Minar was a stubby, tenacious structure. The bloody grey cells of the past seemed to have imbued its stone walls with a strength that bore the onslaughts of urine, excreta and graffiti with fortitude.

The rough rubble walls today protected rather than betrayed homeless junkies. Could it be true? Was this the liberalization they spoke of? Protection in the Tower of Beheadings? From rain, from cold and...from the police. He'd caught Sajjan Kumar taking a tenner from some poor slob once and been enraged beyond belief. When he'd opened his mouth to scream, he realized he just couldn't. Silent rage.

He didn't call many people over either. Laziness? Perhaps. Also, little desire to proffer explanations. Besides, when was he ever home?

He didn't have much by way of hobbies either. To his ever-shuddering horror, he'd once told a girlfriend his favourite music was the latest. She'd been impressed, which had been the point of the whole excercise. That left him with the Chor Minar and cigarettes. And sex.

The latter was an increasingly rare commodity, he reflected on his way out. The life of a swinging bachelor was hard. One had to fight to stay in circulation, to be remembered on people's invitation lists. Sure, one could cruise for sex but the fare on offer was usually commercial.

Conversationally it left him quite limited. Then there was the possibility of this wretched AIDS they were all yapping about. What was the point of being a man if you couldn't have wild promiscuous sex every night? Though tonight could bring some much needed relief.

Rajiv and Geetu were old friends. Well, Rajiv was and today he came with a wife. She was all right, not much in the brains department. Rajiv said she was hot in bed. Knowing Rajiv that meant she was willing to have *it*. Like all of his friends Rajiv was the usual mix of guilt, conservatism and voyeurism.

Indians had perfected the art of silent sex. Literally and metaphorically. Where sex could only be had in a one-room hovel shared with parents, siblings, children – sex had to silent. It also had nothing in common with foreplay, love or any other fanciful notion. It offered momentary relief and a whole lot of grief nine months later, when the eleventh brat popped out.

But even in his elevated class, where a bedroom of one's own could be expected, there was little talk about it. Talking wasn't actually the problem. There were endless jokes, digs and other obvious ways of showing how comfortable one was with sex. But it seldom translated into any real openness. Rajiv was a typical example. They'd giggled and wanked over endless *Playboys* but there was no question of any serious discussion. Rajiv had always wanted to know if he, Juneja, had done *it* with the lady in question, wanted to know if she put out. To the best of his knowledge Rajiv hadn't been put out before marriage. Juneja was certain that Rajiv was gay. He also harboured the suspicion that Rajiv cruised for gay sex in his gym. But, but, but he is married, sir, Joseph would say.

Geetu, the fair, buxom Geetu was a parental find. Geetu was another Indian affliction. She was the girl *mother* brought home. She could cook, sew and take care of live-in parents and bring up perfect children. She could make a ten-course meal for your friends and wouldn't complain when it got served at midnight because your pals were piss drunk. She drank only Coke and could recite Sanskrit hymns with your – in Rajiv's case also live-in – grandmother. And according to Rajiv, she did *it*.

Not that Geetu was always placid. She was capable of being quite acerbic. He'd heard her blast Rajiv in a tone of voice that left little doubt about exactly who the boss was. Juneja had realized the boss may or may not wear pants but she certainly did have boobs and could chop your prick for breakfast. Thanks to this early revelation and subsequent obsequiousness on his part, Geetu liked him a great deal. She also did not subscribe to the view, that he was gay, because he was single. Instead she believed staunchly in the healing powers of matrimony – one shot cures all. She'd often told him, 'You know, Nikki...'

Women often called him by this silly diminutive. He was expected to simper.

'You know, Nikki, all the guests go home when the party ends. But for us couples, the party goes on. I feel about this, Nikki. Your party shouldn't end.'

The first time he'd heard this pithy summary of his predicament, he'd been sure her coke was spiked. The second time he'd gone so far as to try her drink, pretending it was a mistake.

Pure Coke. Cent per cent. Maybe her single friends would put out. Cent per cent.

Joseph wasn't sure whether he was happy or sad about how the day had turned out. He'd felt quite complacent about the way Gupta sir had prevented any further problems. Juneja was an evil person. Joseph decided to go to Church before he went home.

They were lucky the Mar Gregorius was in Janakpuri. Joseph had been awestruck when he saw the huge red cathedral the first time. Although Joseph's heart belonged first and foremost to Blessed Kuriakose Elias Chavara, St Gregorius of Parumala was a close second. Blessed Kuriakose Elias Chavara was someone, he felt, he knew. In Kerala he had felt himself to be on first-name basis with him, his very own namesake. St Gregorius was a glittering star so beyond him that Joseph swallowed before saying his name, even silently to himself.

The church Mar Gregorius was thus the way it should be. Huge, commanding respect and getting it. The massive black cross in front made him weak at the knees. He crept in, feeling small and insignificant. The inside was equally magnificent. The massive red altar, the corner where the vestments of St Gregorius were preserved, the chequered green and white floor...it was all so stunning, it was hard to feel comfortable here.

He had been immensely grateful to find the Mar Gregorius. He'd thought it was a small piece of Kerala in Delhi. Even the service was in Malayalam. Confession was in Malayalam. But he still didn't feel at home. Nobody wanted to know him and after the service he'd go away.

None of the girls came here with him except Glorious. Jamuna Elizabeth and Kamla Doris didn't understand much Malayalam. The priests in any case intimidated the children. In his village he'd been scared of Father Pereira too, but in the way one is scared of a stern uncle. The priests here were *big people*. They spoke English and went abroad. It was hard not to stammer, when you greeted them. Mar Gregorius performed the Holy Qurbana in English once a month so the girls came once a month, but it wasn't the same thing. Mary attended a church, where the service was in a mixture of Punjabi and Hindi. The priests of Mar Gregorius had been scandalized when he'd said in confessional that he felt lonely because he came alone to church. They told him that if necessary he could resort to 'harsh measures' if Mary continued to refuse to attend the Malayalam service.

Mary had downright refused. She said Malayalam was all right in Kerala but why should one have to speak it in Delhi? As it is they were different because they were Christian. People thought they ate cow's meat and other disgusting things. Just because they were Christians, Mary had told Jamuna Elizabeth firmly, didn't mean they could wear short skirts and flirt with boys. Mary didn't want the girls to learn Malayalam. They should learn English, do a computer course.

He found himself a pew in a corner and tried to sort out his feelings. Gupta sir had taken care of him. But it meant working with Juneja.

Joseph despaired.

A priest walked past majestically. Joseph offered a tremulous greeting, which was graciously acknowledged with a slow nod. Joseph sank back.

He hated this feeling of being inferior. Of being dependent. It was what had been hammered home from the beginning. Delhi was an anonymous village. You were dependent on people. The electrician, the plumber, the carpenter, the garbage man, the postman...the list was never-ending. Each of them did their work if and only if you paid them. But was it also necessary to give them presents for Diwali or to serve them tea and give them sweets even when they were three days late?

He closed his eyes. Always standing in queues only to find that someone had got in through the back door, always being lost and not knowing what to do, who to say what to, not to say certain things.... He was going mad. Mary said they were lucky because Joseph was a policeman. Other people were much worse off. Joseph's being in the police meant that he could pay back favours in kind. That people treasured favours they did him, like insurance policies which could be cashed in the future, when required. And everybody, everybody needed the police. Please get my son admission, get someone beaten up, get my son off for beating up someone....

In the village people helped each other. In Delhi no one did anything for you. Not even his colleagues. He smiled wryly to himself. All said and done, he himself got into the police force through the backdoor. Father Pereira had helped him. Maybe the next time he went to Kerala, Father would also demand his pound of flesh!

He wished he'd never joined the police. Some people were nice, like Gupta sir. But most of them didn't understand him, nor did he understand them. Almost all of his colleagues pitied him because he had only daughters. That he had compounded his misery by adopting yet another daughter was a sure sign of his stupidity. Joseph couldn't find the words to say how much he loved his daughters. His women, he called them. Their small hands and feet, the way they looked at him, the little things they came to him with, they were what he lived for.

Mary had asked him, if he wanted a son. A *son*. She had been toubled by a urinary tract infection for years. In fact, had he known, poor Kamla Doris would never have happened. The pregnancies had been agony for her. He would never put his very own Divine Mary through such an ordeal again. So when she asked, he'd been shocked and shaken his head. Then the Sisters asked them. Since he had a regular income and because they were both so active in the Convention of Mary Immaculate. Mary had asked him if they should take the child only if it was male. He'd been nonplussed by her question. And then asked her what she wanted to do. Mary had grimaced and said that women had a hard life. A harder life. Also, if it was a girl, it would be cheaper for them. A boy would not be able to wear the outgrown clothes or use the books of the older two. Now she berated him because he would still buy little Glorious new clothes. And here he was cowering in a church instead of being strong for her.

Rajiv's background wasn't dissimilar to his own. Punjabi, rich, conservative, joint family set-up. He'd joined his father's metal works business. They had a huge factory for car spare parts. He had one sister, who'd been married off at age 19. The family had had hopes of Juneja marrying her, but were probably quite relieved in retrospect, considering his apparent disinheritance.

The house itself was a set of flats. Rajiv on the second floor, his parents on the first and his ghastly grandmother on the ground floor. She got up at the crack of dawn every day and had to say her prayers in the central courtyard. The sacred fire bit was okay, but she also went in for singing in a big way. Rajiv's parents had gradually managed to worm their way out and Rajiv himself had refused outright. But all the servants had to join her as she yowled at the top of her lungs at 4 a.m. For this, they had to be paid extra. They also demanded and had got an extra hour off during their lunch break, to compensate for getting up so early.

Geetu, of course, also shot out of bed, resulting in severe heartache for Rajiv, who apparently felt inclined to put out in the morning. He'd jawed about it to Juneja who'd told him to put his foot down with his grandmother. After all, did she want great-grandchildren or did she not? Rajiv's answer had left him sweating. The grandmother hadn't expected it of Geetu. It was Geetu's idea. Also, having sex in the morning was immoral. How could one think of such a thing? In the morning one must have pure thoughts. And nothing but pure thoughts. Besides, what was a house without ELDERS? Juneja could hear the capital letters. A house was a house, opined Geetu, where you could hear a child's cry in a corner, smell mother's cooking in another and rejoice in grandmother's blessings in yet another. In Rajiv's house his child would have not only his grandmother's blessings but also his great-grandmother's yowling.

Juneja tottered up the stairs bathed in sweat. He'd been telling Rajiv to get a lift installed - bloody miser was intent on killing him! The gin intake wasn't helping either. Upstairs the ACs were thankfully on full blast and so was the party.

'Nikki, there you are!'

'Hi Geetu.' Warm, boob avoiding, only shoulder touching, womanly embrace.

' Why did you take so long? Rajiv, loook!'

'Hi pal!' Back thumping, chest rubbing, manly hug. 'What'll you drink?'

'Anything cold, man, anything on the rocks!'

'What a summer, man, I tell you, I died today. Four hours in the afternoon, no electricity in the factory, man. Bloody workers in a stinking, foul mood. I thought I'd go mad. And then the traffic, man, unbelievable. Traffic lights at the Ashram crossing collapsed. Stupid cops appeared after 20 minutes man, total fuckers...'

'Rajiv, really, mind your language. You're so insensitive!'

Juneja smiled.

Rajiv rolled his eyes. 'Sorry man, why'd you become such a fucker, man? Never mind, c'mon, let's go over. Geetu, tell the servant to delay the food a bit. Nikhil's just got here. Let him have a drink in peace. C'mon, man, it's good to see you!'

Juneja could feel Gupta, Joseph and all the other fuckers disappearing. The vodka was chilled through. Rajiv knew his drinks.

'What's this stuff, man?'

'Finlandia, great stuff, man. I just got a carton full from my source but listen, don't let the others touch your glass. I'm only giving it to you. The others are drinking some Pushkin shushkin crap!'

Juneja grinned back happily. Friends, they made life worth living!

It was the old crowd. 'Hi guys!'

'Hey Nikhil, how's the policing going, man? You guys are such a bunch of corrupt assholes! Do you ever do any work?'

Deep Verma. Bloody good-for-nothing slob had been living off the fat of his father's land and had put on a considerable amount of weight.

'Oh c'mon Deep, you do enough work for the both of us! Why should I work? Tell me, have you managed to get your dick out of your pants yet? That's what your dad pays you a salary for, isn't it?'

The others whooped. Juneja, the life of every party, had arrived. Rejoice!

Dinner was great. When they finally got to it. At two in the morning. Rajiv was sozzled beyond belief. And for a change so was Geetu. Juneja had introduced her to the joys of Rum'n'Cokes. She'd gotten so drunk that she'd thrown up. Amateur. Luckily this meant she was packed into bed. Granny'll have to carol alone tomorrow, sniggered Juneja to Rajiv, who was looking morose.

'She'll kill me man, this is really the end. She'll freeze and tell me to sleep on the sofa. Man, this is really bad, man, really bad. You shouldn't have done bottoms up, man, she'll be really angry!'

'Man, just pretend she has a migraine.'

'Huh?'

'She'll be sick in the morning?'

'Yeah, so?'

'So you pretend like she never drank. You say darling Geetu are you feeling better? Have a cup of tea. All the others left early after you were gone. They felt so bad, that you had a migraine. Nobody even ate anything. That'll make her feel guilty and give you head!'

'Bastard, the servant will tell her and these starving migrant workers from Bihar have cleaned out the fridge! I don't know, why I call these shameless assholes. Don't they get any food at home?'

'Rajiv, think with your head, not your dick. Give the servant a hundred bucks and tell him to shut up. Tell Geetu you gave me the food. Because I'm not married, because my fridge is empty, because I'm a needy, unmarried fool, who misses home cooked food, okay? Have I fixed your problem or what?'

'Nick, man, man...you're a genius, man. You just saved my ass, man.'

'Chill, Rajiv.'

Sunil Malhotra came over. He and Deep and Sunil's current arm fluff were all that remained of the migrant labour force. She was an emancipated, smoking, short-skirted slut called Sonia. Geetu loathed her.

'What are you idiots laughing about? C'mon guys, one last one for the road!'

Sunil wasn't a bad guy. Handsome and rich. Women like Sonia were his natural accompaniment. Only child. His parents had been killed in a car crash. So plenty of cash and no nagging.

'Man, Sunil, how do you put it away?' Rajiv tottered to his feet.

New glasses all round. Deep, the bastard, noticed immediately. 'What's this stuff, Rajiv? It's much better than the other crap you've been poisoning me with.'

Sunil stepped in. 'Relax, Deep. Why're you always pissing around? I gave it to Rajiv. He's just opened the bottle.'

'Yeah man, thanks Sunil, man. Really good stuff. What's it called?'

Sunil dimpled and Juneja watched Sonia melt. 'No sweat, Rajiv, my pleasure entirely. Finlandia. Much better than Absolute.'

This was the best part of every party. All the idiots were gone. Well, almost all, but hopefully Deep would pass out or piss off. The alcohol was reaching its most sublime level. The conversation had mellowed into meaningful murmurs.

'Great evening, Rajiv, thanks a lot.' Sunil was a well-mannered guy.

'C'mon, man, let's chat a bit. Tell him to hang on, Sonia. You know we hardly see each other these days. Man, when we were younger, every weekend, man. It's these bloody women!' Rajiv collapsed into a depressed heap after this fiery speech. Sonia giggled unoffended, and lit up again. Deep was nodding off.

Juneja figured this was the time to try out a theory. He went to the bathroom and got a lukewarm glass of water. Deep had sunk lower into the sofa. His hand was almost touching the floor. Juneja smiled evilly. Sunil looked at him, but Juneja put a warning finger to his lips. He crouched next to the recumbent form and put the glass on the ground next to the sofa. Gently, centimetre by centimetre, he lowered Deep's hand into the glass. The other three were looking at him and waiting for an explanation, but Juneja just smiled and gestured they should wait.

It didn't take long. Slowly but surely, a growing wet patch emerged in Deep's crotch. Sonia squealed with delight. Sunil started laughing and Rajiv, who had taken time to cotton on, roared. Deep woke up with a start.

'Whaa...? What's happened?'

'You've wet your trousers,' Juneja explained kindly.

Deep looked down and shot to his feet. 'Shit, Rajiv, I'm sorry man, I'm really sorry.' He saw Sonia giggling and ran for the door.

'Nick, you are the best, man, the very best.' Rajiv had tears pouring down his face.

'What're you going to tell Geetu ?' asked Juneja, anxious to spread more cheer.

Sunil started laughing again, but Rajiv wasn't having any of it. 'I don't care, man. I'll figure something out. In fact, I'll tell her he did it. That he was the only one who didn't go home although she had a migraine and then he pissed on her sofa. She always wants to invite him because he's such a sanctimonious bastard. That'll fix him good and proper!'

Juneja choked and accidentally managed to fall on Sonia and touch her boobs.

'Arre, what is this, Juneja? I told you, they want to have the cremation tomorrow and now you leak it to the press....This is not what I expected from you!'

Juneja looked at Jt. Comm. Gupta, banking his anger. What the hell was he supposed to have done about it? Bloody Miss Talwar had managed to have sex with sundry men all by herself, without any help from him, and had then got herself killed. He, Juneja had little to say about either, other than good riddance.

Khurana had declined to send the body home and said he'd talk to Gupta about it. Juneja was nursing a major hangover from the large quantities of vodka he'd poured into his gullet yesterday. He'd arrived home at three in the morning. He'd woken up to the sound of the brat next door screaming. It was 4:45. The newspapers came at 5 a.m. They brought further cause for grief. Screaming headlines: *Talwar Daughter Murdered, Made to Look Like Suicide – Police Not Fooled.* Quite funny, actually.

He'd tottered off to get sober and think of an excuse. The Talwar family was a big patron of the ruling party. What the hell was Saudamini Talwar thinking of, letting men access her body, which should by rights have been virginal?

Evidently someone at the morgue had seen fit to talk to the press. There was no mention of the pregnancy. In fact, Juneja didn't know if Gupta himself knew anything.

And here was Gupta going on like a banshee.

'Sir, we haven't talked to the press. It must have been one of the lab assistants from the hospital. They're absolutely corrupt.' That was Sinha, trying to be loyal.

Gupta looked at him balefully and snorted, 'Of course they are corrupt. We are pure as snow, hmm? You know Nikhil, this city is a woman. She is a beautiful woman. And you know, now and then she bends over to comb her hair.'

Juneja maintained a politic silence.

Undisturbed by Juneja's lack of enthusiasm, Gupta went on, 'She combs her hair, Nikhil, with a fine-tooth comb. You know, what we call a lice comb. And then and only then, Nikhil, do the lice come out.

'We are that lice comb, Nikhil. We, the police, are the lice comb, combing out the lice in this society of Delhi. Do you understand? Anyway, where is this boy Joseph? What does he say?'

Juneja was dumbfounded. The thought of being a lice comb sickened him, and anyway why couldn't they be Licil and annihilate the lice of Delhi and what should Joseph have to say? What the hell, it was no skin off *his* nose. Let Gupta see first hand how daft the fellow was. 'Sinha, send Joseph in.'

Joseph arrived, looking anxious to please. He'd spent the evening regaling Mary and the kids with stories of the fabulous wealth of the Talwars. He was quite thrilled to be asked in to this conference.

'So, Joseph, what did you see yesterday?' asked Juneja, quite kindly.

Joseph swelled with pride. 'Sir, the Talwars are a very important family. They have a security man. He has two daughters. He has been getting dowry demands.

'Otherwise the Talwar servants love their employers very much. They are very sad. But it is not good that yesterday chicken was made in the house of loss.'

Juneja smiled cynically. Trust the sod to shove in a paragraph into even that mini piece of crap.

'No, no, Joseph,' said Gupta soothingly, 'the chicken must be a mistake –'

'No, sir, I smelled it myself. The servant offered me a piece. And sir, they are all very upset, very angry about Mr Talwar being in hospital for such a long time. His daughter was staying with him.'

'Arre, Joseph, very good, very good. Now, you go and have lunch. Sinha, you can also go.'

Gupta waited till they had left. 'Did Khurana tell you about the other things he found?'

So he did know. 'Yes, sir.'

'Juneja, that information is only for you. I have told Khurana to take it out of the autopsy report. It is too dangerous.'

Juneja looked thunderstruck.

'Arre, Juneja, you think teenage pregnancies happen only in America, hmm? Premarital sex is becoming more and more routine.' Gupta grimaced, he looked exhausted.

'R.K.'s father used to talk to me. The family, or at least the older boys, also know – the younger fellow is a duffer. When the people who need to know already know, what is the need to put it in the autopsy? But it could be the reason, why this happened. Blackmail gone wrong? I don't know.'

'Sir, if we find the fellow, it won't be very difficult. Under Section 375, we can arrest him for rape and then under interrogation, he'll certainly tell us the rest.'

Gupta smiled. 'Arre Juneja, this is not a game. The Talwars have political aspirations. The fellow you beat to pulp will have a lawyer. If nothing else, the Opposition will ensure he gets one. Then the fat will be in the frying pan!'

'Sir, if I can't talk to anyone, and if no one should get to know anything, how should the investigation proceed?'

Gupta got up slowly, his joints creaking rhythmically. 'You will have to arrange a meeting with the older sons. See what they can tell you. Also talk to the women. Even if the men don't know anything, the women will know about her friends.'

'Sir, she was three months pregnant.'

'I know, Juneja. Arre, what should I do about it? It wasn't my child she was carrying!"

Juneja studied Gupta's back. He was standing at the window, looking at the resplendent trash heap just outside the compound wall. When there was an electricity breakdown, Gupta could choose his preferred form of death: leave the window closed and drown in sweat, or open it and drown in the stench of rotting garbage and fresh dung. Today was another scorcher. It was barely eleven o'clock and the temperature was touching the forties. The eyes hurt to look at the yellow, dusty heat.

'Also, Juneja, look into this Joseph thing.'

Would this Joseph thing never end? What did Gupta see in him?

'If Joseph is saying they had chicken cooked yesterday,' continued Gupta, 'it means something. Had old man Talwar been at home, it would never have happened. If it's a deliberate slight to Saudamini, who arranged it?'

'Sir, it's just chicken!' exclaimed Juneja.

'Juneja, this is your biggest problem and your biggest bonus point. You know nothing about tradition and the Indian way of life. Because of your father, you refuse to think traditionally!'

Juneja could feel his face stiffening. Why should he have to take this nonsense?

'Juneja, listen to me.' Gupta seemed quite oblivious to Juneja's discomfort. 'After a death, in no traditional house is food cooked. More than that, the question of non-vegetarian food does not arise. The Talwars are a very traditional Punjabi family. Who disliked Saudamini so much? You send Joseph to the kitchen again. Tell him to ferret out the information.'

Juneja sighed. 'Sir, the fellow is a fool – it's impossible to have a half-way serious conversation with him. He talks rubbish.'

Gupta smiled, 'He's a very simple fellow, Juneja. But he's honest, very honest. They won't be able to buy him. In this case that is going to be very important. If I had known how it was going to turn out, I would have been more careful from the beginning. In any case, you'd better get going now.'

Juneja needed to go to his own office to pick up his things before leaving for the Talwar house. Gupta's last words had been quite cryptic. Was he (rightly) accusing Juneja of corruption? Or was he saying that Juneja was not good enough for the investigation?

It was a hard nut to crack. Was he corrupt? Was it wrong to think of the future? On the one hand everyone talked about planning the future, investing in the future, hard work – no one told you it wasn't enough. But you had to know the right people at the right time. And they had to like you. Things had to fall into place. It wasn't enough to work – you had to work hard at the right things.

No one was talking about breach of security or anything. God knows, there were enough politicians and bureaucrats who received kickbacks from arms deals – so called facilitation money. But if some rich guy drove over a bunch of poor people, they died. And that was it. If Juneja helped him get away with it, the relatives of the dead got some money, and he, Juneja, got a lot more money. On the other hand, one could throw Mr Big Bucks into jail, then the poor guys got nothing, Juneja got nothing, the BB's family had nothing to show for their money, *and* the state paid for BB's upkeep. Was this murder a way of making sure that the news of the pregnancy got out or was it only about Saudamini Talwar? *Who* was being targeted?

Joseph was waiting for him outside. Juneja smiled feebly. 'Let's go, O Honest Soul!'

Joseph smiled back shyly. 'Sir, the car is waiting outside, this way. I have also brought food from home, sir, so you don't get indigestion from the dirty canteen food. Nutritious food from home, sir, with little oil and spices. Very wholesome, sir.'

'Sir me the car, Joseph!'

The short journey was hot and dusty, as expected. Juneja smoked incessantly. Gupta's new avatar surprised him. He was used to seeing him behaving like a jovial jackass, this intelligent policeman was a surprise, as was the strange turn to honesty, or was it a test? Juneja sat up with a start, causing Sajjan Kumar to look askance at him.

'No, no, keep going.'

Could that be it? Was that what it was all about? Was Gupta testing him? Checking to see whether he was clean or not? And what was the correct answer? Was Gupta looking to see, affirming that he was a discreet, tactful accomplice or was he from the Anti Corruption Bureau? The only person he was relatively sure of was Khurana.

The jeep screeched to a halt in front of the Talwar residence and Sajjan Kumar leaped out to open the door for Juneja. Juneja stomped out the cigarette and turned to Joseph. 'You go to the kitchen. Find out more about the servants, where they were when it happened and all that. Also this chicken business, okay?'

'Yes, sir,' answered Joseph, seemingly unhappy.

As Juneja turned on his heel to go to the house, he saw that the older two Talwar brothers were waiting at the door.

'We have been in touch with Jt. Comm. Gupta,' started N.K. Talwar immediately. 'I find the behaviour of the police inexcusable. We have to find out about the supposed murder of our sister through the newspaper? What kind of nonsense is this?'

Juneja squared his shoulders to take the bullet straight in the chest. 'Mr Talwar, I am very sorry. Yesterday I was in the morgue till late in the evening, talking to the forensic pathologist. I wanted to come here then itself, but it got late. This was an unforeseen leak. Most probably from the lab.'

'Look, Juneja, that's is no excuse. These bloody journalists have besieged the Golf Links house, my brother had to fight his way out. How can this be? Do you know what it's like for my father? I mean, he is ill, and then to find out about his only daughter's murder from the papers? I mean, he could have had a heart attack!'

'Raghav's wife is pregnant, she could have lost the baby!' This was R.K. Talwar, putting in his bit.

Juneja prepared to move in for the kill. 'That's what I want to talk to you about, Mr Talwar, the baby.'

There was silence.

'Why don't you come inside and for God's sake, no more leaks, Juneja.'

Achtung Baby!

Inside, the house had been cleaned. Carpets were spread out and the furniture had been moved along the walls to make place for the inevitable stream of mourners. A garlanded photograph of the deceased, as Joseph would say, had been placed at one end on a sort of small podest. Incense burned sweet and thick.

'The arrangements for the cremation,' offered R.K., by way of an explanation.

'Yes, well, I'm afraid that is going to have to wait a little.'

The scions exchanged a quick glance before R.K. again said, 'Look, Juneja, let's be reasonable about this entire thing.'

'Mr Talwar, we have been quite reasonable about this entire thing from the beginning, but if we can't expect any cooperation from you then I don't see why we should continue to be reasonable,' countered Juneja, feeling rather cocky.

They entered the landing, where they had been last time. Rags was striding up and down, laughing into his cordless. 'Because sheep can't bring beer from the fridge. That's a good one!' He looked at them and turned on his heel and left.

'Please take a seat. Ram Singh,' R.K. hollered. A youngish fellow in uniform, with red eyes, came in. He turned again to Juneja. 'Tea, coffee, or maybe a sweet lime?'

'Thank you, a lime soda with salt, please,' condescended Juneja.

'Now, Mr Talwar, how long have you known about the pregnancy?' *Go straight for the jugs with women and suspects, that's my boy.*

R.K. blanched. N.K. looked the other way. He turned back again towards Juneja and seemed about to speak, when R.K. raised a forbidding hand.

'Juneja, this is not a matter of joking.'

'No, this is not a matter of joking at all. A girl from a good family, an unmarried girl,' Juneja paused meaningfully before continuing, 'is pregnant. This is nothing to joke about. But the pregnancy was almost in the third month.

Very soon an abortion would not have been possible. You told me about a November wedding. That would have been too late. So since when have you known? Why didn't you tell us? Who is the man?' Juneja screwed his eyes to mere slits and tilted his head to one side.

'Hi Yul Brynner!' said Rags, slapping him on the back.

'Raghav!' R.K. shot to his feet. N.K. shook his head in opprobrium.

'Raghav, if you don't know how to conduct yourself, please leave.'

'But I just wanted to...'

'Leave please.'

For the second time, heel turning, leaving.

Juneja studied his toes. 'Like I was saying, the police need honesty from you.' Pathetic attempt, Nikhil, all that good drama ruined by one Yul.

'Juneja, look, you have a mother, sisters. Can you imagine what this must be like for us? N.K. looked at him pleadingly, Gilbert like. It was R.K.'s turn to look sad and shake his head.

Juneja refused to buy the Sullivan act. 'I'm an only child, Mr Talwar, and my mother died in childbirth. Why did your sister do something like this?'

R.K. took over again. 'I don't know, Juneja. They were so much in love.' N.K. shook his head, bemused.

'I don't know what they were thinking of. I mean, he's a lovely boy. Shattered. This sort of thing happening to your fiancée. I mean, he's just broken down completely. God knows, if they had said anything, we would have preponed the wedding immediately. They are, were children. Mistakes happen.'

And pigs fly. 'His name and address?'

'Of course, you'll want to talk to him. Pratap Singh. N.K. will write down his contact details for you. I must ask you to be gentle with him, this is very traumatic. Look at Raghav. These young people lead lives untouched by tragedy, so they take refuge in humour. But on the inside? They are hurting inside.'

'Of course, Mr Talwar, I can understand, it *is* a dreadful tragedy.'

He turned to thank N.K. for the scribbled address. 'I'll leave for Mr Singh's house immediately.'

'Juneja, we are prepared to be quite reasonable, you know.' It was R.K.

'We understand how cooperative you have been. I mean, working extra hours and keeping our sister's honour and our good name out of the newspapers – we are really very grateful, you know,' chipped in N.K.

'Yes, very grateful and also very thankful.' R.K. again.

'Thank you, sir. We are always pleased to be of assistance. It is our duty, what we are paid for. By the government that is,' returned Juneja, who knew the code better than anyone else.

R.K. exchanged wary glances with N.K., leaving Juneja feeling rather smug over his repartee – foxed you, didn't I? Was this acceptance or polite refusal? Will he, won't he? Who could tell?

Juneja politely requested the return of Joseph and enigmatically smiled his way to the door.

Ram Singh handed over the fresh lime soda to the balding policeman, feeling rather dour. It had been a harrowing week. The death of Pinky Baby had contributed further to his work load. Papaji in hospital meant special food had to be cooked for him every day. The entire routine of the house had been thrown off balance.

Now the ladies of the house, R.K. Bhabhi and N.K. Bhabhi (they were really called this) were so upset, that the entire burden fell on him. Also there were arrangements to make for the cremation and after that for all the ceremonies that were to be conducted. He really didn't have the time to attend to sundry other guests who were inconsiderate enough to drop in at odd hours. This other fool Joseph had also appeared again to poke around his kitchen and insult Papaji.

Joseph wasn't feeling very good either. The whole thing had started off on the wrong foot. He'd carefully omitted telling Mary anything about his faux pas. It had been so utterly unpardonable that he really didn't know what to say or do. Today of all days Juneja seemed to be warming to him. If he failed, Juneja would have him hung. He touched himself protectively and turned to Ram Singh, who gave him a disgusted look. Joseph hastily removed his hand and tried his best lamb bleat. Unfortunately, tension had loosened his bowels, resulting in surprisingly loud flatulence. Ram Singh tried for a replay of disgust but then started giggling. Joseph shyly joined in. 'Look, I'm really sorry about yesterday.'

'It's okay, but you shouldn't talk like that.'

'I know, I'm really sorry. You mustn't take it badly. You're looking very tired, can I help you?'

Ram Singh smiled wryly. This policeman was like no other he'd met or heard of. Offering help!

'No. Thanks anyway. Come down, we can have some tea.'

The kitchen was surprisingly quiet. Nothing on the fire except a huge aluminium kettle put on sim. Ram Singh opened a drawer to get a packet of glucose biscuits. They drank the tea from thick, squat glasses.

'Hmm, cardamom, no? Tastes very good.'

Ram Singh smiled teasingly. 'Better than what you have been eating!'

Joseph blushed and studied his fingers. Now, what did Juneja want to know? Yes, the chicken. He tried for a discreet approach.

'Yesterday was such a sad day. Why did you make chicken?' He leaned back, relieved it was out of the way.

Ram Singh might have been surprised by the query but he didn't show it. In fact he seemed more embarrassed than anything else.

'I feel so bad about that, you can't imagine. R.K. Bhabhi told me to make it because she said that Raghav was coming for lunch and everyone knows he won't eat any vegetarian food. So I made. But I felt bad all the time. Then N.K. Bhabhi came down and shouted at me and told me to throw the chicken away. I was planning to take it home in the evening –'

He broke off to look the other way.

Joseph shook his head understandingly. Obviously. No one would want to throw away chicken just like that. It cost money, which didn't grow even on the money plant, much to Gloria Godaveri's dismay.

Ram Singh continued to look more wretched with every passing minute. 'I had packed the chicken into my tiffin, when N.K. sahib came down with R.K. sahib. After dinner. They wanted to eat the chicken. I told them N.K. Bhabhi had told me to throw it away, then they started shouting at me. I think they were drunk! But I didn't give them the chicken.'

Joseph tried to smile understandingly again.

Ram Singh whispered, 'Maybe I should have. But their sister had died. It's my duty to not let them commit any further sin. You know, even drinking is not good. Their father would never have allowed it.'

This time Joseph was wholehearted in his agreement. 'Absolutely. This is no way to behave, how can they be drinking at a time like this? They are in mourning. They should be weeping at the loss of their only sister, not celebrating!'

Ram Singh nodded, 'They were always funny with her. Pinky Baby was very simple. Very innocent, like a little child. She was so happy when I made her favourite dishes. So pleased.'

Joseph looked down, knowing his eyes were filming over. The thought of something like this happening to his darling trio made him choke.

Ram Singh sighed heavily. 'I don't know what this house will be like without her. R.K. Bhabhi and N.K. Bhabhi were never very nice to her, but as long as Papaji was at home they never dared to be openly mean to her either. No wonder she preferred to stay in the hospital with him.

'Only Raghav Bhaiya was friendly with her. Always playing with her and buying her chocolate and sweets. But after he got married that changed also. His wife never got along with the other two women and they moved out within months of the marriage.'

Joseph tsked his way through that passage. It was true, in no house could two kitchen fires burn at the same time. Today one has to divide up everything. How sad it was to think not even old respected families like this one were immune to this evil malaise.

Joseph sank back in his chair. What was their future? Would his daughters move out some day, leaving their ageing parents to fend for themselves? Would their husbands be unable to bear him and Mary? Was this where it was all leading?

Ram Singh leaned forward. 'Have you seen the film *Hum Aapke Hain Kaun*? Raghav Bhaiya got married just like that! So many functions, one after the other!'

'Really? Tell me about it!'

'Well, it was....'

Juneja decided to go straight home after another useless day. This case was getting on his nerves. All these fools beating around the bush. This wretched Pratap Singh.

He looked at the slip of paper. Either this was some particularly exclusive address no one had ever heard of, or the man lived in the back of beyond. Bloody Sajjan Kumar would hopefully find it. He had relatives in every corner of the city.

It was five o'clock.

Time for a drinky-poo. He called up Rajiv, who was still in the factory.

'Hey man, how did it go?'

'Nikhil man, you are wasted in that frigging job. Dump it, man, just dump it. I'll get you a job as a sex arranger!'

Juneja laughed. 'I told you she'll fall for it!'

'Fall? Man, she's drowning in it! She called up that asshole Verma and screwed his happiness! Just screwed him through and through. I almost crapped myself when she asked him why he didn't go home, even though she'd had a headache. I thought he'd say she was drunk. But the bugger was too embarrassed. And she wants to thank you because the food would have been wasted otherwise. And she hopes the food is okay. And man, she is so grateful to me! Ever so grateful! She's going to have a lot more aches by the time I'm through! I can't wait to be home.'

Juneja grimaced. That was the end of their drink together, 'Tell me man, do you have Sunil's number? I thought we'd get together for a drink tonight.'

'Shit man, you wanted to go for a drink tonight? Look, I'll tell Geetu...'

'Tell her to take everything off and wait with parted legs! No, you asshole! Don't be ridiculous. Sunil's a nice guy and I thought we should meet more often. I'll tell you all the gossip, man. You go get your head!'

'You're a pal, Nikhil. Seriously, you are the best. Sunil's a decent guy too. Thank him for me for that Finlandia bit. Tell him next time he's over, he's in from the beginning, okay?'

'Will do. And Rajiv? I want the gossip tomorrow as well, okay?'

Some insanely filthy talk later, Juneja found himself with Sunil's telephone number. He liked the guy but he'd never gone with him on twosome dates before. What the hell, Nikhil, time to lose your virginity. Sunil had no such reservations. They agreed to meet at a bar near his flat. Sunil said it was on his way. Juneja was only too happy to comply. He'd be able to have a quick one beforehand and in any case, he was beginning to hate driving.

Fortunately Sajjan Kumar drove during the day. This wretched Maruti phenomenon meant all these bastards who couldn't drive a bloody cycle to save their lives were strutting their stuff in Maruti vans today. Choking the streets with their poisonous presence. Parking was a nightmare. People had taken to getting their servants to guard parking places near their homes. People rioted over parking spaces. The entire city was a temple that worshipped at the altar of illegal construction and now there were all these cars squeezing the air out of the roads as well. It was true. A road was like an artery – to block either was dangerous.

He'd got this piece of knowledge from a street guide. Along with the information that the undertaker loved overtakers, to say nothing of becoming a hell's mate should he choose to go without a helmet.

Maybe Rajiv was right. Maybe he was in the wrong job. 'Sex arranger' certainly sounded better than thulla. He wiped himself roughly with the towel and walked to the wardrobe. His reflection in the mirror underlined his glum state of mind. Lousy job, poor salary, being called thulla, which sounded like thug, developing a paunch and meeting Sunil tonight. C'mon, Juneja, pull yourself together. How bad could life be? It could be so bad that you're hot and have money and have a date with a paunchy, corrupt thulla. Take that Sunil, I may be a loser but I have a date with you and you only got one with me!

Cheered by this thought, Juneja decided to go in for the cool Indian look. Kurta-pyjama, soft fresh muslin with decent looking silver buttons. Leather slippers to underline the intellectual look. A touch of...what should it be? *Azarro*, too horny, *Aramis*, too conservative, *Old Spice* – which idiot gave him that, *Fahrenheit*, too warmly feminine, didn't he have anything normal? *Jazz*, hmm. Smelled a little pretentious, but what the hell – he was feeling quite pretentious today.

It was probably best to walk rather than drive. On the other hand, crossing the main road was a death-defying act. The cars were driven by homicidal maniacs determined to make it home at the speed of light on roads made for buffaloes. By the time he reached the *Cedar Bar* (weren't cedars some kind of trees?) his feet were light black. Grey, his art teacher in school would have said, but the truth was light black. Grey would have meant they weren't very dirty. They were actually fairly filthy and therefore light black. Like his skin colour. In India, it was fair, wheatish, in the white world, brown, in reality, light black.

Sunil was probably gorgeous everywhere, thought Juneja sourly. His Gorgeousness hadn't arrived though, so Juneja allowed himself to order a large gin and went towards the back in search of the cedars. He'd never figured why Indians were so obsessed with British flora, to the extent that Gulmohar Park, named after the indigenous Gulmohar tree, had a 'Poplar Villa'. The 'Cedar Bar' had no trees of any kind.

He summoned a waiter. 'Why is your bar called Cedar?'

'Sir, it's the name of the owner, sir.'

'The owner's name is Cedar?'

'Mr Champaklal Dar, sir, Mr C. Dar.'

'Hey, Nikhil, what're you doing skulking at the back, man?' Sunil relieved the waiter from Juneja's interrogation. 'Waiter, one large vodka. Nikhil, another one for you?'

'No thanks, I haven't even started this one! Good to see you.'

Sunil looked a bit tired. It had evidently been a long day after the short night.

'Better to see you, Nikhil! That was one wild night.'

Juneja tried for the same sincerity. 'Yeah, we don't do it as often as we should.'

Sunil smiled. 'It's the women! Seriously, it was a great evening. I must call Rajiv. And your Deep stunt!' Sunil broke off and started laughing. 'How could you, Nikhil? How could you? Where'd you get the inspiration?'

The waiter appeared with Sunil's vodka. 'Cheers Nikhil, to many more evenings!'

'Salut!' tried French Juneja.

An awkward silence set in.

'So, how was the day?' asked Juneja, going in for the housewifely bit.

Sunil smiled. 'Good, it was good the way all my days are good. What about you?'

'Ditto.'

'Ditto good or ditto they're all the same?'

'Ditto, I don't know either!'

They started laughing.

'You know Nikhil, I feel good about not being married. Sonia's been hinting a bit but I don't see it working out. In fact I feel strange about this entire relationship bit. How does Rajiv cope? Geetu's lovely, don't get me wrong. But I can't imagine being with one woman for the rest of my life.' He took a long draught of the vodka and grimaced. 'After yesterday I don't know how I can stomach this stuff.'

'The older you get, the lower the tolerance level,' agreed Juneja. 'I know what you mean. Geetu thinks I should get married too.'

'God help the woman and her sofas!'

Juneja laughed. The evening would be good.

It *was* good. The way yesterday should have been. Gossip replaced the embarrassed jokes, leading to confidences. In a rare fit of bonhomie, he invited Sunil home. The walk back wasn't in the same city. The streets were almost bare. A lone car drifted by. The traffic lights were on yellow blinker. Small groups of men stood near the paan vendors, listening to the latest Hindi film songs, gossiping, smoking and spitting out the red tobacco juice that marred every public corner in the city.

It was a balmy evening. The harshness of the sun was snuffed out by the tubelight brilliance of the moon. The soft, gentle breeze was cool and his skin prickled delightfully as the sweat dried.

He deposited Sunil in a folding chair on the balcony and pulled out a vodka bottle and two glasses, plonked ice into the ice bucket, assembled a small bowl of salted peanuts and tottered forth.

The Chor Minar glistened threateningly in the bright moonlight.

'God, Nikhil, what's with the pygmy tower?' demanded Sunil. 'It looks positively evil!'

'It's the Chor Minar. You know they used to hang up the heads of thieves as a deterrent. Maybe we should be doing it too!'

'I know, these bastards don't understand anything else. I really think hanging is too good for most of them.'

Juneja was surprised by his vehemence and it must have shown.

'No, man, I'm serious. Look at this girl who's been murdered, Saudamini Talwar.'

Juneja froze. 'You know her? Knew her, I mean?'

'Not directly. My aunt is Sunita Malhotra. Her son, my cousin, Vineet was.... Well, actually, he wasn't anything, but they were considering an engagement with N.K. Talwar's daughter, Bahar.' He grimaced involuntarily.

'Just the name, or is it the girl?' asked Juneja, perspicacious as ever.

Sunil smiled. 'The name's pretty gross, isn't it? The girl's worse, if that's possible! But seriously, Nikhil, it seems so ridiculous. I called up my aunt to ask what the scene was. Apparently Vineet is obsessed with this Bahar. She's quite hot in a crude sort of way but my aunt is now really worked up. I mean, you don't marry your son to some chick whose aunt's been murdered!'

Correction, whose single, pregnant aunt has been murdered, smiled Juneja to himself.

Sunil didn't notice any lack of attention on his part. 'Vineet says, why should our life be ruined just because of this woman? Apparently she was pretty hideous and basically incapable of getting hitched up. There was some scandal that my aunt was going on about but I didn't listen. Families are the pits. Hate 'em, can't leave 'em! In any case, that's what I mean, hang the SOB who did it and stick his head up here!'

Juneja opened a bleary eye to look at the morning sun. After his meeting with the Talwars two days ago, little had happened. He had wanted to meet the fiancé of this wretched girl but due to the visit of Madeleine Albright, the city almost stopped functioning, at least the police force did. Typical. All the politicians were out, all the policemen were out, two days down the drain. He scratched his chest, running his fingers luxuriously through the abundant foliage. Not really down the drain – a lot of alcohol had been poured down *his* drain. Devyani Talwar had called up and left a message with the servant. He hadn't bothered returning that call either. Evidently Rags had finally figured out who he was and was making his wife do the dirty work.

Didn't look like there was going to be much happening in this case. Why should it? The only people who were in a position to kick ass, the Talwars, seemed highly reluctant. In which case it was unlikely that any one else would. Maybe this boy Pratap Singh might fall at his feet and beg for justice. Juneja smiled, this had actually happened to him. Some idiots had actually thrown themselves at his feet, begging him for justice, asking him to swear by his mother's milk. Juneja had felt sick – milk in any form was disgusting.

He dragged himself out of bed. Shower, breakfast, perhaps a shave? A visit to Devyani Talwar, wife of Raghav Talwar, daughter-in-law of the Talwars and most importantly, gossipy bitch sans pareil, could not be made in a stubbly state.

What did Devyani want to discuss with him? Was she acting at the behest of the Talwar clan or was it just Rags? Juneja didn't believe for a minute that she was concerned for her late departed sister-in-law. Devyani was a rich bitch in the truest sense of the word and didn't care very much for any one except herself. Interesting thought, though – what did she care about enough to have called him? Maybe he would condescend to visit her. Not that he needed to call. Devyani never breakfasted before noon. And one should never underrate the element of surprise.

That left Pratap Singh to question. So much work in one day? Juneja called the police station to tell Joseph that he'd be going straight to Devyani Talwar's house and would report to the police station only after he'd finshed the interrogation. Joseph need not bother waddling his fat ass over. Joseph guffawed politely as all junior colleagues must, and inquired if he might go shopping with his wife instead. But of course, was the answer. Devyani with Joseph out of the way was an even more delightful prospect.

Golf Links is one of the older colonies of Delhi. Located near the Delhi Golf Club, south of India Gate, it is a colony of 220-odd houses. *A quiet and elegant neighbourhood with mature trees, well maintained parks. A very dignified and posh area, a mix of large and small plots. Khan Market, a market that offers practically everything to the expatriate, round the corner*, say the real estate agents.

Unlike colonies like GK 1 or 2, Golf Links offers a uniform neighbourhood. Houses in GK may all look more or less the same, the inhabitants can be horrific. As a swinging single you would pay a crazy rent for a cool penthouse bachelor pad. The problem was the demented Hindu rightwingers on the first floor. The second floor was infested with violently loud South Indians. And a real Delhi penthouse meant the landlords would be secreted somewhere in between, telling you when to bathe and how much water to use. One thing you don't get are Muslims because, after all, you know, they aren't one of us.

But Golf Links offers uniformity. It's rich. Everyone is rich. No one aiming to be, no one hoping to be, everyone just already is. A fair number of whites, otherwise called expats, makes the landscape even more beautiful. The houses are large and spacious. The best Delhi has to offer. Everything one could possibly desire is around the corner – hotels, schools, restaurants, and that commodity so rare in Delhi – safety. You can walk on those clean, broad streets and not be pinched or attacked or mugged. Though, one may well ask was there to attack? For in this haven, only servants walk. The whites, browns and blacks are quite united on this front – air-conditioned cars, fleets and fleets of them, stand parked in front of each house. Why walk?

Devyani Talwar would certainly never have dreamt of anything of the sort. She looked at herself critically in the mirror. She was turning 30 this year. Despite increasing pressure from Rags' she'd avoided getting pregnant. Her friends had told her she wouldn't be able to avoid it indefinitely but Devi, as she was called by her near and dear ones, had been quite hopeful. Rags was besotted with her. And rightly so, purred Devi to herself. She was an extremely lissome lass. Tall, slim, very fair, with lustrous green eyes, which gloomed with lust at the sight of diamonds. They glowered sullenly at the thought of the pregnant months ahead. She'd had to give in Rags had insisted. Still, Kavita said, it was a minor problem of a few months and then that was it. Devi had seen a doctor to make sure it was a son to begin with. Rags was unlikely to make any further demands once he'd got his son.

That wretched Shivani, R.K. Bhabhi, had already had a son. They named him Rajvansh – the Royal Heir, if you please. Bitch. Roma, N.K. Bhabhi, had two ghastly daughters, one of whom was already 19. Devi shuddered.

Although the age gap between the three sisters-in-law was relatively small, they lived in different worlds. The two other brothers were of the old school. They'd just about finished school, then joined Papa. Rags had studied in the US and could speak fluent English. N.K. and R.K. Bhabhi were totally sari-clad, Hindi-movie-lapping cows. Devi loathed them. They'd treated her like a low-class slut when they lived under one roof after her marriage.

The arrangemant had been doomed from the start. N.K. Bhabhi was the First Lady of the Talwar clan. At the age of 40, she was the mother of two daughters, Bahar, 19 and, Khushbu, 15. R.K. Bhabhi also had two children, Shira, 15 and Rajvansh, 12. In fact they had been pregnant at more or less the same time, and had delivered within weeks of one another. So the bonds were well in place when Devi married Rags some ten years later. The older Talwar daughters-in-law were what one expected of an industrialist Hindu family – dutiful, fat, fair and pretty. They were born housewives. And they had bred as housewives do.

Devi was different. As was Rags. The difference became more and more obvious when Papaji, insisted on playing *Happy Families*. The evil sisters had been quite clear where Devi's place in the hierarchy was – right at the bottom. Devi had been equally clear – that was where they belonged. Devi had been brought up to have fun, none of this housewifely nonsense. She came from a family as rich as any of them. The difference was in the packaging. Her dowry hadn't consisted of thick gold necklaces – she wore only diamonds, designer diamonds. No brocade saris from Benaras, only designer-matched outfits from Hauz Khas Village – the new urban village where all the designers were showcased. No three-day honeymoon in Agra to gawk at the Taj – no, they'd flown to Italy for two weeks.

They'd also stopped talking within a week. Devi had worked on Rags, going so far as to deny nuptial rights, till the family had bought the bigger house in Vasant Vihar. That left Devi the Mistress of All She Surveyed in Golf Links.

Devi looked at her lithe figure and was glad she'd waited till she told Rags. Today, she felt like white. White diamonds and gauzy organza. In the evening a chilled Tropicana white rum shot. That should impress little Nikki.

The Golf Links house was all that the Vasant Vihar house wasn't, thought Juneja ruefully. Impeccably maintained, the servants snobbish and English speaking, the air perfumed. Western rather than Indian. Décor straight out of *Good Housekeeping*.

Devi had apparently been checking out trends on her European jaunts and was into the Swedish look this year. This was one of the things that Juneja missed. Moving out had meant no more access to Daddy's bottomless pockets. Devi certainly had access to someone's fairly limitless pockets, Rags' or her father's, supposed Juneja. Large crystal vases filled with lilies were tastefully arranged; colourful rugs flung carelessly on the white marble floor, and of course, the hallmark of the nineties – the Indian artist. No cheap, tacky copies of the Mona Lisa adorned the walls here. Instead Anjolie Ela Menon, M.F. Hussain, and a priceless Jamini Roy smiled benevolently upon the visitor.

The servant had been told by another servant to guide

Juneja to the morning room, where coffee waited. He was served a rich fragrant brew. The room was at the back of the house, and opened onto a lush, green private garden. The garden too had been landscaped. In one corner was a bamboo tree. A species Juneja had never seen before – it was in full bloom. Seeing a gardener weeding a bed, he stepped out to inquire about this flowering mystery.

The gardener didn't seem to be too thrilled and looked at him rather sorrowfully, 'The bamboo tree blooms only before it dies. I will replace it with a jasmine bush. So many years it took to grow. This is the way these bastards pay you back for the care you shower on them!'

Juneja fled back into the room. Devi still hadn't appeared. He was turning to refill his cup when she flowed into the room. Dazzling in white, she looked ethereally beautiful. The chikankaari salwar-kameez was embroidered in white and silver. Fine appliqué work along the seams emphasized the delicate wrists. Tinkling anklets for the feet. A diamond stud for the nose and massive solitaires in the ears. She had pinned up her long hair, so that tendrils seductively framed the long chiselled face. Juneja swallowed. Devi had come to wage battle.

'Nikki.' Devi stopped in her tracks to stretch out her hands to Juneja. 'You've finally come. Why didn't you call me? You know it's been ages since we met.'

Juneja smiled back. 'Ages is right. When was it? At your marriage? One of those parties?'

'Nikki, just because I'm married doesn't mean we can't meet, does it? Stop being so mean! Come and sit here and tell me what's going on.'

'Other than your sister-in-law dying, you mean?'

'Uff, Nikki, now don't be irritating! That girl was very dull, I never understood why Rags was always running after her.'

'So dull, that you don't even want to talk about her?'

Devi paused in mid-pout. 'Is that why you've come to see me?'

Juneja sat back, trying to gain time. What the hell was going on? Had she really called him to gossip?

'What do you think?'

'Oh Nikki, the moment Rags told me that you were in charge I knew it was going to be okay !'

Juneja sagged. And straightened up hastily before she noticed.

But Devi was glaring at an errant gardener. 'Hang on! Silly fool, uprooting a flowering tree!'

She strode out, abandoning the flowing Ganges look for militant banshee, giving Juneja a precious few seconds to recuperate.

Juneja gulped down more coffee and tried to think what was it that Devi was hinting at.

'Yeah, so where were we?'

'What should be okay ?'

'You're right. Let's get this nonsense out of the way and then we can chat in peace. I've told the servants you'll stay for lunch, all right?'

'Great!'

'Now, where were we?' asked Devi rhetorically. She settled back on the blue settee and started her not very well prepared speech.

'Well, Nikki, you know. This silly girl went and got pregnant and panicked. That's really it. Rags is very fond of her, so I can't talk in front of him, he keeps calling her my baby, which gets on my nerves because she was *really* a baby!'

'What do you mean?'

Devi sighed, her bosom heaved gently. 'Nikki, she was the youngest. You know what men are like, especially three older brothers. And they'd spoilt her rotten. After Mummy died Papaji insisted on cosseting her and made everyone in the family do the same. I wasn't here then, but Rags told me. The problem was that Pinky, Saudamini I mean, was really stupid. All that attention went to her head.'

Juneja smiled, more than a trifle bemused. 'Devi, sweetheart – surely being stupid doesn't warrant getting murdered. I understand she got on your nerves, but is that why you killed her?'

Devi burst out laughing. 'You know, this is what I miss! You're lovely, you really are. You look so serious and so strict and then you say such funny things! No, obviously not. I think that silly boy, Pratap must have killed her. Really, he's too local. I don't know why they chose such a local character, he's totally like, poor and such a lower-class background. I asked Rags why we had to be related to him but Rags said there was no choice.'

'Because she was already pregnant?'

'Obviously, silly. How could have been so stupid? But she was sooooo ugly and really retarded, you know. And quite frankly, I know I shouldn't say it, but she was quite fat.'

Juneja nodded – it was true. She had been plain. Those thick features were no match for Devi's perfect beauty. Admittedly, her calculating eyes made her look a little tarty but Devi was nonetheless spectacularly good looking.

'See, even you admit it.' She continued, 'So, Rags said, beggars can't be choosers. I think they were offering Pratap,' she shuddered at the name, 'quite a lot of dowry. And also he's, hmm, I think a little, you know, not totally legal!'

'So she had to be married in a hurry.'

Devi grimaced. 'The big problem is that ghastly daughter of N.K.'s, Bahar. She wants to get married. Her boyfriend is the scion of Malhotra Industries. Obviously the brothers are quite keen that everything works out. The engagement is planned for December. The cards will be out soon.

'Now, how would it look if the niece got married before the aunt? Vineet's dad, that's Bahar's guy, had already asked why she wasn't married. And...' Devi paused to take breath.

Juneja seized upon the chance. 'But what does Rags want me to do?'

'Arre, that's what I'm saying. How will it look, marrying some girl whose silly, pregnant and also very idiotic aunt has got murdered? Maybe by her very own fiancé? Imagine what a scandal it would be. Disgusting, too local! So now, you please handle it so that it all works out and this ghastly Pratap disappears from the horizon, okay? You know, maybe he killed her because she was so dumb.

'Now enough, I can't keep talking about this nonsense. Did I tell you about Leila's party? The silly girl served partridge! Can you believe it? Partridge.'

Juneja sat back. Fishy or just very foul?

Joseph left for the bus stop feeling rapturous. He loved sitting with Mary in the kitchen. The idea of beating your wife or being unfaithful to her or in any way deliberately hurting, what to him, was his very own personal angel, was utterly abhorrent. It had made for endless difficulties with his colleagues. They were nowhere near the evil monsters all those women's groups made them out to be, but they weren't angels either.

It had been very hard for Joseph to understand that being a policeman had little to do with justice or truth. He had wanted to be a postman like his father. Over the years his parents convinced him to change his mind. Joseph's entire village had been in considerable awe of the local policeman. A policeman wielded power, commanded respect and was a friend of the common people. Joseph himself had been quite taken with the idea. Unfortunately his parents never lived to see their son in uniform. They were 'secular' god-fearing people. Being financially unable to make the pilgrimage to Santiago de Compostela, they decided instead on a pilgrimage to Mt Kailash in the Himalaya. The heavy rains that year were responsible for more than one landslide. The rescue forces couldn't even recover their bodies. Instead Joseph had had to bury a photograph from their wedding album. Luckily after a few years he met Mary. There was nothing to hold him back. Not that anything could have!

It had only been thanks to the help of Father Pereira, the local priest, that Joseph had at all got this plum post. But life in the police force was unlike anything Joseph could have imagined. Delhi too defied his imagination.

Delhi, as Joseph discovered, was no melting pot. The erstwhile meeting ground of Afghans, Mongols, Mughals, Sikhs, Jains and Buddhists seemed to have smelted into solid Punjabi. The language, the people, the food, the music, the dance – the entire culture of Delhi was Punjabi. While, in the past the city had absorbed the invader, making him one of her own, today she had been taken over by a devious insider. Joseph wasn't quite sure about his feelings for this Punjabiness. Mary revelled in it. She was more Punjabi than a Keralite in every sense. Or was that just another example of the takeover?

Joseph still felt ambivalent. Not that he had anything against them. No, no, some of his favourite neighbours were Punjabis. Mrs Gupta, the Khannas, the Chhabras – they were all very nice people. Just so aggressive. Was this because Punjab had once upon a time been a border state? It still was, but Joseph didn't think that Pakistan was such a big problem. Like many Indians, he hoped that one day India and Pakistan would reunite. If there had been no Partition, there would have been a cricket team, the likes of which the world had never seen. Kapil Dev and Imran Khan, Sunil Gavaskar and Zaheer Abbas!

The bus arrived. The temperature inside was explosive. Joseph thought he would melt and fade away. Maybe that was the reason behind their aggression – this unbelievable heat. People were fighting and screaming on the roads. In the beginning he had been unable to hear anything in the bus. The assault on his ears left him feeling like a zombie.

Not that Kerela was cold, no, no. The temperature in Kerala could be unbearable but there was the ocean, the cool breeze, the sight of that water and tall green palm trees – they cooled the soul. In Delhi there was concrete everywhere. True, Lutyens' Delhi had green trees, but who could afford to live there? Only millionaires and politicians. In Janakpuri, where Joseph lived, the landscape was considerably different.

Illegal constructions and electricity connections dominated the skyline. Their house too was illegal but Sinha sir had seen to that. Janakpuri was the largest unauthorized colony in all of Asia. Among other things it also housed the largest jail complex India had to offer – the Tihar Jails. This had been pointed out to Joseph right in the beginning. Now that he had had occasion to step inside, he felt a little less awestruck. Other than Tihar, Janakpuri had little to offer in terms of cultural entertainment or scenic beauty. It was also teeming with people.

It was this aspect that had so jolted Joseph when he looked out of his second-floor window. The vast number of people, the noise, the ceaseless motion. It wasn't as if everyone was doing something. Movement – endless movement, like so many millions and million of ants. Drunk ants, thought Joseph sometimes. Nobody seemed to have the need to do anything. But no one could do anything because everyone had something to do.

In the summer heat it all looked more bleak than ever. The cheap yellow paint, the sad trees struggling against the daily onslaught of betel juice and urine, so generously supplied by passers-by, flies buzzing around the water vendors, the people themselves seemingly immobile in the eternal heat.

Heat, aye, the scorching, unending heat. Burning your soul, sucking it out only to drown it in a sea of sweat more acrid and corrosive than the Dead Sea. Diarrhoea, dehydration, death. The cycle repeated itself endlessly, every summer, every year. For years politicians had promised 'clean drinking water'. It was a catchline. Basic civic amenities, they called it. 'How can you spend money on defence/culture/ whatever the government wanted to spend money on, when half the population doesn't even have clean drinking water?' It was asked by the Opposition, by indignant journalists; the new NGOs demanded an answer equally vociferously.

Joseph shook his head. He'd told his girls never to drink water outside. Only boiled water at home. No sugarcane juice. Only green coconuts straight out of the nut, just like at home.

Mary had protested at first. She really was a Punjabi! Ever the hedonist. Summer was the time for endless golguppa rounds. Sugarcane juice was a must. You only got it in summer for Christ's sake, she'd said to Joseph. He'd been appalled, that she could take the Lord's name for such a trivial thing. It had been a big fight – the first where he had asserted himself. Only when the Sisters had confirmed his standards of hygiene had Mary grudgingly consented.

Maybe the new God, *Liberalization*, would change things. Liberalize clean drinking water. Make it available. Wasn't that the meaning of liberalization? Liberal – many, liberate – free.

Please God, let there be free water for many people. Many, many people.

After his evening with Devyani, Juneja was determined to go and see this wretched Pratap Singh. It had been a long lunch with Devi. By the time Rags joined them they had had quite a few SoCo shots, as Devi had insisted on calling them. He didn't stay for dinner but it was around eight by the time he left.

He'd remembered Devi's advice about Rags being quite besotted with his sister and had steered clear of the subject. Rags himself had only said, 'Man, Nikhil, just do things, man, just do them. My bloody family will screw my happiness if my niece's marriage doesn't come off!'

Interesting. The grapevine had it that the Talwar family fortunes were a wee bit shaky at the moment.

A lot of companies had over-extended themselves, post-liberalization. The sudden end of the License Raj had been quite bewildering for most people. Until then, business had really meant liaising with the right people and bribes. If you didn't know anyone, well then, you weren't getting rich in a hurry. That all this import-export business should all of a sudden be without licences and certificates and clearances was quite a shock. People were even talking about hundred per cent convertibility of the rupee. The real estate market was rocketing like never before. Every slum dweller in Bombay was a millionaire. Delhi wasn't far behind. The point was, one had to get off the giant wheel at the right time, otherwise one could get catapulted into financial oblivion. But why think about oblivion, when there was easy money to be made?

The Talwars would of course have to cough up a pretty packet to finance the marriage, but in the long term it would definitely pay off.

Juneja thought about the plans of dynastic expansion, that Daddy Dearest had had for him. Juneja Sr. was a cloth merchant. Unlike the other old fogies, he'd had his eyes on the *big time*. During the License Raj, he'd paid careful attention to detail and to the necessary officials. Today they were personal friends. Anyone who said the License Raj was over knew nothing about the Indian system. Licences were just an excuse.The truth was, money made money, with or without a license.

And more money always came in handy. That had been the reason behind Daddy's insistence, that Nikhil nuptially align himself with another dynasty. Actually, he'd been all right with the idea. He'd grown up knowing there were girls you screwed and there was one whom Mummy would bring home to you, or Daddy would in this case. It wasn't even a bad system. Arranged marriage didn't have to be about child marriage or cruelty or any of the other nonsense the West was so fond of. It was a reasonable arrangement, one which satisfied everyone involved.

Nikhil would have gone with the circus but for an

unfortunate remark which he had seen as a challenge to his youthful idealism. Nikhil stormed out never to return, swearing he would make it on his own. Today, more than ten years later, he quite regretted it. Going to Devi's place reminded him of what could have been his. Maybe it still could. Maybe the old man would take him back. After all, Juneja Sr. had a multi-million empire. His cloth mills provided fabric for the domestic and the overseas market. Their slogan, *The Fabric of India*, was a slogan Nikhil and several generations had grown up with. Like Amul, Thums Up, Bata and the Ambassador car, Juneja & Sons was a household name. These were brands that defined India and your Indianness.

Juneja smiled. For keeps. That was really the problem. Everything was for keeps and momentary, all at the same time. India, Delhi, the police, were all momentary and permanent lapses of reason. Nothing changed but the faces kept changing all the time. Like the rotation and revolution of the earth all at the same time. Things changed in a groove but the groove remained. It didn't even become deeper.

His father could take him back. He'd often toyed with the idea. The idea of all that money was particularly appealing, the aged father less so. Nikhil liked to think of himself as a self-made man. Sure he'd managed the exams himself, but all the quick promotions in the world don't compare with a leg up on the greasy pole. No, he'd not needed to climb, there had been any number who had wanted to do Juneja Sr. the favour. To say nothing of the large dollops of money, that were regularly transferred to his account.

He'd go back and have to eat humble pie for a while. Then he'd marry a wealthy homemaker. Have kids. Papa would finally kick the bucket. And he'd take over. Expand the business, make the fabric of India the fabric of the world. The kids would grow up and marry other fabricators. He'd have to ensure that. The homemaker would want it too. New faces, old motions. Nikhil smiled, a trifle derisively. Maybe that's what held him back. Why become an old face?

Like this bloody Pratap. Randy boyfriend gets fiancée pregnant. Old story. Juneja figured today, Wednesday, was a good day to see him. Wednesday's child is full of woe. Wednesday, which dawned scorching and dusty like all the others.

Juneja sauntered into office to be told that Gupta had been demanding to know exactly, repeat *exactly*, what progress had been made on the Talwar case. Juneja grimaced. Of all the times to start being conscientious, the summer was the worst. He backtracked out of the office, telling Sinha to send Joseph out to him.

Joseph looked his usual benign imbecilic self. 'Morning, sir!'

'Have you met Commissioner Gupta this morning?'

'No, sir, he wanted to meet you, Sinha sir told me, but I didn't go on my own to meet him, sir, that would not have been good, sir, so...'

'Good, then you go inside and tell the Commissioner's PA that I have come to pick you up to go and see the man Ms Talwar was engaged to.'

'Really, sir? We have an appointment?'

Juneja paused. Was Joseph really so daft? Only Time, Death and the Delhi Police wait for no man and boldly stride in, where none have ever wanted to go.

'Yes, we have an appointment. With great difficulty we have got one. So hurry up. I'll wait outside with Sajjan Kumar.'

Pratap Singh lived in the back of beyond. Delhi with a whopping population of 10 million and another 15 million strolling in to work every day needs every inch of its 1500 sq. km. Not that these kilometres are evenly spread. Certainly civilization hadn't spread to Delhi's borders, reflected Juneja. Delhi shared a border with the neighbouring states of Haryana, UP and Rajasthan. All three states were largely populated with testosterone hardware. Rajasthan burnt for its right to burn widows, Haryana vied with UP for the highest female infanticide rate in the world and UP most certainly was the crowning jewel in the so-called cowbelt.

He'd told Gupta's secretary they'd be gone for the day. Hell, they'd probably land up doing overtime. If this hadn't been such an important case, he'd never have undertaken this ridiculous journey. He'd had no idea where the place was – a very bad sign. Sajjan Kumar claimed he knew because an uncle's neighbours' mother-in-law had a relative who lived there. Or somewhere near there. This particular part of Delhi had not been properly mapped, a constable at the local police station informed Juneja when he telephoned for directions, because there were no macadamised roads. It was mostly farm land. Interesting character, this Pratap Singh, the constable had added, at some stage the police was going to get to know him better – no chargesheet yet, but a lot of interest.

Juneja drew a deep nicotine-laden breath, bought an extra pack of cigarettes for the journey, loosened his belt and hoped for the best.

Sajjan Kumar had propelled them through the usual traffic jams with his customary delicate touch. But now they were approaching areas unperturbed by him. Crowds did not part like the sea before Moses, cars adamantly stayed in front of them and trucks derisively honked their way past.

Joseph, though used to the deafening mayhem, was unprepared for such wild masses. He'd been unable to stay out of the way of a spittle-hurling bus passenger and had a fine spray of red betel juice across the front of his shirt. He wasn't worried about the stain – Mary was a genius. Besides, this was an occupational hazard of living in Janakpuri. But, this time the man who'd done it laughed. Joseph thought he'd fall on his knees and cry for mercy. But this man had just laughed, leapt off the running bus, telling Joseph what he'd do to his sister, and disappeared into the much amused crowd. Joseph had looked to Juneja for help – at least the old ogre would be good for something, but Juneja had looked the other way, pretending not to notice, only Sajjan Kumar responded – with a guffaw.

Juneja had, in fact, seen. He really couldn't be bothered. It was too hot and the public here was spoiling for a fight.

Joseph could beseech all he wanted. Juneja lit up again. His throat was aching and he was feeling quite light-headed from all the tobacco.

He blew out the smoke slowly, settling into the comatose state only a summer afternoon in Delhi could induce. The crowds, screaming and shouting, receded into the background like a dull ache. The loud film posters, the screaming billboards, became part of the ever-flowing, raging colour. He retained nothing, he saw heads, no faces. The very air ceased to move. Dust motes peopled the sun beams, glaring so fiercely upon the glass windows as the jeep crawled forward. He could almost see the sweat flow with maddening slowness down his neck, trickling its way through the folds of his belly.

It was surprising how ugly the city could be. In the centuries to come, when the Red Fort and the Old City had ceased to be, would these ugly, yellow, human and animal excrement-besmirched constructions be our only legacy? Not all of India, no, but Delhi certainly was an old city, a beautiful city, at least partly an architectural wonder. The only thing wondrous about the jaundiced monsters was the utter lack of imagination and love, that had evidently been the building force behind them. The makers hadn't lacked talent, they had wanted not to use it. Instead they had employed a distorted, malevolent arrogance and put the poor firmly in their collective place. You think you have enough money for a house? Here, live in this smelly, filthy hole. Eat, shit and die.

Thank God for childlessness, Juneja shuddered. At least no one will remember me! He looked up at the bit of blue sky he could still see. Only the sun managed to find its hateful way through the crisscrossing maze of electric and telephone cables. Cable upon cable – blatant electricity theft. Who cared? Certainly not this behemoth of a government that only spent on its bloated politicians. Bodyguards, armoured cars, police protection, foreign junkets, free housing, telephones and naturally, electricity and water. They got it all for free. And so did he.

So did he. It made him feel sick. How had it all gone so terribly wrong? Here in the wilderness he had to be careful himself. The crowds bayed for water, electricity, food, a life beyond a pathetic existence. Failing all this, they settled for blood. A poor substitute. Blood meant weeks and months of police brutality after the deed. Curfews, interrogations, custodial rapes and deaths. But if the poor bastards could think, they wouldn't buy the pale excuses their masters sold them at every election, would they? Generations of eating dust, drinking black water, and baking in the sun made you stupid, deferred your dreams. Everyone craved instant gratification. Somewhere, sometimes, one time – it must surely be possible? Give them blood, Marie, not biscuits.

Sometimes, he'd thought, why not poison the lot. Contaminate the water, get rid of this vast bunch at one stroke. Slaves, masters alike. Nothing remains round the colossal wreck, yellow, crappy, decrepit. The lone and level sands stretch far away.

The jeep moved on. The crowded streets made way for agricultural vistas. Cows, buffaloes, naked children, women carrying water on their heads, others squatting, making dung patties. Juneja opened the door and spat copiously.

The slap of dung-ridden air woke Joseph. He sat up groggily. They were truly lost. This couldn't be a part of

Delhi. Neither did it like a village in his beloved Kerela. It was so ugly. Joseph shuddered. What must it be like to live here?

He had exchanged his existence in the village for life in the big city. When he went home now, for a marriage or on the odd vacation, everything seemed so small and subdued. Delhi was life on a large scale. Everything was big. People drove big cars, lived in big houses, like the Talwars, even the traffic jams were massive.

But here there were none of the advantages of the city to be felt. There was only a feeling of loss. Joseph averted his eyes. He couldn't bear to look at people so utterly deprived, so poor, so stripped of their dignity. What kind of person must this Pratap Singh be? Why did he live here?

Sajjan Kumar slammed on the brakes as a dog scooted across the road.

He looked at Juneja ruefully. 'Sir, I'll have to ask. I don't know from here.'

Juneja nodded.

Sajjan Kumar came back beaming from the street café, 'Sir, no problem. Looks like he's a big man here. Everyone knows him. I think he's a rich farmer. His house is not very far away. Just three or four kilometres more, the man said.'

It was a large, sprawling mess. Juneja looked at the house and then turned on Sajjan Kumar. 'Are you mad? I thought he was an important man. This is a bloody slum. Go and find out again. NO! You go on foot. We'll wait here. What is this bloody nonsense?'

Sajjan Kumar cringed. It was Joseph's turn to look away. He couldn't blame Juneja. The heat was a living force. He could hardly sleep at night thse days. The fan pushed the air through the room but it didn't cool. The children said most of their friends were sick. Mary had already had a bout of diarrhoea from that wretched sugarcane juice she was so fond of.

Many of the men at the constabulary suffered from something or the other. Food poisoning, rashes – flatulence and diarrhoea were the least of it. It was true – in Delhi rich people had dogs, the poor were lucky if they could eat a dog! Certainly the lives of those rich dogs were better than theirs. Air conditioning, soft carpeted floors, plenty to eat and drink. The average constable got a pittance as allowance for the day. With that, they were to pay for their food and drink. The men were like hungry beasts, starved so that they could serve their masters better. No wonder the police were brutal. People were killed everyday in the city. Every minute a rape and all the other crimes the newspapers raged on about. But wasn't it a crime to treat them, the police, this way? Was it surprising when the policemen like cornered rats turned on the victims? They had nothing except a token uniform, a badge. All these silly Hindi films, prattling on about pride in the khaki. It was just cloth. It didn't feed you and it didn't send your kids to school. People like Juneja could talk. They had money. The system would help them.

Who would help Joseph? Why, if something were to happen to his own family, his Mary, his girls, Juneja was hardly likely to help him – no one would.

Joseph had yet to take his first bribe. Mary was terribly proud about it, but Joseph knew it was just a matter of time. At some point the need would be too great. Even now, when Jamuna Elizabeth had demanded a new bicycle, it had broken his heart to say no. Sinha had said he could come along on the traffic beat – there was plenty of money to be made with parking tickets. But Joseph couldn't. Not yet, not for a bicycle.

As it is the girls shared clothes, shoes, books, everything. They couldn't share a marriage or a husband. So all their money went into saving for those three marriages. Maybe next year he could buy a cycle, a second-hand one, perhaps.

'Joseph, what the hell are you looking so serious about?' Juneja was looking sourly at him.

'Sir, it is very hot. But I need to buy a bicycle, sir.'

Juneja paused. Little had prepared him for this answer. 'Why, Joseph?"

'To play. Sir, you know for the children.'

God help him. Children, pestilent brats. A pox on them all. The ghastly boy who lived next door to him had been plaguing him for the past two weeks.

The previous tenant had left a brand new cycle in the garage.They'd also conveniently left a shit load of filth on the balcony for Juneja to dispose of. The cycle, he'd said to Juneja, was a small present for Junior. Juneja had told him that 'Junior' preferred to ride things other than bloody cycles, which the fool hadn't understood. The brat next door had been irritating Juneja ever since, but Juneja saw no reason why he should be giving him anything including the time of day. Gifting Joseph the useless thing meant pissing off the neighbour for good.

Juneja grinned at his own brilliance. 'Come to my house on the weekend. I have a cycle I don't need. Brand new. You can have it.'

Joseph's mouth fell open.

Juneja grinned some more. Wonderful, another problem out of the way. Now he only needed to ensure that that ghastly child from next door saw him giving away the bike.

Sajjan Kumar reappeared. He brightened up at the rare sight of a beaming Juneja.

'Sir, this is the house. It is like a slum, sir, but it is the house.'

Juneja cocked an eyebrow. 'If it isn't, I'll chop your balls off.'

The house, or rather the row of shacks, was filthy and broken down. It just didn't make sense. How could Ms Vasant Vihar marry into Slumsville? The shacks turned out to be stables. Full of buffaloes. In one of them squatted a woman. She was shovelling the steaming shit.

Juneja turned to Sajjan Kumar again. 'You better hope she knows something otherwise you're joining her in there.'

The woman looked up at the sound of Juneja's voice. The sight of three men, two in uniform, startled her. She immediately pulled at her sari end, covering her face. Juneja sighed. This modesty would be the death of him. Half naked, the sari hitched up to her thighs, but of course she covered her face. Joseph opened his mouth to speak, when he caught Juneja's baleful stare. Sajjan Kumar spoke up, his Hindi so accented that Joseph barely understood a word. But the woman did. She pointed towards the end of the shacks. Did she mean they should go there? There was nothing else to be had from her. She stood like a mute statue, not trusting herself to tremble, waiting for them to leave.

At the end of the row, a narrow dirt path led to the open courtyard of a large house. It was a house typical of small towns and villages. A double ended, single-storied, L-shaped structure built along a courtyard, which in turn functioned as the kitchen, drawing room and reception area. The rooms were all bedrooms for the various family members. Community life took place in the courtyard, under a huge tree. A group of men sat on charpoys under the tree, smoking, drinking tea. Lunch was over. Juneja could hear the women on the far side. Chattering, bangles and utensils clinking.

It was his turn. Sajjan Kumar and Joseph knew it instinctively this time round. Their pace slowed as Junejas's stride lengthened. They walked a step behind him. The men fell silent. The sun glared into their faces as they marched from the shining light into the soft shade.

'Pratap Singh?'

'Inspector, we are Pratap Singh.'

Juneja swallowed. The man was huge, moustached and there was no other word for it, lewd. He defined lewdness. The others could be categorized into equally lewd sidekicks and old father/uncle types, who didn't count. This was bad timing. Given the situation, Pratap Singh would play to the gallery. He'd have to.

Juneja looked pointedly at the mattress, waiting to be asked to sit down. He'd handled such situations in the past. This was class war at its best. There was no point being nice or speaking in Hindi and trying to make an effort. These bastards understood an Oxonian accent and arrogance best. In any case, it was what they expected. Why disappoint them?

Singh guffawed. 'Hey, you silly cow, can't you see we have guests? Bring some chairs!'

He looked at Juneja again, his head lolling back. 'Will you deign to drink tea with us? Real buffalo's milk. Only for men.'

Juneja was up to the challenge. 'First we talk, then we can drink tea together.'

'Is that right?'

A sidekick giggled. The rest smirked. Juneja majestically sat down on the proffered chair and shot off his first salvo: 'When did you last meet Saudamini Talwar?'

'Who?'

'Saudamini Talwar. The woman you were going to marry.'

Pratap Singh's face tried to show puzzled lewdness but had a hard time of it. 'I don't know this person. Besides, I'm married and I have five children to prove it.'

Juneja tried again. 'You know the Talwar family?'

'Talwar family?'

A sidekick butted in. 'I think he means the Talwars, you know, the people whose daughter died.'

Singh's face cleared to plain lewd. 'Pinky Baby?'

Juneja looked mystified but Joseph came to the rescue. 'Yes, sir. Her pet name was Pinky.'

'When did you last meet Pinky?'

Singh looked thunderstruck. Lewd gone. Clearly this required analysis. 'I don't know.'

'Weren't you going to get married in November?'

'No. I told you, I'm married.'

Juneja changed tracks. 'How do you know her?'

'She's the daughter of Talwar sahib. His father was an old friend of my grandfather. Pinky Baby came here with her father to pick up mangoes. The next-door plantation belongs to them. We take care of it for them. Our mangoes are very good. You want some?'

Juneja paused to think. Bloody fools, unable to even carry on a conversation – Joseph, Sajjan Kumar and now this goon. What should he say? Yes, I want mangoes later.

'Yes, I will take mangoes later.'

Singh looked flattered. In a lewd way.

'But first tell me, weren't you going to marry her?'

'But Inspector, I'm married!'

Juneja felt the familiar wave of helplessness rising, 'Okay, but did you want to marry her?'

Singh tried again – evidently this policeman was slow on the take. 'Inspector, she was a child AND I'm married.'

Juneja took a deep breath but Joseph spoke up before he could expel it. 'Mr Singh, who was Pinky Baby going to marry?'

Pratap Singh was amazed. He'd thought the bald fellow was the boss but the other one was apparently the chief. His English was impeccable!

'There was some plan for her marriage but we were not told any details. Do you want any mangoes? Sir?'

Juneja cut in, 'When were you told about these plans?'

'It's like this. Last month Talwar sahib came with his daughter to pick up the mangoes. She was very happy and dancing around everywhere. So we asked, what was the happiness about. Then she said we shouldn't tell any one but she was going to be married. It was her secret. You know she was a child, we didn't take it seriously, what would she know about marriage? These children don't understand anything.'

He paused and bellowed threateningly to the side, 'You bloody cow, do we have to tell you again, that we have guests? Where's the tea? Or do we have to make it?'

At that moment the woman who had been tending to the cows made an entry. She looked at Pratap Singh. 'If you don't want your guests to drink shit, then shut up. I have only two hands and both of them have been up a buffalo's ass!'

The entire company including the far-off women and Sajjan Kumar collapsed with mirth. Joseph had only partly understood her accented Hindi and looked askance at Juneja, who in turn sat frozen to the spot. Was there no end to these humiliations? Was this what he'd become a policeman for? These ghastly crude people and their even coarser sense of humour. Juneja closed his eyes. Ye gods, she was going to make tea!

'What else did Pinky say?'

'Pinky? Oh, Pinky. She said she was going to get married but it was a secret. That was all. We thought it was a joke. You know how children are. We didn't say anything to Talwar sahib. In any case, it's not our place to say anything. They are big people. How can we ask them anything?'

Juneja heard a threatening clink of cups in the background. 'Come on, show us the mangoes, or was that just a joke? The Talwars told us they are very good.' They had to be better than the tea!

They walked over to the plantation some boys were lounging around and were promptly ordered by Singh to climb the huge trees. The mangoes were large and smelled ripe. Pratap Singh swilled one in a bucket of water and tore it apart with his teeth before offering it to Juneja.

Juneja blanched and stepped aside, gesturing towards Sajjan Kumar and Joseph, both of whom eagerly took a half each.

'Excellent mangoes!' praised Joseph. Sajjan Kumar nodded, his mouth too full to speak. Singh beamed. 'All of you will get some!'

Laden with mangoes, they made their way back to the waiting jeep. A bunch of little boys was herding back a mass of black buffaloes. As Juneja closed the door, one lifted its tail, showing bulging pink flesh and released a mass of viciously green excreta that copiously sprayed the door.

'Let's go back, Sajjan Kumar.'

The mango party disbanded in front of the police station. It was just before five. Juneja walked straight from the parking lot to his own car and shot off without a backward glance. He'd been silent on the way back. There wasn't very much to say.

The morning brought little respite. The sun blazed on, Juneja's headache gnawed on and Saudamini Talwar remained unmarried, pregnant and dead. Juneja arrived at the station at nine o'clock. Instead of waiting for Jt. Comm. Gupta to summon him, he went directly to the Commissioner's office. No, the big boss wasn't in as yet, but yes, he would be told that Juneja had developments to report.

Juneja retired to his room. His head had been pounding since the disastrous meeting with Pratap Singh. The Talwars had wanted him out of the way. They had led him up the garden path and now he was sitting pretty counting flowers, waiting to be sacked. Why had they lied to him about Pratap Singh? Lovely boy, they'd called him. It didn't matter how rich you were or how distanced from reality,

Singh was a local goon. The idea of anyone marrying him was appalling. Five children, he'd said. Juneja closed his eyes at the thought of so many fecund Pratap Singh Juniors polluting the planet for generations to come. Why were goons so brutally potent? To say nothing of his own neighbour. Yesterday the brat had appeared again, calling him 'uncle'. Juneja had glared at him so savagely that he'd run away whimpering.

He cheered up at the memory and tried to come back to the task on hand. What should or could he do now?

The Talwars had themselves, voluntarily, offered the scapegoat of Pratap Singh. He was firmly married. Married to a woman who put her hands up buffalo posteriors *and* answered back Singh in public. Unlikely that he would lie in such circumstances. Pratap Singh was a common enough name – but not that address. He'd got it from the Talwar brothers personally. No possibility of a mistake there.

So it was the right person. Yet it wasn't. Even if Pratap Singh hadn't been married, the idea of Saudamini Talwar or dear Pinky Baby marrying him was ridiculous. Such things might happen in the West perhaps. Rich Princess Marries Stableboy. Here they didn't speak the same language – literally. Saudamini Talwar could not have been expected to milk buffaloes or to muck out a cow shed. They lived in separate eras.

When he'd been in Europe, Juneja had been been appalled at the ease with which people consorted with bus drivers and their ilk. Waiters, taxi drivers, postmen, vegetable sellers – the low life wasn't quite as low as it was in India.

No wonder liberated diplomats were pawing the domestic staff in Delhi in that silly way. They evidently thought servants could sit at the table with them. Any number of foreigners had told Juneja how sweet or cute or shy their servant was. So different from the rest. Only to come weeping to him in the end, saying they'd been burgled silly. He'd always had to hold himself back. Juneja knew that slaves are slaves and masters, masters – sometimes bastards but always masters.

The Talwars also knew this. It was part of the breeding process. It made you Indian. An understanding of the finest social nuances. Cleaner of bathrooms, sweeper, servant, maid, senior servant, cook, watchman, driver, secretary, PA, subordinates, children, and finally your wife. Depending on how many of those you had. In that ascending order. All below you, you Tarzan; all above you, you Jane.

That in this hierarchy, money and qualifications tended to go together was coincidental. Like blacks being slaves. Had history deemed otherwise, they'd have been blonde slaves.

Pratap Singh was a senior servant. An old trusted family retainer. No more, no less. For him no further upward mobility was possible. Unless he suddenly became a millionaire. Juice vendors could become billionaires, so it *could* happen. But it wasn't very likely. Though it was certainly more likely than the daughter of the house falling in love with him, and much more likely than the family actually approving match.

That Pratap Singh hadn't grovelled enough was another disturbing factor, Juneja ruminated. Neither in front of Juneja nor in the face of the Talwar family. When Saudamini Talwar's identity had been established, he'd merely said that he was married and that she was a child. He should actually have said that she was far above his station and a flower to his dung, gold to his tin etc. etc. and that the question didn't arise and *then* said, O Great Policeman, she was just a beautiful, tender child, like a sister/daughter to me and incidentally, this insignificant person also has a wife and five children – not that that or they matter. Had this been his idea of standing up to Juneja in front of his cohorts or was he a self-confident hooligan or was there an altogether deeper, devious reason for his behaviour, like his being able to blackmail the Talwars?

The telephone rang. Female nasal tones told him he could pay his respects to the commissioner now. It was 12. Juneja dragged himself to his feet.

Outside Joseph was waiting. He'd been anxiously looking out for Juneja. Juneja had given him and Sajjan Kumar all the mangoes. He had taken none for himself. When Joseph asked him about the bicycle, he'd nodded. Because he'd looked so tired, Joseph hadn't wanted to press any further. The journey back had been rather morose despite the fruitful booty. It had been clear to everyone that this long journey to the ends of the city had been useless. Sajjan Kumar had done his best to get them back to the station as soon as possible, but the crowds had been dense and rowdy.

Joseph had gone home in a pensive mood. Maybe Juneja was a devil with a heart of gold. He would have liked to show Juneja that he understood, that Juneja had to play the hardhearted boss.

At home the children had been wide-eyed at the sight of such huge mangoes. And so many of them! Although they regularly bought fruit (the nuns said it was healthy), it tended to be bananas because of the price factor. In summer Joseph would indulge the kids with mangoes but considering what mangoes cost, the kids would choose ice-cream for the same price. That night, after a sumptuous dinner, the children had happily done their homework and gone to bed without a fuss. Not that Kamla Doris or Jamuna Elizabeth were difficult, Mary would glare, it was Glorious. Joseph had spoilt her rotten, she would grumble.

Joseph and Mary had also had a relaxed evening. Mary had peeled an extra mango for him and fed him with her own hands. He blushed at the memory. She was so wonderful!

He'd asked Mary what she thought of Juneja. She'd said, maybe he was all the time under pressure. Like Joseph, maybe he also had a hard time fitting in. After all, he wasn't a typical policeman like Sinha or Sajjan Kumar, was he? He'd not answered. How could he tell her that the rest of the policemen loathed Juneja for being arrogant and uniformly rude? He was having difficulty figuring out what he himself believed.

And here was Juneja, looking so tired and depressed. Joseph caught up with him and ran forward to open the door to the office of the Jt. Commissioner. He had taken a special prayer for him from Mary.

'So, Juneja, what progress do you have to report? Joseph, we'll call you when we need you, all right?'

So that's the way it was going to be. Brass tacks and straight to business and no small talk.

Juneja burnt. He hadn't been asked to sit down and Gupta was looking at him with almost the same insolence that that idiot Pratap Singh had confronted him with yesterday.

'I went to see the supposed fiancé of Saudamini Talwar yesterday. He can't be her fiancé. He's married and has five children. Also, he's an old family retainer.' Gupta would understand this logic.

'So who is the father?'

'I don't know.'

Gupta allowed the silence to develop. He turned to his file, fiddled with a button, took a telephone call from his wife and all the time refused to meet Juneja's eyes.

'This case exploded six days ago and you don't know. What do you know?'

Juneja found himself speaking through clenched teeth. 'Sir, I have visited Devyani and Raghav Talwar – that is the youngest brother and his wife. They say that the family wanted the girl to hurry up and get married so that the niece could get married. The daughter of the oldest brother. The industrialist family Malhotra has expressed an interest, they said.

'The older brothers gave me the name of Pratap Singh, whom we saw yesterday.'

'And he is not the father of the child? Yes, this has already been established.' Gupta looked through his files and papers again, leaving Juneja to stew.His anger had given way to confusion. What should he have done? And why was Gupta being so...so professional? Where was the avuncular idiot?

'Sit down, Juneja. I told you before about being professional. You only think with your head. You don't see what is in front of you. Did you really think that you can ask a question and these fellows will tell you?' Gupta sat back in chair. His eyes looked amused although his mouth was under control.

'Arre Juneja, you turn on the English accent and shoot off some questions. All right, that impresses some people.

You get some local thugs and some other riffraff. The Talwars are neither.'

Juneja tried to answer, but his terribly dry throat didn't allow him to. In any case, Gupta was already holding up an admonishing hand. 'Be quiet and listen to me, Juneja. I am like your father. In fact, you should see your father, but that is a different story.

'If you want to go far in this business, you will have to learn to deal with people like the Talwars. You don't become Head of Delhi Police by catching a pickpocket. Even if you catch a hundred it won't matter. But one single Talwar case will always make headlines.

'So tell me, why haven't you spoken to the women of the house?'

Juneja who had begun by turns to seethe and sulk was caught off guard. 'Women?'

'Yes, Juneja, the women. Good, you spoke to Devyani Talwar. But she doesn't live in the same house. What about the other women?' Gupta looked at Juneja, speaking slowly, as if he was talking to an imbecile.

'What should I say to them?'

'Juneja, I keep telling you. This is still India. Not your dream America or any such silly place. Women talk to women, not to men. Do you really think that between going to the office and working, those men had anything to do with their sister? Their wives sit at home the entire day, surely they must have some idea what their sister-in-law did, who she met, by God, who she whored around with!'

Juneja gulped. What was wrong with Gupta? Where had the kindly uncle gone?

'Sir, I mean she was 23...'

'Yes, Juneja, she was 23 and she was pregnant. She was unmarried and she was pregnant. If she was my daughter or my sister I would have horsewhipped her. By God, what is the world coming to? Obviously these foolish fellows gave you the name of some fellow, saying he was going to marry her. Next time you meet him, he will say it himself and so will his wife! Never mind the fifty children. He doesn't need to leave them now, does he?

'The point is, the Opposition will not let the Talwars get away with it. And even more importantly, they will not let us get away with it. We have to act. We have to *know* how to act. Before you find out who to arrest, you need to know who not to....'

Gupta broke off in mid-sentence to take yet another call from his wife. Evidently they had house guests. Juneja gulped discreetly, trying to get his throat to work again. What should he do now? What was Gupta saying? Was there money to be made here? Was Gupta honest or was he testing Juneja?

Juneja shot off his first question, the moment Gupta put down the receiver. 'Sir, how can I ask the women anything? The men always answer.'

'Juneja, tell me something. Are you at all Indian? Don't you understand anything about the way Indian homes work? You cannot wish away your own roots by pretending they don't exist. But this you will find out for yourself.

'Take Joseph with you, he should talk to the staff. Go to the house when the men are at work. Who do you think will receive you? Huh? Talk to these women the way you would speak to your gossipy aunt. Curl up on the sofa under a quilt and chat with them. Drink tea, not beer. Eat samosas, not bloody sandwiches. Listen to what they say.

Listen to what they want to say. Do you understand what I mean, Juneja?'

Suddenly his demeanour changed. The voice which had been jeering became serious. 'Look, if you can't, all right. I'll get someone else.'

Juneja shook his head. This had never happened to him before. He had been offered cases where others had failed. Never had his competence been questioned before. The Talwar case was a time bomb waiting to explode. The point was where and when it would. In his face or for his face. But the question of giving up the case did not arise.

'No, sir. I'll change my way of, of speaking and of asking questions also. Sir, please don't take away the case from me.'

Gupta refused to make it easier. 'You're sure you can cope with this, Nikhil?'

Oh god, now the first name avuncular crap!

'Yes, sir. I'll start immediately.'

This time Gupta let him go.

Now what?

Joseph came running towards him, worry and concern writ large on his face. The man was genuinely concerned.

'Sir, I have been praying for you. I mean all my family, sir. This...,' he thrust a slip of paper into Juneja's limp, astonished hand, 'you must read and keep it at all times, sir, especially times of trouble.'

Juneja tried for a smile and ran to his office. He cares about me, Juneja thought with a pang and shuddered. Any moment now a small comforting/confiding/or was it a trusting hand would find its way into his. I'm losing it. I am genuinely losing it. No wonder this bloody case is slipping out of my hands. Instead of dealing with murder cases, I'm praying.

He looked at the sweaty slip of pink paper,

The LORD is my shepherd,
I shall not be in want.

He makes me lie down in green pastures,
He leads me beside quiet waters,
He restores my soul.
He guides me in paths of righteousness
for his name's sake.
Even though I walk through the
valley of the shadow of death,
I will fear no evil, for you are with me;
your rod and your staff,
they comfort me.
You prepare a table before me
in the presence of my enemies.
You anoint my head with oil;
my cup overflows.
Surely goodness and love will follow me
all the days of my life,
and I will dwell in the house of the LORD
forever.

Your rod and your staff comfort me? Was this real? How can I possibly fear evil, when your rod is comforting me? Indeed, my cup is more than running over. Juneja groaned. In fact my brain is running away with itself and my balls.

Be Indian? It was one of those things that was never said. Amend that, had not ever been said. Intersperse it with meaningful pauses and let it rest. But it had been said. How could he possibly throw off the mindset of a lifetime and suddenly accept the greatness of the Indian culture?

Juneja sat down slowly in the big swivel chair and lit up. The chair had been his only addition to the office furniture. Unlike Khurana, who had gone to considerable lengths to personalize his surroundings, Juneja was sure that an office was only a transitional space. If Gupta was right, however, then this was going to be it. Maybe he should start off with potted plants and get ready to get rooted.

The cigarette calmed him down and he reached for the phone. Sinha looked in.

'Get me a coffee.'

If Gupta was right, then all this had to stop. No English, no coffee. The future held Indi-Pop, Bollywood, Chicken Tikka and milky masala tea. What had the past been all about?

Childhood may not have been quite as westernized as he was now making it out to be but there had never been any doubt about the superiority or to be more precise about the desirability of the West. Music was Police, Eagles, Tull. If you were stupid, Abba, but it had never been Kishore Kumar. Why should it be? In a world where speaking English with an Oxonian accent was better than a PhD in Hindi, how could it be? The stupid thing was, if you spoke English, fluently, the way We did, it earned you a lot more money than the Hindi PhD as well. Sure a lot more people speak Tamil or Gujarati than they do Russian but Russia was white. And when you wrote Russian, Microsoft didn't mark it with a curly red line. In fact it was Juneja not Joseph, who was a marked man.

It was Joseph, not Sinha, who popped his head in with the coffee.

'Sir, coffee. I am the only other one, sir, drinking coffee here. It is very good. Much better than the tea. They are boiling the kettle whole day, sir, without changing leaves. It is orange...'

'Thank you, Joseph. I am fine, you know. No need to babble.'

'No, sir, yes, sir. Shall I stay here, sir?'

Juneja smiled. It was a heroic offer to stay in the smoky lair of the dragon.

'No. I'll call you later. We need to look at this case again. I'll work out a new strategy and call you.'

'Yes, sir, okay , sir. I'll be outside, sir.'

'Yes Joseph, go.'

So was this intermission? The Big Pause? That moment in every Hindi film when the hero finds out the beggar he's been spitting on every day is actually his father, and the millionaire he's been ass-licking is the guy responsible for making his erstwhile billionaire beggar dad a pauper? Ergo, second half of film means reducing millionaire bad guy to rubble and adoring spat-upon dad.

Was this his end? Say good-bye to your life, Nikhil, say hello to India. To festivities and tradition, culture and family, responsibility and shackles, Daddy and arranged marriages, relationships and subtexts, religion and ash-smeared foreheads.

It wasn't that any of this *really* bothered him. It just disturbed him. Slightly. Only very slightly. Otherwise he was totally under control.

It was the lack of dignity, the lack of possibilities, the lack of reason. How come Western kids spoke about sex to their parents and that was fine, but Indian children came with the stork? None of his acquaintances had learned the facts of life from anyone other than *Playboy*. Now that's real tradition. From secretive father to secretive son. Rajiv's father had hidden his copies in the small temple in the storeroom, under the deity. Considering the mother cleaned the room, she must have known.

Or maybe *that* had been the idea, contemplated Juneja. Maybe *that* had been the bloody idea the whole time. A hidden code. Leave the magazine open at the desired position. Talk, the only four-letter word for intercourse, that Indian couples didn't indulge in.

Was that his future? All fucking, no talking? No English, all Hindi? He looked down at the crumpled pink slip. Their God spoke English and didn't have a problem if trouser-wearing women prayed to him after eating meat. He didn't have a problem if you didn't have kids, if you heard rock music or had long hair, hell, he'd done it all himself. No kids, long hair, hung out with tarts, didn't speak Sanskrit, the list was endless.

That was the other thing. The western God lives in church. Huge Gothic churches and modern, crappy ones. Indian gods live in storerooms, kitchen corners and, in particularly inspired cases, kitchen cupboards. They also live in huge, crappy temples. The big beautiful ones were all monuments, not places of worship. So Indians who were spiritually further advanced, found gods only in cupboards, stores and carnival-inspired temples. Was it being Indian to do this or was it being Indian, if one chose to reject the temple and looked for Indian culture in the monuments?

The new cigarette tasted as foul as the last but at least provided a change of thought.

Why could one smoke in front of one's wife and kids but not in front of your father? How could smoking be *disrespectful*? It was bad for your lungs but how was it a lack of respect and why only to the Indian elders? Why were women who smoked loose moralled or fast? Were male smokers slow? Or faster?

He closed his eyes against the tide of smoke.

His throat was uncomfortably dry and the untouched coffee was already tepid.

He moved the spoon carefully, easing the thick, milky skin unbroken out of the brown liquid. The coffee was like the tea. A stew. Cook milk and water in equal parts, add sugar and coffee till a spoon can stand in it, voila, you have Indian Nescafe. Unknown to the grateful Rest of Non-Indian. The RNIs. A dying species. The entire world was being invaded by Indians. They smelled and stank up the room while they were at it. Now they were knocking on his door. They could smell the non-Indian air inside through the crack in the door. They were knocking, no, battering at the door. His head pounded. They were breaking down the door, they were in–Aaaaaaaaaaaaaaaargh!

'Sir, you called?'

'No, Joseph, the, the... I stubbed my toe against the table. I'll let you know when I need you. And get me another cup of coffee.'

Juneja waited at the window till Joseph had exited after bringing the second cup in. He sipped it before the skin and any funny ideas could form again.

Okay, Nikhil, nice to know you can get in touch with your female side at a pinch. Now start working.

'Okay, Joseph, get in here.'

When Joseph walked in, Juneja was opening the windows to ventilate the room a little. The cross-ventilation blew the papers off the table. The pink slip fluttered to the floor. Joseph quickly picked it up before any one stepped on it. It would be a bad omen if some one walked on Juneja's prayer.

Juneja's room was full of smoke. Although the poor man was airing it, it still stank. Juneja had been locked up inside his office since his meeting with Gupta sir. How he could drink so many cups of coffee in this heat amazed Joseph. That was one thing he really missed. Green coconuts. Nothing like them in summer. In Delhi there was only the awful sugarcane juice. The stuff itself wasn't bad. But the flies, the dirt were awful. He'd been aghast to see the enthusiasm with which Mary leapt upon it. At night they slept on wet sheets. The sheets dried in minutes. The trick was to fall asleep while they were still cool. During the day there was little respite to be had. The girls tried to stand in front of air-conditioned shops. Every time a customer opened the door, for a short second they'd be in paradise! Then there was the dust. Mary fought a losing battle against the thick yellow dust that was everywhere. When the wind blew, it was hard to tell if it was a blessing or a curse. It dried the sweat and replaced it with a crust of acrid, salty dust.

He wasn't surprised that everyone was so short-tempered in this heat. No wonder Gupta sir had been so curt with him. The heat drove everyone mad. Only Juneja had become more bearable. Maybe he was the Devil and living in hell made him feel better.

Joseph gulped. Maybe that was it. Juneja was a devil. Not Satan, of course, he didn't seem senior enough. The mangoes could have been a way of tempting his soul or maybe it was just hot and he was out of his mind. Mary would laugh at him. Either way, she wasn't here and it couldn't hurt if he crossed himself.

Juneja turned from the window to see Joseph looking tremulous. He was holding the rod-cupping prayer. His hand was moving towards his head. Juneja blinked. Was Joseph trying to bless him? He turned back to the window. He should feel touched but he didn't. This ghastly maudlin Indian spirituality turned his stomach. Which in turn made him feel guilty. If a fellow prayed for you, you have to be grateful in some way or at least look it.

'Okay, Joseph, before I forget, come to my house tomorrow. Sinha will give you the directions. I'll get the cycle cleaned up. Come at nine o'clock tomorrow, okay?'

Joseph was stunned. Was this another temptation or was Juneja actually a misunderstood saint? He must give a noncommittal answer. After all, one can't risk the Eternal Soul for a bicycle.

He choked.

Juneja looked the other way. He felt sick.

'Look Joseph, have a look at the bicycle first. Maybe it's the wrong colour or size or whatever. Come over on Saturday and then we'll see, all right?

'Now we need to get down to this case. We will go back to the house today. I want you to talk to the domestic help. Find out what they have to say about Saudamini.'

'The deceased, sir.'

'Yes, Joseph, yes, the deceased, the very same. Her name was Saudamini. The name means a hundred volts of lightning in Sanskrit.'

This was rubbish. Juneja didn't know Sanskrit to save his life. But Sau meant a hundred in Hindi. And he knew that Damini meant lightning. A nightclub dancer he'd once met had called herself Damini. She claimed she'd cause thunderstorms between his legs. It had been a gentle rain – not too bad.

But it was sure to impress Joseph.

Joseph *was* impressed. Juneja must be a highly educated man.

'So, Joseph, you will find out what the domestics think of the situation in the house. What is the relationship between the people in that house? Do you understand what I mean?'

Actually it was Juneja who wasn't sure what he was saying or demanding. He'd never had to give instructions of this kind. Sinha or Sajjan Kumar were not people you could give instructions to. Only commands.

Sajjan Kumar thought with his dick. Saudamini Talwar could therefore only be seen in some sort of sex light.

Since she was dead, Sajjan Kumar couldn't screw her. That was the end of his thought process.

Sinha was incapable of thought. He could fetch files and coffee. And cigarettes.

Juneja had never needed this sort of information before. His cases had been the kind, that could be handled with the sort of commands he could give Sinha or Sajjan Kumar. Screw her, bring the file and some cigarettes. Or screw her and bring the file, while you're at it. Sajjan Kumar had in a rare confiding moment informed Juneja that given the chance he would swing both ways. After all, one doesn't get many chances and one does become lonely, he'd added bashfully. Sajjan Kumar could drive as well. He drove probably the same way that he had sex. Juneja drew in a deep breath. Was he seriously thinking about Sajjan Kumar's sex technique?

Joseph rose to the occasion. 'I will get the inside story, sir. Servants see a lot of what happens in the house, sir. But this one fellow, sir, they are asking him for dowry. Sir, this is against the law. Dowry is a crime, sir.' As the father of three girls, dowry was a crime Joseph felt particularly passionate about.

Juneja felt reassured. Clearly success was destined to be his. Playing Sherlock Holmes was getting him nowhere. This bumbling fool was going to be the end of him.

'Joseph, get me a coffee, okay?'

Juneja collapsed in his chair after Joseph had gone. Maybe he should take Sajjan Kumar instead? He'd screw the shit out of all the domestics and make sure they signed whatever fantasy Juneja had concocted by then.

It was the last option. If nothing else, one could get a scapegoat. A servant raped her and then killed her. They'd have problems with Khurana, but quite frankly, in a case of this magnitude, money would play no role. Gupta himself would have to intervene and make sure that Khurana shut up. Or maybe Khurana already had. Why whould he otherwise not release the information about her pregnancy?

Joseph returned with the coffee to find Juneja looking calmer.

'Tell Sajjan Kumar to get the car out. We'll leave in fifteen minutes and...'

The telephone rang. Nasal tones demanded he appear again in Gupta's office.

Leaving Joseph with the coffee, he walked out into a wall of noise outside his room. The police station looked like a rubbish heap crossed with the interstate bus terminal, which was a garbage dump. The corridors were lined with files, piled one on top of the other. Over the years the heaps had begun to reach the ceiling. Indian wallpaper, some wise guy had called it. The few windows the builders had allowed, were grey. People were everywhere. Policemen, minions, peons, secretaries or PAs, as they were called, and of course the public. The Honourable Public. The police were the servants of the public. Servants, masters, secretaries, everyone was screaming. Maybe it was the heat, or the fact that no one was listening anyway.

The public's screams were mostly of supplication. Please, please, please take down my report so that I can get a new driving license issued. The entire thing was so farcical and the police so corrupt. Most people preferred to get a new license/bus pass/ ID card or whatever it was they had lost. To go to a police station, endure lecherous glances, nudges and innuendos and then pay a bribe for the privilege was more than most of their Public Masters could bear.

The policemen in turn, were screaming to be heard and also because roaring became them. Besides, if you're taking the pants off someone in public, you might as well get as much attention as possible. Take down your bloody report? Can't you see it's my official lunch break? What do you mean you're here for the third time today? Are you saying I don't do any work? You can file a complaint. The complaint book is always available to the public. The last utterance was accompanied by a leer of gigantic proportions.

Juneja smiled. At least here things were normal. Police work, the way it should be done. Not guesswork and silly running around, the way Gupta wanted him to do.

At the commissioner's office, the PA informed him that Gupta had gone for his lunch break and left a note for him.

'Nikhil, the Talwar brothers claim they have found a letter from their sister, saying she loved a man called Kartik Varma. He is the father of her child and she would rather die than marry Pratap Singh. Kindly confirm.'

Juneja confirmed it silently. He too would rather die than marry Pratap Singh. He turned to the waiting PA.

'Joseph is in my office. Tell him to get Sajjan Kumar and the jeep. I'll see them outside.'

The drive to the Talwar house was mercifully short. The heat was driving Juneja nuts. It was high time he got an AC-d police car.

They were automatically waved in through the gates. Sajjan Kumar looked inquiringly and beseechingly at Juneja, who heaved a sigh. 'All right. Joseph, you take him with you. Sajjan Kumar, I expect you to be polite. Try and get some information out of them, all right? About this chicken thing, okay ?'

Sajjan Kumar grinned and grunted assent.

Dizzy from the heat, Juneja strolled into the house. The servant marched him up to the landing. There was no one there. Juneja ordered a chilled glass of water. 'I want ice cubes in the water, okay ? You understand? Not just fridge water. Make it with ice, do you understand?'

'Sahib, the ice is finished.'

'What the hell do you mean? You want me to get you fired? You lazy sods keep all the ice for yourself. Get more ice, understand? Now move it, move it, fast!'

N.K. Talwar entered on this unfortunate note. His raised eyebrows made Juneja feel slightly uncomfortable. Ordering other people's servants around was bad form, but what the hell, he hadn't got this bloody girl knocked up and you never knew, maybe this ghastly skinny servant had. Bastard, serves him right. All these fellows were the bloody same!

'Is there a problem?'

'Not at all, or there wouldn't be if your servants didn't think getting a glass of cold water in this weather to be an affront to their dignity!'

'Ram Singh, get the water. Immediately.'

'Yes, sahib, I'll get it immediately.'

Juneja waited till the man returned with his glass of water. It was cold but there was no ice in it. Juneja contented himself with a savage glare and turned the same glowering face to Mr N bloody K.

'So a new letter has surfaced, has it?'

There was no trace of appeal or supplication on N.K. Talwar's face. 'I don't understand what there is to be so surprised about. I knew from the beginning that this could only be suicide. My poor sister was so mortified at her mistake that to save the family's honour she committed suicide. I don't know what kind of doctors the police employs. Maybe it's a political conspiracy against us. The Opposition...'

Juneja interrupted him rather wearily. 'Look Mr Talwar, there is nothing wrong with the police doctors. They are highly qualified people and they haven't made a mistake. Your sister cannot have committed suicide. Do you understand me? Can not,' said Juneja, enunciating clearly. The time had arrived to expound on the intricacies of modal verbs.

'Do you understand me, Mr Talwar? "Can" means to possess the *physical* ability. The physical ability, Mr Talwar. So it's not the question, "can you tell me the time", it's "will you", if you're polite, "would you". Subjunctive, you know? It's not "can I come in?". Of course you *can*. The question is, of course, if you *may*. May you...'

'Juneja, what are you talking about?'

'Mr Talwar, she could not have killed herself. She was bound. She was hit on the head. BEFORE she died. Now, you please tell me how she managed to hit herself on the head and then tie herself up and then jump on a chair and finally hang herself?'

'She was tied up and then hit on the head?'

Juneja was taken aback. The somewhat crass description of his sister's death didn't seem to disturb N.K. Talwar overtly. His inquiry had been quite unperturbed. Almost as if he were ascertaining facts. Facts perhaps hitherto unknown to him, but not facts that really meant anything to him.

'Yes, Mr Talwar. She was tied and hit. Hit on the head. And then someone strung her up and murdered her. In cold blood...'

'Juneja, you're talking about my sister and I would appreciate it if you showed some consideration for my feelings. Please note, "would". The subjunctive, you said, hmm?'

Touché? No, it's only check, Mr Talwar. In other words, only half touché, a passing shot, a flesh wound.

'Yes, Mr Talwar, the subjunctive. I'm glad you can discuss your sister's death so objectively.' Another half touché, Mr Talwar, but for me this time and wait for the second half because here it bloody well comes. 'I appreciate it very much. But I don't appreciate getting information at the last minute. Especially misinformation. Wrong information,' added Juneja, for emphasis.

'You sent us off to meet Pratap Singh. Pratap Singh, who had never heard of his marriage to your sister. Pratap Singh, who is married and has five children. Who shows no sign of getting divorced and also shows no sign of any kind of discord with his wife. So Mr Talwar, if you want me to consider your feelings and I would be subjunctively happy to, why did you send me to Pratap Singh?' Double the half touché, makes one full fatal touché for me.

'Juneja, you're being ridiculous. Do you really think I lied to you? You think if any one had touched a hair on Pinky's head, I wouldn't have their rip their head off? My God, Juneja, my father would rip my own head off, if I didn't!'

Juneja screwed up his eyes. Reel, reel under my touché. Reel, damn you, what the hell are you babbling about?

N.K. ran a hand through his thick hair. Bastard.

'Look Juneja, I told you about Pratap because this is what Pinky herself told me.'

'Pinky told you that she wanted to marry that goon and has now written a letter that she would rather die than marry him? Was your sister a schizophrenic? Or just mad?'

'Mind your bloody tongue!' N.K. glared at him. 'This is no way to talk about my sister. She was an innocent...' He drew in a deep breath. 'It's a bit complicated, Juneja.'

Tell me about it and reel while you're at it.

Oblivious to Juneja's sullen derision, N.K. continued, 'She came to me some time back and said she was in love with Pratap Singh. As you know, he's an old family retainer. We were quite taken aback. But Pinky was adamant. We thought, after some time the infatuation will blow over. Then Pinky went to my wife, Roma, and told her they had made a small mistake and had not been able to wait. So we had no choice. If that was what the two of them wanted, I said, we will fix it with Pratap's wife and everything else as well.

'Now I think Pinky lied about Pratap in her desperation. Then when she saw that we would arrange the marriage, she got into a panic. She felt caught in her web of lies and that drove her to this extreme step.'

'Your sister had another lover? A lover whom she didn't tell you about? She was pregnant by him but thought you would prefer it if her lover was Pratap Singh? Mr Talwar, I would believe you, I'd like to, but I've met Pratap Singh. I have seen him. He's a local thug. What kind of man is her real lover that she thought you'd prefer Pratap Singh? A Mafia don?'

'My sister was a child, Juneja, she was very simple. I don't think she realized what kind of lies she was telling.'

N.K. sat back heavily. He tried to wobble his chin but it wouldn't play along. He went in for hard swallowing instead, and gave Juneja a supplicating look.

Juneja refused to have any of it. 'And you knew from your wife, Roma, that your sister was pregnant?'

N.K. looked the other way.

'Answer me, Mr Talwar. You knew. So why pretend to be surprised, when we told you?'

'Juneja, have you seen the film *Sholay*? A man in it says, the hardest thing for a man to bear is the coffin of his son. Pinky was like my own child. She was twenty years younger. My God...' he broke off as the wobble perfected itself. He swallowed and manfully continued, 'it was terrible, terrible.

'When Roma told me, I couldn't believe it. My baby, she was like a flower, a blossoming flower. I didn't tell my brothers or my father. I'm the oldest son, Juneja, and it's a very heavy burden to bear. And at times like this I, no we, we all miss the guiding hand of our father. He would have been like a rock between the world and us. Nothing like this would have happened if he had been at home. But now, this has happened.' He buried his head in his hands. 'What face should I show my father when he comes home?'

Juneja looked at him. The man was going to start weeping. Judging by the choked squeaks, he already was.

Juneja got up. 'I'll be back in a couple of hours, Mr Talwar. We need to talk again.'

Joseph and Sajjan Kumar were sitting on the steps in front. They looked extremely hot and upset.

'What the hell are you doing here? Why didn't you go down to the kitchen?'

Joseph had leapt to his feet and looked not unlike an indignant pig. 'Sir, we told, we told. But that fellow was very rude and said he didn't have any time for us because he had to go and buy ice. Can you imagine, sir, he left us sitting here! Didn't even give us any water!'

Sajjan Kumar hung his head and looked sad. It would have been a new experience for him to go inside such a big house. That too, air-conditioned.

It was always the same. You give crap to someone's servants. Their servants give crap to your servants. But his servants were the police. The Police.

'Don't worry, Joseph, we'll get back here in a couple of hours and then we'll take these idiots apart. Sajjan Kumar, let's go to the nearest canteen. I'll buy you guys lunch.'

Sajjan Kumar knew every canteen in the vicinity of Delhi. Juneja had personally harassed every single waiter, cook and canteen owner who had ever crossed his way. It was a marriage made in heaven. Joseph looked on stunned from the sidelines.

It was past the lunch hour. But of course, of course cringing of course, there was fresh food. No, no, not leftovers. Nothing of the sort. They would cook again. Now, immediately. Obviously Juneja, their most treasured customer, could not be kept waiting on an empty stomach for so long. No, no and these wonderful people he had brought with him...Mr Sajjan Kumar, was in any case the apple of their eye. Why not just their eye, every canteen owner's eye. Of course it was their pleasure, their honour, their spittle-licking delight to provide him with some small refreshments. And this handsome young man? Mr Joseph is his name? Welcome, Mr Joseph, welcome! So very pleased to meet you! Why have you not brought your families? Mr wonderful Sajjan Kumar had once brought his lovely family! Four boys, two girls and one bashful wife and his honourable mother. How assertive she had been, not at all shy, these old ladies, nowadays. No, no, she had marched into the kitchen and told the cooks how to cook. How grateful they had all been. And the boys had overturned a pot and drunk four bottles of coke each! Boys will be boys after all, the darlings. Whose sons were they after all? Just like their manly dad! Mr Joseph must bring his family too. Expense, what expense? It was every canteen owner's secret (and now not so secret) dream to serve Mr Juneja, the Great Mr Juneja and his associate Mr Sajjan Kumar. It was on the house, this house and every other house as well.

Nonplussed, Joseph sat down at a polished table, specially wiped with a filthy wet rag. Chilled Pepsi bottles were placed before them. Juneja had ordered Sajjan Kumar and him to sit separately. Was this a bribe? Was it a bribe, when you took no money? Or gave no money? If you gave no money, that you should have given, then you were keeping money, that you would otherwise have spent, weren't you? That was a bribe, wasn't it?

Sajjan Kumar looked quite befuddled at Joseph's logic. 'Look, Joseph, we wouldn't have paid in any case. I have been working with Juneja sir for a long time.' This was true. Although the general opinion was that Juneja was a bastard, Sinha and Sajjan Kumar had been his core team for a long time. Everyone knew that Sinha sir was, well, a bit lazy, and Sajjan Kumar just was.

Sajjan Kumar continued, 'He can be quite a pain but he always pays. When you go out with him, he always pays.' *Always*, the third time for even more emphasis.

'Look, Joseph, when we got the mangoes, I knew he wouldn't take them. He never does. It's like he takes the bribe but he doesn't. And Sinha sir said to me that if he is taking it, then we are not taking it, are we? You can't be taking the same thing two times. We are taking it from him and that is not a bribe. Why should Juneja sir bribe us? You tell me that.'

Joseph shook his head. This was Delhi. A big city with big problems. Questions that had no answers. Juneja took the bribe but didn't keep it. They got the bribe but didn't ask for it. If they were caught by the Anti Corruption Bureau, who did they catch?

Joseph thoughtfully bit into his reheated samosa. The owner had apologised for it. But till the fresh food came, maybe they could make do with this. The owner, called 'hey you' by Juneja, had also switched the usual Hindi film music off. Juneja had said so. Fans had been brought to their tables. Juneja had said so. The salad was to be washed and the hands of the people who made it were also to be washed. Juneja had said so. Joseph was amazed. Was this also taking a bribe?

He had often had to pull Mary away from such an enticing wafts. The flies also find the smell lovely, he'd joke with her. Jamuna Elizabeth and Kamla Doris would also nod. This is what the nuns said too. But Glorious, who had just started school, was easily led astray. Mary would smile smugly. She knew he couldn't say no to Glorious Godaveri. But he would say no rather than ask, no, order the owner to make fresh food or move the fans or put off the loud music he didn't understand. Not that the girls would agree to the last in any case.

Besides, where no money had exchanged hands, who would they believe? Who was to know that Juneja had ordered them to move the fans? Maybe they had done it of their own free will. And even if one ordered them to move a fan and turn off the music, was that corruption? Misuse of power, misuse of position? Was it corrupt to demand that food be hygienic or that water be clean?

Sajjan Kumar mock-boxed him on the arm. 'C'mon Joseph, yaar, stop worrying about these things. Juneja sir will take care of us. He might be a bastard but he won't hurt you.'

'Why not, Sajjan Kumar? If the Anti Corruption Bureau catches us, maybe Juneja will say it was us? What will happen then?'

'Joseph, are you mad or what? The ACB because of a bloody samosa? Are you mad? Have they ever caught anyone? They catch as many people as we do!', Sajjan Kumar guffawed.

'Sajjan Kumar, you are a clown,' retorted Joseph severely and grinned. There was no point being serious with this man.

At his own table near the window, oblivious to this discussion, Juneja angled over another chair with his feet and crossed his legs on it.

The discussion wouldn't have meant much to him in any case. He took bribes as a matter of principle. If he didn't need them himself, he gave it to other needy souls. If they didn't need them, he would keep the bribe till he met someone who did. Like the bicycle. But all bribes were to be taken. That's why one worked, yearned for power. What was the point of having the power and doing nothing with it?

But none of this this was important. The Talwars would be very generous if the case went the way they wanted it to. And that was the point. Which way did they want it to go?

N.K. Talwar had sent him to meet Pratap Singh. Why? Because he had been told by bloody Pinky that Pratap Singh was the father of her unborn child. Which may or may not be true. In fact, both statements were dubitable: had Pinky told him this and was Pratap Singh the father? If he wasn't the father, who was? Kartik Varma? And whose word did he have for that? With any luck Kartik Varma would say that he'd been bonking like a horny rabbit with Ole Pinks. Otherwise he'd have to look for another sucker.

It was the other question that was much more difficult. If Pinky hadn't told N.K. and the family, who had? How had they found out that she was pregnant? That was really the crux of the matter. Her pregnancy.

So what did the Talwars want him to do? Keep quiet about the pregnancy, that was obvious. But if they had wanted to keep quiet about the pregnancy, why not arrange for an abortion? God knows every bloody woman had them.

Delhi was supposed to be one of the most conservative cities in India. Yet the preferred mode of contraception was abortion. All the women Juneja knew had sown so many wild oats that they should have enough muesli for a lifetime by now. Devi was a case in point. She had such a laid-back attitude. Laid back, get it? Juneja snickered, causing the canteen owner to jump to his feet and collapse again in the quivering-heap pose people assumed at the sight of the Juneja–Sajjan Kumar combine.

The food appeared. Decent vegetables, hot dal, and really good rotis straight from the tandoor. Juneja picked up a raw onion and chomped reflectively. The resultant mouth odour would be a handy side effect. Nothing like a stench to squeeze the juice out of N.K.

Juneja burped for dessert and got up to go outside. Joseph wanted to jump to his feet but Sajjan Kumar stopped him. He kissed two fingers silently and kept eating. Joseph looked at him blankly.

Sajjan Kumar grimaced. 'He's going to smoke outside, he always does. If he wanted us to go with him, he'd have said so.'

Joseph was impressed. How gentlemanly!

Outside the canteen, Juneja squinted at the blazing sun and looked for some shade. There was a bougainvillaea tree ablaze in the corner of the courtyard. Just looking at the garish colours made Juneja feel hotter. He hunkered down on the stairs in the open entrance, feeling somewhat discomfited. On the one hand it didn't really go with his image of being the master of all he surveyed, and on the other, the steps weren't too clean. But on the third hand, neither were his trousers. And he was only crouching, not sitting, on the ground. Standing in this bloody sun would kill him even if the fag didn't.

Hygiene, the presence or absence of it, was a useful tool. Like his redolent mouth odour. It helped to keep the classes under control. The masses couldn't care two hoots, they stank in any case, and had developed noses that were amazingly resilient.

People lived in garbage heaps, in slums, they worked in police stations and in the kitchen of this canteen. No one could afford a nose here. On the other hand, people like the Talwars had a nose that could cut through the air like a sword! It could distinguish between the finest perfumes. The onion should have them reeling, wanting him to leave as soon as possible. Juneja grimaced. The stuff had a foul aftertaste. Ah, the sacrifices one made in the line of duty!

Since the interview, he'd been trying to remember something. Something N.K. had said, that didn't make sense. N.K. wanted it to be suicide but Khurana had said it couldn't be. Juneja had been rude to him and insisted it was. He'd said it has to be murder because she had been hit on the head and been tied up. N.K. had blanched and subsequently heaved. Okay, so what was the problem?

Begin with the bloody body, Nikhil. It had been found tied up etc. Khurana had performed the autopsy and said injuries prior to death. Who had found the body? I don't know. His mind went blank. Am I serious? I don't know? How can I not know? Gupta had introduced the case as suicide. Velvet gloves all the way for the Talwar family. Okay, he'd tried to comply. Meanwhile, Khurana had dropped his bomb, forced his hand. Okay maybe it hadn't been Khurana, it had been the Opposition, a foreign conspiracy, the CIA or terrorists – it didn't matter, the affair had been leaked to the press. It was murder. And he'd found sodding nothing since. He'd gone where no man had ever wanted to go, to the lair of Pratap Singh. And had been buggered royally this morning by Gupta. Yet no one knew who had found the body or in what condition? And had Mr I-am-such-a-royal-dick-Juneja just told N.K. Talwar all about it? Juneja lost his crouched balance. The cigarette dropped from his fingers. To stop his fall he put out his hands and found himself on all fours, inhaling the noxious fumes of his own cigarette mingled with odiferous horse shit from someone's shoes.

The canteen owner saw him and came running out. He helped Juneja to his feet. 'Sir, so sorry, sir, I'll sack the sweeper, sir, he is such a lazy bas...' Juneja cut him off with a wave of the hand.

It had been a bad idea from the beginning. Squatting in front of a third-rate canteen, what had he been thinking of? He groaned, making the canteen owner look sicker. Juneja glared at him. 'Get some water. A bottle of Bisleri. Cold. Go.'

What had he been thinking of? How had this happened? In this entire case normal policing had been thrown out of the window. The owner appeared gibbering, with a bottle. Juneja took it. The owner took one look at his grimacing countenance and fled. Juneja didn't notice.

Okay, darling Nikki, before you start to grind, go through the sequence. One more time.

Had he asked? No. Gupta had said something about suicide. At the time there had been no talk of murder. So who cared about the body? Now that it was murder, he'd better find out.

Joseph and Sajjan Kumar sauntered out. Sajjan Kumar looking like Garfield, Joseph bemused. The canteen owner gulped in the background. Juneja sighed. What the hell, make his day, it wouldn't cost him much. He pressed hundred rupees into the quivery hand and left. Joseph looked distinctly complacent, Sajjan Kumar cockeyed.

The drive back to hell began.

Juneja marched into the mansion like he owned it. Sajjan Kumar looked particularly evil. His was a spirit easy to revive. Joseph went in for a self-abasing look – it was second nature to him.

The servant at the door managed to look sullen and triumphant at the same time. 'N.K. sahib has left for the office. He said it was urgent.'

'So who is at home?'

'Only N.K. madam.'

Had the bird flown or had it left the nest unguarded? Go Nikhil, chat with your bloody smelly aunt and get the juice.

'I'll see her.'

'But sahib, she is, she is just finished with lunch. She sleeps in the afternoon.'

'Her sister-in-law has been killed and she can sleep?'

Sajjan Kumar guffawed appreciatively. 'Juneja sir, she must not have liked her very much. All these wives are the same, sir. Hate your mother and don't want to give any dowry for the sister. Maybe she only bumped her off! Saved the dowry.'

Appalled, Joseph tried to intervene, but Juneja and Sajjan Kumar were old hands.

'Is that right? Your mistress had her bumped off?'

'No, sahib, how can you say...'

'How can I say it? I'm only saying it. Your bloody mistress is doing it! You think I sleep when my sister dies? I don't even sleep when N.K. Talwar's sister dies. That's why I'm standing here in front of you, you fool! Now you had gone to get ice, hadn't you?'

Juneja continued without waiting for an answer, 'Then you must have enough now. My fellows, my colleagues will come with you to the kitchen. You will give all of us ice water, okay ? And before that you tell Mrs N.K. Her afternoon nap just got disturbed.'

Juneja smiled meaningfully. The cheesy lines really turned him on. His voice was gentle, tremulous as Barbara Cartland might have said, 'Go, tell her.'

Pause for effect.

'Now.'

Humming softly to himself, Juneja made his way to the landing. No one was there, as expected. He carefully started blowing large breaths of air into the room. Pre-scent the environs for the empress.

The servant appeared with a jug of iced water, looking more sulky than ever. 'Madam is coming. Very bad mood,' he added viciously.

Keep walking, boy, blast her with past victuals. Juneja smiled benevolently back and blew some fragrant air into his face. The servant looked back at him blankly and then left.

Obviously there was no reaction. Poor working class. Jutting lower jaw, narrow forehead, a blunted sense of smell – all distinctions of class. He looked admiringly at his reflection in the window. All right, the forehead was a bit too high now, but it had always been high brow. His well-proportioned jaw made him look like a Roman emperor. And the eyes were piercing. There was no other word for it. He had heard Sinha telling the juniors how Juneja's eyes could bore into you. If that wasn't piercing, what was? Juneja smiled whimsically at himself and discovered from the reflection that he had been joined by a dumpy, short woman, who looked distinctly irritated.

He turned to her. 'Mrs Talwar?'

'Who else would I be?' she answered grumpily and called loudly for the servant, who appeared running.

'Put on the AC, you fool! You want to kill me in this heat? Idiot!'

Juneja was amazed. Mrs N.K. Talwar looked like a square in a sari. She had to be under five feet tall and at least four feet wide. She was as fair as her husband and also had virulently black hair, pulled back into a wispy bun. Devyani's wisps had been carefully contrived. Her sister-in-law looked like she'd been pulled backwards through a hedge. Her sari was cheap nylon. The diamonds, dull and huge, had long passed from the brilliance of sparkling youth into the banality of everyday wear. Ears, nose, neck and three diamond-studded bangles. Some make-up would have improved matters greatly. She looked like a mean white pig.

After the AC was running to her satisfaction, she demanded a glass for herself and settled herself not unlike Madam Heap on the sofa, leaving Juneja no choice but to stand if he wanted to face her, or take his place next to her. He chose to take a wooden chair from the dining table and drew it over.

'Since your husband has gone to work, I will have to speak with you,' he tried.

'All right. Speak with me!'

Let's try the traditional method. 'First of all I want to tell you how much we, in the police, feel for you and your family's loss.'

She snorted. 'What loss? Huh? You tell me what loss? Loss of our good name? If you feel sorry, then, then...' she drew in a deep breath, paused to consider what they could do if they felt sorry, and then it came.

'Then, then understand that Pinky committed suicide to protect our name,' she blew at him a breath that not only smelled of onions but was an onion, the whole onion, the theory and the practice and the abstract idea of an onion.

Juneja swallowed in anguish and felt sick at the aftertaste. Low brow, jutting jaw, why hadn't he taken a photograph of the family in advance?

'Mrs Talwar, were you at home when Pinky was found?'

'You don't feel sorry, huh? Now you don't care about how we feel?'

'Mrs Talwar, she could not have committed suicide. The medical evidence does not allow it.'

'What medical evidence? Medical evidence from your Khurana?'

'Your husband must have the report.' Like hell, but by the time Mrs N.K. onioned Mr N.K. about it, Juneja would be in the next city. Juneja paused. How did she know who Khurana was?

'Mrs Talwar, were you at home when it was discovered that Pinky was dead?' Best avoid all homicidal and suicidal words.

'No.'

'Who was?'

'You don't know?'

'Mrs Talwar, do you know?'

'No.'

This was going nowhere. Take off the bloody velvet gloves and Sajjan Kumar her. 'All right, Mrs Talwar, would you please call your servant? Perhaps he would know? I would prefer to ask him in front of you. I am sure someone must have been at home. After all it has now been discovered that she was murdered.'

She looked back sullenly at him. 'I don't know why we have to talk like this. This is not important. You know my daughter is getting married to Malhotra Industries? You know who they are? This is no time for us to be hiding. Please understand.' She suddenly became serious. He could see this was really important for her. More important than tense or adjectives, for example.

'We are a very respectable family, you know. My husband is a well-known businessman. My father-in-law is a very important person. He was a freedom fighter, you know? With Gandhiji? You know these things?

'My father did not want me to marry into a commercial background. But because my father-in-law, Papaji, was so great freedom fighter – he only wears white you know – that's why my father allow. Only that's why he allow. I said no, first, but my father he say, when Papaji is so great it is your good fortune to marry into such good family.

'Now you come and our good name is in the newspaper. Our Good Name. What Malhotra Industries will say? What everyone will say? This is not good.'

'Mrs Talwar, I understand completely. But if your sister-in-law dies under strange circumstances, we have to investigate.'

'No. You don't have to. You can stop. If you want to.'

'But if I stop, others will come. The government is involved.'

'You see? It is a conspiracy against us. We are innocent. She was also innocent. Just one small mistake and look, they are throwing mud on our name. On Our Good Name.'

Juneja closed his eyes. She breathed heavily, exhausted by the strength of her convictions. He opened his eyes and straightened himself up and out of the way. Too late. Onion breath moves faster than tiger can jump.

'Now you don't care any more? Huh? Huh?'

Be still, my beating heart, don't breathe, don't speak, don't swallow, O all-in-one monkey of Gandhi. What should I *do*? He switched to Hindi. 'Your Divine Other told me that Pinky confessed to you about her small mistake.'

She turned her face away as if he had slapped her. Bloody hell, she'd told him off as if he were a snotty brat on the streets, but the moment sex got mentioned she turned coy. But she hadn't. When she looked at him after scrutinizing the sofa for long seconds, her eyes were brimming. 'Mrs Talwar,' he spoke urgently, 'please, I didn't mean to upset you.' Hang the Hindi, he couldn't be expected to emote in the language like Amitabh bloody Bachchan.

'Mrs Talwar, I don't want to upset you, please, please understand.' God, they were running down her face and her nose was turning redder by the minute. He fought and lost with himself. 'Mrs Talwar, please.' Must I do this? You must, came the implacable retort. So he pressed his Irish linen handkerchief into her hand and sat himself down next to her. She must live off wretched onions to have achieved this effect. She turned helplessly towards him and he gingerly rubbed her shoulder. God, let her not react like an outraged virgin. But unlike her Divine Other, her grief was genuine. She didn't heave, but she did take the Irish linen handkerchief and blow her nose with it.

'Could you get me a glass of water? The servant has left the jug on the table.'

He complied.

She thanked him sadly. 'You know I should get up. You are the guest. But I have such severe pain in my knees. I am very fat, you know. Pinky was saying to me, Bhabhi, we'll go to the gym together. She was like....' She floundered and again a tear escaped. 'Not like a daughter, like a small sister. You know, she was so simple. Not like other people, not money conscious or anything. Very simple. Finding her like that was horrible. But poor girl, my poor girl, there was no choice.'

She wasn't speaking to him so much as to herself.

'Yes, I found her. You can ask anyone. I called Ram Singh and then I called my husband. He was not at home. My brother-in-law was also not at home. I was all alone. With Ram Singh.'

'What time was it?'

'Time? Time, I don't remember. But it must have been morning. They had gone to office.'

'I will need to talk to Ram Singh.'

'You can talk to who you like. They will all tell you the same thing. The same thing, because I am telling you the truth. But please understand, whatever your doctor-wockter is saying, Pinky wanted to protect Our Good Name.'

She was back to glaring.

I can glare too.

'Okay, then I'll be going. We will need to take a statement from the servant. He will accompany us to the station.'

She looked surprised but not unduly alarmed. 'You do what you want. I will tell him you want to take him. Please call me after you are finished. I will send the car to pick him up. Otherwise these wretched servants never come back on time.' She staggered to her feet.

Juneja stepped back. It had been an edifying meeting.

But she wasn't finished. 'You want, I keep your hanky?'

Before Joseph and Sajjan Kumar could start with their daft stories, Juneja held up his hand. 'Look it's very hot and I'm very tired. Joseph, you come to my house tomorrow. At 9 o'clock. Sharp. Sajjan Kumar, you drive me home first so that Joseph knows how to get to my house. After that take the jeep back. And no taking the jeep home or anything. I'm making a note of the kilometres, so don't think you can try it!'

Juneja felt mentally and physically exhausted. They could pick up the wretched servant tomorrow. Maybe the threat would have more of an effect after twenty four hours. Or maybe it would make no difference. To him or to them or to the entire wretched affair.

Diwan Singh was surprised to see him home so early, but only too ready to serve dinner immediately. Juneja went for a quick shower and reappeared to find dinner waiting, fresh and hot. He ate and went to brush his teeth almost immediately after the obligatory cigarette. Diwan Singh looked questioningly at him but Juneja just wanted to sleep. It was barely eight in the evening when he tumbled into bed.

He was up the next morning at six. He hollered for Diwan Singh, feeling much better. In celebration of the day, he stirred himself to make a gigantic pot of freshly brewed coffee. Diwan Singh only made tea. He'd informed Juneja early in the relationship that Juneja would get what he, Diwan Singh, ate. So coffee had to be a self-production.

He had a massive breakfast of coffee, eggs, toast, and more coffee. He sat back with the newspapers and yet more coffee and told Diwan Singh to clean up the bicycle, when the bell rang. Juneja got up. It couldn't be Joseph, it was just going on 7.30. But it was.

Joseph looking the way Juneja had felt yesterday. Dishevelled, although he was shaved and bathed, eyes bloodshot and wild.

'What's the matter?' Oh God, let me not have ruined everything. There had been nothing in the newspapers. Maybe he could do something if Gupta found out that he'd stopped Joseph from reporting yesterday.

'Sir, sir it's my daughter, sir.'

Juneja looked at him and struggled for control. 'What is the matter with your daughter that a bicycle won't cure?' Bloody measles, probably.

'No, sir, it's not my eldest,' said Joseph, who'd only heard the word bicycle in this sentence. 'Sir, it is my youngest, sir, sir, I, sir, she came home with blood, sir.' There, it was out.

Juneja sighed and opened the door and took Joseph inside. Was he now going to have to explain menstruation to this dodo? What was the immaculate Mary doing?

'What kind of blood, Joseph?'

'Sir, sir, from her bottom, sir. Sir...' Joseph spoke with his eyes closed. 'Sir, my Glorious has been raped.'

Joseph went home feeling quite benign. Although Ram Singh had been surly and bad-tempered to begin with, Sajjan Kumar had sorted it all out. He had spoken to Ram Singh in his own language, a dialect of Hindi, and Ram Singh had started smiling straight away. After that not only did they get iced water, Ram Singh gave them cold Coca Cola as well. Ram Singh said that he would tell the big Memsahib, N.K. Bhabhi as he called her, that the policemen had demanded it! Joseph had been highly distressed by this slander but Sajjan Kumar had laughed loudly and slapped Ram Singh on the shoulder, so it was probably just a joke. By that time the bottles had been empty in any case.

Joseph had tried to get them to talk about the Talwar household but then Sajjan Kumar had discovered a TV in the corner. Ram Singh shrugged modestly. 'Yes, Raghav sahib said we should also have a TV of our own. You know, otherwise we had to stand in the corner and watch TV in the big room, when there was a Hindi film, but Raghav sahib said this was not good.'

It was cable TV. Joseph and Sajjan Kumar had never seen the likes of it. On one channel there were lots of foreign girls all wearing skimpy clothes. Sajjan Kumar had been enraged and said that women like this deserved to be beaten up. But Ram Singh said even N.K. Bhabhi's daughter, Bahar, dressed like that. Not in front of her parents, but at night he had seen her sneaking off to go out with boys. Why don't you stop her, demanded Joseph aghast at such duplicity. Because she stops his mouth, said Sajjan Kumar, catching on immediately. Ram Singh had also laughed, much to his amazement, and offered them more biscuits. After this they had zoomed through all the channels and had been surprised when it was time to go.

Thank God Juneja had said he should report tomorrow! There wasn't anything to report in any case.

Janakpuri seemed quieter than usual as Joseph walked down from the bus stop. Jamuna Elizabeth and Kamla Doris were paying hide-and-seek with Glorious in the street. Joseph patted them and went Marywards. She was at home.

'You've come home very early today. Tea?'

Joseph laughed. He'd had Coca Cola!

'You know today I saw lots of naked girls on TV!'

Mary also started laughing as he continued, 'Have you finished dinner? Come, I'll tell you all about it. Their clothes...'

'I thought they were naked!'

They took the small wooden chairs and went out onto the small balcony. Mary took a glass of tea for herself.

He regaled her with stories about the channels. Mary being Mary of course knew all about it. Cable TV, she said to him. It was quite expensive but Mrs Chadha, their neighbour, had said prices were bound to come down and maybe they should also think about it because there was BBC and the nuns had said BBC was the best English the girls could learn. But obviously they would have to be very careful. Not only because of the money but also because the girls could not be given access to all these naked girls. This had Joseph giggling again.

Dusk began to fall as the girls came up. Mary told them to go and bathe before dinner. She had filled buckets for them. The water out of the tap came only twice a day for an hour each. The girls would each use half a bucket. On days when they had a head bath, this would increase to a full bucket, much to Mary's dismay. Glorious needed only a half bucket, her curly hair refused to grow long!

Joseph staggered to his feet, drunk on the intoxicating evening air. The sky never achieved the spectacular colours of Kerala but the bruised, mottled pink and lavender hues soothed his soul. Mary withdrew into the kitchen. Jamuna Elizabeth would be the first to have her bath so that she could then help Mary with the roti-making. Joseph went to see how Glorious was faring with her homework. But Kamla Doris was sitting alone at the desk. Gloria was in the balcony, wasn't she? She had been tired and had stopped playing and gone upstairs or so she had said. Jamuna Elizabeth emerged from the bathroom and confirmed what Kamla Doris had said. Joseph ran to Mary. The nightmare began.

Joseph ran down the stairs. A couple of hours ago, the children said. What did that mean? How many hours ago? The girls didn't have a watch. They didn't know. Dusk deepened, bringing with it the darkness of shadows hiding trysts with destiny, both willing and unwilling. Glorious crouched behind the vendor, no, it was a dog scratching its ear. She was hiding behind the fat Aunty, no, it was a sack, she lurked in the doorway opposite, no, it was a dustbin, she beckoned from under the tarpaulin, no, no it was, no, it wasn't, it just wasn't her. He ran down the street dodging, weaving through the crowd.

Jamuna Elizabeth and Kamla Doris tried to keep up with him and cried out finally when they couldn't. He shouted they should go back home. And then stopped in his tracks and turned around to take them back home. Where was Glorious, demanded Mary, standing in the doorway. He started running again. People abused him as he pushed past. He tried to say what was wrong but the words wouldn't come. The shadows lengthened, the street lights came on. That would help, he prayed. It didn't. In the silvery light everything got twisted. Men leered lustfully at him, women mocked him. The cry of the vendor bellowed out its victory. He ran to the bursting bus stop and almost came under the wheels of the screeching bus that bore down upon him like a modern day T-Rex. He found himself standing on the road divider. Which side had he checked? Where should he go? Call the police? He closed his eyes. Mary would have to tell him what to do.

He turned into the street to find Mary talking animatedly with the neighbour. She held a small bundle in her arms. No, that was the light deforming everything, playing tricks on his bruised eyes. No, it was a bundle. It was Glorious. He started running.

The neighbour, Mrs Khanna, was laughing. She had found Glorious hiding behind a vendor's cart. Mrs Khanna had gone to the vegetable market around the corner. Trying to select some mangoes, she had dislodged some from the heap. Bending down to pick them up, she'd discovered to her amazement, Glorious! A big mango, she laughed. Mary was also laughing. Joseph held the wall, unable to speak. All was well. He smiled gratefully at Mrs Khanna and taking Glorious from her arms, went up the narrow stairway. Glorious was very tired. Her eyes were drooping.

Mary came up, still pale from the shock but smiling, 'Na, do you know what a shock you gave us? Look at me!'

And Gloria opened her eyes slowly and closed her childhood out.

It was Juneja's turn to close his eyes. He slumped in his chair.

He picked up a cigarette and inhaled deeply the moment it was lit. Expelling the smoke as slowly as he could, absorbing every shred of the life-giving nicotine, he turned to Joseph who was still standing in front of the sofa. 'And you know who has done it?'

'No, sir, yes, sir, I can't understand anything. We have taken her to the nuns and they have arranged for a doctor, sir. Sir, I don't know what to do, sir, sir...' and before Juneja could answer this fairly dispassionate plea, Joseph broke down into a series of dry sobs.

Juneja hollered for Diwan Singh. 'Take him to the kitchen and give him some tea, breakfast, toast, you understand.'

Joseph tried to protest but Juneja waved him away. And Diwan Singh, who knew his wilful master well, led him away gently.

O God. Was there no end to this? No end at all? What was to be done now? Most of all, what was he to do? First these wretched Talwars and their silly promiscuous brat and now Joseph and his misbegotten idiots. In all fairness, Nikhil, the wretched child can't have been misbegotten. If nothing else, the Immaculate Mary would have ensured it, to say nothing of bloody pious K. Joseph. Nothing misbegotten in the Castle of K. Joseph, reflected Juneja sourly, if incorrectly.

But their problems are misbegotten, by God! Now this fool in his fatuous way would expect some revenge vendetta. Well, it was going to have to wait.

'Diwan Singh! Bring that Joseph here.'

Joseph emerged looking more dazed than ever.

Juneja spoke in a bracing tone, 'Look Joseph, I want you to give Sinha the full details...'

'No, sir, I can't. How can I go to the police, sir? Her future will be ruined, sir, Mary made me promise, sir...'

'Okay , okay , okay . Hang on. Let me think.'

Not go to the police? Man, Joseph, you *are* the police. I am the police, and that is the reason why you have come to me. Or isn't it?

'Joseph, if you don't want to go to the police, then why have you come to me?'

'Sir, everyone knows, sir.' Yes, this was the tricky part, what did everyone know?

'Sir, everyone knows, sir, you are better that the police, sir. Sir, please help me, sir please...'

Joseph started wobbling alarmingly on his feet.

Juneja turned desperately to Diwan Singh, who had been looking on as dispassionately as ever. 'Diwan Singh, has he eaten anything?'

His servant gave him (or was it the suggestion?) a disgusted look and answered in a surly tone, 'I will take him into the kitchen and feed him, if you stop calling him. You finish your breakfast. Now.'

Juneja gratefully collapsed. A Gold Flake would help. He poured more coffee into his cup. It was actually a beer mug. It belonged to his grandfather. The old geezer had drunk lassi from it. Useless stuff. Not that these quantities of coffee were good for him. He'd be better off drinking the same useless stuff, instead of the enormous amounts of poison he was currently ingesting. But what good would that be? Well, for that matter, what good was the coffee? It wasn't going to make bloody Joseph or his daft children disappear. Perhaps it would relieve the headache he was rapidly developing.

He felt completely empty. What the hell was he supposed to do? On the one hand Gupta was taking his ass in this wretched case, which he had to get right. Apparently he could get it right only if he worked with Mr I-am-a-grade-A-Ass-and-let-my-kids-get-raped. The Talwars refused to come clean about what their even more ridiculous sister had been up to and he, Nikhil Juneja, was getting rogered, any which way you looked at it.

So what could he do? Send Joseph packing, for a start. And figure out this chicken business. How? Ask Rajiv. Or Sunil. Or the servants. Had life come to this? He would now be hobnobbing with the wretched servants? Okay, what were the other possibilities? Ask Devi. She'd know but would she tell him? Ask Raghav. Drinking with the man must give him some rights. Or ask the Onion. No, no, no. No asking the Onion. Besides, he could still taste the wretched thing.

Go back to the beginning. How to send Joseph packing?

'Joseph! Joseph, come here!'

It was Diwan Singh who appeared instead, looking even more dour than usual. 'He has gone to sleep. Let him be.'

The missive was followed by the usual silent departure.

Juneja drew in a deep breath and called up the kotwali. It was only 8.15 but Sinha would be there. He was.

'Look, Sinha, I am going to be visiting the Talwars and I will come in late into office. You tell Gupta sahib's office, if anyone asks. Also fill out some forms for Joseph. Sympathetic leave. There has been a...a loss in the family.' It was one way of looking at it.

'Death of parent, sir?' asked Sinha, knowing full well it couldn't be. But Juneja was an old hand.

'No, a female relative, who has been with them from the beginning.' And never mind whose beginning, thought Juneja, feeling quite smug.

'Yes, sir. When is the funeral, sir? Should I go to the house, sir? I mean, as a member of the police?' That was Sinha, ever ready to dodge work solicitously.

'No. Not unless you're going to Kerela on your own. He got a telegram yesterday and will be going home. So just fill out the forms, all right? Now go, okay ? Let's say tentatively one week.'

'Okay , sir.'

Feeling quite satisfied with this form of telephonic delegation, he gave it a second shot and called Rajiv, 'Hi Geetu, How're you?' It was the typical Delhi greeting. If you were a really old hand, you dropped the 'r' completely and it came out *howvyu*, but Juneja abhorred such shortcomings.

But Geetu certainly didn't. '*Howvyu*, Nikki?' she demanded enthusiastically, emphasizing the you or the 'u' as it were.

'I hope I didn't wake you up,' knowing damn well he hadn't, but maybe Geetu would edify him with a story about Beginning the Day with a Prayer on your Lips.

Geetu cooed deliciously, 'Nooo, Nikki, I get up early. It's your friend who's the sleepyhead. But even he's surfaced by now. Hang on, I'll call him. I don't know what he's doing in the bathroom for such a long time. You know, he wants to get the bathroom AC-d. Can you imagine, he's mad, absolutely mad! Just wait a sec!'

Grouchy tones filled Juneja's ear. 'What d'you want, bugger?' Geetu squealed her protest against such familiar address, in the background.

'Listen, I need to get some info from you. Can we meet in the evening? Or maybe for lunch? Today's your half-day, isn't it? And bastard, who're you calling bugger, you constipated bastard?'

'Okay , bugger, we'll meet for lunch at the Haveli, okay ? And why the hell am I constipated?'

'Then why are you living in the bathroom?'

'Man, Nikhil, don't you screw my happiness as well, man. Why d'you think, man? I'm starving! My happiness and my ass get screwed, only I don't, and stop laughing, you bastard!'

'Okay , Rajiv, hang loose, we'll figure out something at lunch. One o'clock?"

'Cool, man, see you then. And Nikhil?'

'Yup?'

'It's on me, okay ? Don't even think about arguing. Bye.'

'Rajiv, I'm the one asking you...'

'Nikhil, shut up, I have to go and Bye.'

Juneja delegated for the last time. 'Diwan Singh!'

He waited for the silent arrival.

'I won't be in for lunch. When Joseph wakes up, tell him to go home. I have filled in forms for one week. He should come here tomorrow. No, make that the day after tomorrow. Or no, let's say Wednesday. He should come here on Wednesday, Okay ? And he shouldn't go to work, okay?'

There was silence.

'Okay ?'

'Okay , Wednesday. I will tell him.'

The Haveli called for an entirely different look. A touch of Azarro. After all, lunch meant cruising chicks. Tight jeans that, emphasized the crotch, and an expensive white shirt. Shit, it was too hot. A Polo would fit the bill better. Man, Nikhil, you're developing a bloody paunch! Time to cut down on the vodka. He sighed. What the hell. Maybe he'd get the woman of a lifetime with a paunch. She hadn't made an entry all this while, so why should the appearance of a paunch make her disappear?

Shoes, now, that was a problem. Slippers made you look like an overweight Marwari dick. On the other hand, he was decidedly too old for sneakers, no matter how foreign or expensive. Leather shoes made his sweat, soaked soul cry out in protest. Besides, the mixture of formal leather shoes and jeans and a Polo was the pits. That left sandals. And they left Juneja feeling queasy. He'd bought them in a mad fit last summer and never worn them. He put them on rather gingerly and beheld his reflection. The sandals were beige and made of leather of some sort. Leather that was soft and like suede. Or maybe it was suede. They made him look like a wimp. Or gay. Or a gay wimp. Or just blind. And if he looked blind then no one could blame him for looking like a gay wimp, decided Juneja and tore himself from the mirror.

Okay , that was everything done. Now, money, credit card, and cigarettes. He needed to pick up petrol. The bloody car drank even more than he did!

Thank God he could use the police car so often. The way petrol prices were shooting up, he couldn't drive his Contessa as often as he'd like. Okay, that was crap. He had enough money to do most things but it was nice to pretend to be poor. He often did with his colleagues, who'd never figured out, whether he was talking BS or whether he meant it. His address was fancy. On the other hand, Sinha had told everyone there was no furniture in the flat. This being the reason why he'd called Sinha over in the first place. Sajjan Kumar had also entered the holy portals, but he was too thick to notice anything except the amount of liquor available. Sajjan Kumar's visit had in any case been more of a revelation for Juneja. The varieties and crudities of legal and illegal sex available in the city had been hitherto unknown to him. He'd informed Rajiv, unable to keep such hot stuff for himself. The two of them had spent an afternoon on the net checking out all the possibilities.

Juneja started laughing. Rajiv had been enraged. 'Man, there's so much to do, man, so much, and I get so little. How can she do this to me, Nikhil? I mean, I thought she loved me. But she's starving me, she's just bloody starving me!' It had become a code between them ever since.

The parking was going to be full, but Juneja had no qualms about handing over the keys to the flunky from the hotel. All the fools knew him. More importantly, they knew he was in the police.

Rajiv was sitting in the lobby trying to look nonchalantly at some foreigner's boobs.

'What's up, dude?'

'Man, Nikhil, just check her out! I mean, how can she go out in public like this? I swear man, that top is transparent. I swear it is!'

'Rajiv, she is going for a swim and that transparent thing you are orgasming about is going to come off. Want to get ringside seats?'

Rajiv grinned at him. A friend in need...They marched into the restaurant and informed the maître d' they had to sit at a window overlooking the pool. The eyes felt better looking on water, Rajiv informed the man, who was trying to lure them in the opposite direction. Suitably seated with both able to look in the direction of the pool without breaking their necks, they immediately decided on a pitcher of beer and kebabs for starters, the main meal and dessert. Green stuff was for women or for Rajiv, when Geetu was around. The blonde woman had appeared as well. She sat down on the white lounger. It had a dark blue cushion. The transparent shrug came off revealing a fairly modest orange bikini.

'Mmm,' murmured Rajiv without missing a beat. He took a long thirsty gulp of the iced beer. 'Good colour, highlights the contrast.' Juneja nodded agreement. Detailing, that was what made the senses tingle.

At that moment the Technicolor extravaganza got more colourful. As if feeling the burning intensity of their gaze the woman looked around inquiringly. Juneja grinned evilly at Rajiv. She couldn't see them through the glass – it was too dark. Rajiv smiled back and then swore. The woman had found what she was looking for. She beckoned to the two-bit shit waiter passing by and gave him the bottle of sun-tan lotion. Before Juneja could manage to look the other way, he saw her unhook the bra.

Rajiv changed his seat and sat down with his back to the swimming pool. 'Don't look, man, it hurts. I wouldn't let the asshole clean my loo and she let him paw her. In public.'

'For free,' Rajiv added bitterly after a short moment's reflection. It was disgusting.

Juneja looked down. It was true. Here they were, starved for a good piece of meat. And this silly bugger, who spent his life serving tea and checking out white women, got a feel for free.

'Maybe it's a good thing, Rajiv. You wouldn't have heard a bloody word otherwise!'

'Too true, man, too true. I met our pal Verma the other day on the street. He told me a bizarre story, man. Apparently there was this French guy. Like, in medieval times. And he was like a monk. And, man, he screwed this chick, who was a nun. In a church. Man, and you know what her family did? They castrated him. So, Nikhil, what's the moral of the story?'

Juneja looked tolerantly at him. 'I don't know. Don't screw nuns in churches, that's only for God!'

'No, man, check it out: Verma originally came from France!'

Despite himself, Juneja started laughing. 'Good one, Rajiv, really good one!

'But the story is true, man. Can you believe it? A story like that? I thought the French were cool!'

'Man, Rajiv, nobody's that cool. And people who do weird things like that, well, what d'you expect? Anyway can we talk about other things?'

'Wow, man, you're really serious today! And what's with the sandals? Are you gay? Or maybe blind?'

'Thanks, Rajiv. You look like my girlfriend. Now, can we get serious?' retorted Juneja as Rajiv started giggling again.

'Okay, pal, you got it. What's up?'

Juneja wondered, if he was going to sound like a complete dick. He drew in a deep breath and spat it out: 'Tell me, is it a bad thing if you make chicken in a dead person's house? I mean, if someone dies, can you cook chicken in the house?'

Rajiv looked gobsmacked.

'Rajiv, look, if you die, then on the same day if Geetu makes chicken, on the same day, not months later, before the cremation even, is that bad?'

'Is this some detective stuff?' asked Rajiv in an awed voice.

'Sort of.'

'Man, sorry, but I'm not really into this stuff, I mean, you should ask Geetu about whether it's like, really bad or evil or something but man, Nikhil, it's not done. I mean, if I die, then I'd expect her to sit around weeping, not make chicken!'

'Hell Rajiv, she's not going to hang around the effing kitchen! But she could tell the cook to make chicken!'

'No, Nikhil, listen.' And suddenly Rajiv looked very serious. 'Listen, if I die, then she loved me right? So she should be sad. And not thinking about hot stuff to eat. It doesn't matter who cooks it. I mean, even if she were to order food from some fancy restaurant, it would be weird. I mean, if she dies, I'd be sad. I wouldn't want to eat fancy stuff. I mean, if boiled chickens are in the house, I wouldn't have a problem eating them but man, why would I think of eating when my wife's died?'

'Rajiv, you are really making this entire thing sound simpler than it is. I mean, these are Hindu scriptures and stuff like that, man. I mean, no offence man, but maybe I really should talk to your wife or maybe even to your grandmother!'

Rajiv looked down and took time off to spear an onion and another kebab. Juneja also avoided looking at him. This wasn't what he'd planned. Silly bitch's death didn't mean screwing up perfectly decent relationships.

Rajiv took a deep breath and started again, even as Juneja wanted to ask him to drop it. 'You know, Nikhil, Geetu said all these old customs have a meaning. That they have or at least used to have a practical function. I think most of the stuff is crap. I mean, you know what I want Geetu to be doing in the morning!'

Juneja smiled. Trust Rajiv to get sex into everything. 'Bastard, you ever think of anything else?'

'Not often!' answered Rajiv grinning back. 'But to get back to the point, I mean, somebody dies and you hang around cooking food, that's weird. It means, it means like, like you don't care! And I mean, if someone dies in your house, you should care, shouldn't you?' he demanded somewhat incoherently.

'So it's not about good and evil and Hindu tradition?'

'Not for me. Hell, Nikhil, if you kicked the bucket, I'd get drunk, man, not stuff my face with kebabs!'

The rest of the lunch was the usual mix of backslapping fun. Juneja had to cut it short. It would be wise to put in an appearance at the police station. Gupta might be screaming, there might be a new case, maybe Saudamini Talwar would disappear into thin air, whatever, he'd better find out.

But Juneja was feeling quite jolted by revelations he hadn't asked for, much less expected. Was Rajiv perhaps not so thick? Did he, perish the thought, *could* he actually love Geetu? They'd always laughed about it. About Geetu, the sex with Geetu or the lack of it, the way she pushed him around, her desire to get him, Juneja, married off. Hell, what hadn't they laughed about?

Or had the laughter been fake? Men's laughter, the kind that doesn't count in the real world. Girls giggled together, bought clothes and cooked, thought Juneja, men swap stories, thump each other on the back and laugh. Part of the fun is knowing that the stories aren't true but was the laughter, the friendship, the loyalty damn it, was that also fake? Had he believed a Banbury tale? He started laughing. A Banbury tale. Where did that particular phrase come up from? He didn't even know *what* Banbury was! A colonial education and a policeman, an Indian and intelligent, 40 and alone. Maybe the symptom was the cause.

Africa Avenue shimmered in the afternoon heat. It was still. The madness of the first crossing and then the relative calm after he crossed the inner Ring Road. Was that what it was all about? The relative calm belied by the madness within? If he was wrong about Rajiv, was he wrong about everything else as well? Suddenly it all seemed too much. He pulled over on the side, next to the DLTA: Delhi Lawn Tennis Association. His father had had fond dreams of him playing at Wimbledon. Juneja hadn't had anything against it. Short-skirted chicks bending to pick up stuff for him was a cool idea, only it wasn't happening at the DLTA. Rajiv and he had been only slightly disappointed. It was something you got used to. Walking London, talking Tokyo – reading, writing, listening West, doing, living and yes obeying Indian. It was actually quite self-explanatory. All Indians understood it implicitly, only stupid firangis like the silly woman today didn't. Archie and Betty and Veronica were permanently smooching in school and wearing skimpy clothes and eating hot stuff. But their own childhood, the real thing, had been wanking over the same Betty and Veronica – they never got to meet any girls. During the course of one of his many tussles he'd asked his father why he had allowed him, Juneja, to read Archie comics, if he couldn't subscribe to *Playboy* all these years later? His father had been thunderstruck. He hadn't had a clue who or what Archie was. His answer had been a classic one. No more Archie *or Playboy* for you! Juneja started laughing despite himself.

It was one of those self-explanatory things. Your wife was chosen by Daddy or Mummy. So you put up with it. But why would you be sad if she copped it? You weren't supposed to love her in the first place. Thank God he hadn't told Rajiv about Joseph. What would he have expected from him, Juneja? Maybe Rajiv would have cuddled Joseph in his arms and consoled him. Maybe he would have, as a hypothetical policeman, unleashed a revenge vendetta: Nobody gets away with touching a policeman! What a load of bollocks.

A cigarette would help. What was happening? Why was he collapsing like this? It was one bloody case, the Talwars one way or the other didn't change that. Joseph was one bloody sidekick, he and his brats didn't matter one way or the other. Neither did his father nor did Rajiv. Okay, Rajiv did matter, but just because Rajiv had changed or whatever, *whatever*, Nikhil whatever, it doesn't matter. You cannot break down like this. What is going on? It can't end like this. You will go on and life will have a meaning.

He started the car and sent the wheels squealing down the road. It was time to get back to life.

At the police station, Gupta had already left. It was three o'clock in the afternoon on a Friday. He hadn't expected any less. Sinha, less fortunate, was drowning in his sweat in a corner and waddled over at the sight of Juneja marching in.

'Sir, no electricity since morning, sir,' he almost wailed. Juneja nodded his condolences and demanded information about any new developments

'Sir, I have filled out Joseph's leave form, sir, and put on your desk for approval and signature. The servant of Talwars has come over and is sitting with Sajjan Kumar since the morning, sir.'

Yes, of course, the wretched servant. Ram something was his name. The Talwars must be very sure of themselves, if they sent the fellow over instead of letting him be hauled over by the police.

'With Sajjan Kumar?'

'Sir, when he came he said he knew Sajjan Kumar, sir, so Sajjan Kumar is doing questioning, sir, because he knows him.'

This was Sinha at his best and purest. Take no responsibility and you shall receive none. Sajjan Kumar was blameless and so was Sinha, and if there was blame to be attached it would attach itself to the most convenient scapebody. Juneja had long been trying to internalise Sinha's unique turn of phrase and inarticulation for future use.

'And where is Sajjan Kumar?'

'In the courtyard, sir.'

The questioning was taking place in the courtyard, was it?

Bloody Sajjan Kumar had evidently been having a protracted tea break. But he was also an old hand. He'd placed himself strategically in a corner, such that he could see Juneja coming a mile off. The hapless servant, who had evidently been having a pleasant chin-wag, was sitting with his back to the entrance. Inexperienced sod. Sajjan Kumar paused mid-sentence to gauge His Master's Mood before shooting to his feet on seeing the sardonic query in Juneja's eyes. He thumped the servant on the back, sending him flying out of the chair. 'Bloody fool, stand up to salute sir!'

Juneja knew instinctively that Sinha had followed him to arrange for the equitable distribution of opprobrium and encomium alike. He didn't need to turn around. Besides, it reinforced the I-have-eyes-in-the-back-of-my-head-and-am-utterly-godly image he quite liked.

'Sinha, take this fellow down to the cells.' He smoked a cigarette in peace while Sinha waddled past at his slowest, hoping to hear the exchange between Sajjan Kumar and him. Sajjan Kumar stood erect, hoping for the best and slowly beginning to feel the pressure.

Juneja took a last drag and then carefully crushed the butt underfoot. Can't be too careful, these embers could start a fire. He turned to Sajjan Kumar. 'Call the Talwars and tell them we are keeping him in custody till Monday. To assisst in our inquiries. Say Gupta sir has not spoken to the servant as yet and so questioning could be delayed. I will be taking over the questioning. You please come into the office and tell me what you have learnt, so that I can proceed accordingly.'

It had been the 'please'. Sajjan Kumar appeared quaking in Juneja's office. Actually, Juneja wasn't particularly angry with him. It was just good training. Keep them on their toes and all that. Besides, the bloody fellow had done no work today. If the rubbish on his table was to be believed, there were other wretched cases waiting for his kind attention as well. Armed robbery and a small murder. But Juneja knew that Gupta couldn't be kept waiting on the Talwar case.The other crap had to wait. Gupta wanted *action* on this one.

'So what have you found out this morning?' It was an easy thing with Sajjan Kumar. No long words, no sarcasm, no irony, no difficulties: the simple life.

'Sir, actually you know, we...'

'You spent the morning talking to him. It is now almost four o'clock. What have you been doing all this time?'

'Sir, you know...'

'Listen Sajjan Kumar, do I look like an elephant?'

'No, sir, no sir, not at all sir!' It was a cry of anguish.

They had played this game many times and it was the meanest thing Juneja could say to him.

'Then the bamboo you are trying to stuff into me is not meant for my mouth, is it?'

'Sir, no, sir, no sir, no Sir!'

'Have you spent the entire, the entire morning just chatting and drinking tea and having fun?'

'No, sir.'

'Then what have you learnt?'

'Nothing, sir.'

It was a sign of Sajjan Kumar's extreme defeat that he hadn't tried to insinuate a Foreign Hand in the matter. It would have been par for the course to suggest that the fellow had appeared just ten minutes ago or that Sinha or Tom or Harry had done something, thereby causing a delay in Sajjan Kumar's highly conscientious desire to question. There was little point in reducing him to further.

'Sir, they have been given a TV for the kitchen, sir, and on this TV there are naked women all the time.'

Juneja smiled. 'Is this what you have been discussing with him? Naked women?'

Sajjan Kumar grinned back, feeling much relieved, 'Yes, sir.'

'You know, Sajjan Kumar, you are one horny bastard!'

'Yes sir,' answered the aforementioned, looking quite flattered.

'And what should I do with you? Tell Gupta sir you only think about naked women and don't do any work?'

'No, sir,' replied Sajjan Kumar adoringly. This kind of banter he could handle. Juneja understood him and he had no problems with Juneja's little quirks.

No bloody sir. Nothing to stand on other than a TV

showing naked women. Juneja was savvy enough to know it was cable. This wretched MTV was going to ruin the country. It was one thing for white women to parade their bodies, but if Indian women also started, then, then, Geetu had started spluttering, quite unable to go on. If he remembered correctly, Rajiv had given him a look. One of those ones. Meaning, change the subject fast, bastard. Or had that been a sign of his love for Geetu? Juneja had assumed it was evidence of the terror she exercised. Had that not—stop it Nikhil. You are a police officer, not a marriage councillor – so drop this nonsense.

He turned to Sajjan Kumar, who was now looking dopey as usual.

'Did you see any of this MTV?'

Sajjan Kumar cocked an eyebrow to show his extreme incomprehension.

'The naked women, did you see them?'

'Yes, sir, yes, yesterday we saw. The whole afternoon, sir, when we were there.'

'Yesterday afternoon? When I told you to find out about this chicken thing?'

'Sir, sir, Joseph was to ask. Sir, he asked also...' added Sajjan Kumar, ever honest, 'But sir, I thought he will tell you, so I forgot.'

The problem is, you never think, but luckily for you I do. And I am just getting the glimmer of an idea.

'This MTV, these naked women, you know, how does this servant, what is his name, see them?'

'His name is Ram Singh, sir.' This was the easy part. How did Ram Singh see them?

'Sir, he sees with his eyes, sir. He doesn't need glasses.'

Juneja looked at Sajjan Kumar with bitter loathing.

'You bastard, don't be more stupid than you are. Where does he see them? Does he sneak into the room of Talwar sahib? Where is the TV?'

'No sir, I see, sir, no sir, they have their own TV, sir. In the kitchen. They can watch all the time.'

'They have a TV in the kitchen?'

'Yes, sir, a colour TV. One of the sahibs, I think it is the youngest one, said they should have their own TV because otherwise they have to stand in the corner.'

It couldn't have been better.

'Does this fellow like the naked women or does he watch other channels?' Might as well make the case watertight.

'Sir, I don't know. I said to him, these women should be beaten, but he said the daughter of the house also wears clothes like that.'

Geetu and Sajjan Kumar, the pillars of Indian society. Hopefully, a dying race.

'The Talwar daughter? The one who is dead?'

'No, sir. The one who is alive.'

Ah! Miss Malhotra Industries. Or Mrs Malhotra Industries as she wanted to be. Daughter of the Onion. How did the Onion countenance it?

'What do her parents say about this?'

'Sir, they don't know. Ram Singh says she goes out at night, when they are asleep.'

'And this fellow Ram Singh gets a few notes from her, hmm?' It could scarcely get any better. Just to get things in proper perspective he demanded, 'So has he killed this woman?'

Sajjan Kumar was startled. He thought about it. Juneja could see the struggle. But even MTV wasn't worth it.

'Maybe, sir. We should ask him.'

The police station was clearing out. Those blighted souls doomed to the night shift were settling down. Bottles of local liquor, though not openly in evidence, could be smelled by the discerning nose. If it had been winter, there would have been surreptitious lining of chairs with blankets. Thankfully all the officials turned a blind eye on the heaters that ran the whole day for the purpose of making tea as well as for heating. The Holy Budget did not allow for a fridge, which was a sore point with Juneja. There were no ACs and the lack of cold water was simply the pits.

The usual stale smell of sweat, grime and general apathy was somewhat diluted. The lack of electricity meant any and every window had been open the entire day. Juneja usually avoided going to the toilet at work. But today the heat had got to him and he had consumed endless glasses of water, to say nothing of the quantities of beer at lunch time. And lo! wonder of wonders, even the toilet stench was somewhat reduced. Sinha was still lurking about.

'What are you doing here?'

'Official night duty, sir,' Sinha replied trying to look hurt as Sajjan Kumar chortled. Sinha was notorious for unnecessary overtime.

'Are you sure?' Now that Sinha had brought it to his notice, he'd better make sure that all the formalities were in place. 'Have you brought Ram Singh into the cell?'

'Yes sir, but the cells are quite full so I put him in the corner cell, sir. He said it was dirty but I said, we cannot help.'

This was part of the formalities. Sinha had understood that they were going to beat the fellow. Putting him in the corner cell meant the fellow would be considerably softened up. The corner cell was traditional for first-timers. It was used as an additional bathroom and was a paradise for rats, cockroaches and other life forms Juneja had no desire to be better acquainted with. Like all good cells, it was in the basement. This meant windows above the head and bad light. Ram Singh could count his lucky stars, it was evening and the temperature was going down. None of the cells had electricity. For questioning, additional lamps were brought in. Some of the luxury cells had a toilet. Without exception, none functioned. None of the cells had water. But as Sinha would point out, the cells were only for a short-term period. This was no exaggeration. A weekend, in chronic cases a week. In such cases, the concerned policeman could be incited to bring some water to the inmates. A little bonus never hurt. This was a plum job. One for which Sinha's lazy soul yearned on a daily basis. Sit around and snooze, the idiots behind bars, extra money to be made for every exertion. Life didn't get much better.

There weren't many inmates. A few petty thieves, an odd whore or two. Typical really, for a small elite police station in the city. The big work was done in the slums and other seedy parts of town. Sinha had once been threatened by a transfer and had come weeping to Juneja. Sajjan Kumar was never transferred. Every station needed its in-house thug. But, to be fair to both of them, neither looked particularly happy at the approaching questioning. Sinha, probably because it meant work. As for Sajjan Kumar, well, who cares, thought Juneja, mentally shrugging his shoulders. If they all want to become Mother Teresas in their old age, it isn't my problem.

Sinha pulled out the lamps grumbling softly to himself. Sajjan Kumar silently helped him out. Juneja was busy looking for a clean spot to stand on. The place was absolutely filthy. He had them set up the lamps in one of the luxury cells. No way he was going into that hellhole. It probably gave off radiation of some sort.

Ram Singh must have been cowering in a corner. Sajjan Kumar dragged him out and sat him down on the chair opposite Juneja.

It was the classic mafia setup. Light on Ram Singh's face. Sajjan Kumar behind him, Sinha standing in the corner. Juneja opposite. All three were in the shadows. Both Sajjan Kumar and Juneja could see Ram Singh and each other clearly. He could see neither. More importantly, he couldn't see Sajjan Kumar at all. As a result, every hit would be a bull's eye. They had done it so many times it was like poetry, graceful, smooth, cascading. Every time he, Juneja, looked at Sajjan Kumar, Ram Singh would get hit. Suddenly and disarmingly. Need one add, painfully?

'So, you have been working for the Talwars for a long time.'

'For more than twenty years, sahib.' Look.

'That was not a question. When I ask you, then answer, otherwise shut up.' Look.

'Since when have you been screwing Miss Pinky?'

'What are you saying, sahib?' Look.

'No, sahib please no, sahib, she was the daughter of the house sahib, I am a servant.' Bloody hell, this was the way that wretched gangster Pratap should have reacted.

'Servant, huh, bastard? Servant, who looks at naked women the entire day, huh? Instead of cooking, you get horny and then screw Miss Pinky, huh?' Look.

'No, sahib, no...' Look. Keep on looking, don't stop now. Back to life, back to reality. What was the song? He had really liked it. Not keep on looking, keep on moving. That was it. Juneja started with a jerk and stopped gaping at Sajjan Kumar. 'Stop!'

Ram Singh lay on the floor. Sajjan Kumar had been kicking him. Shit, hopefully the idiot wasn't dead. 'Is he all right?'

This wasn't like him. To get distracted in the middle of an interrogation. What was the matter with him?

Sinha answered dolorously, 'All right, sir. He may have lost a tooth, sir. I can't tell. There is some blood and sir, here it is too dark. Also, sir, it is smelling very bad.'

Of your shit, you bastard, responded Juneja silently. And then indulged himself and repeated it loudly.

'Take him upstairs and put him together again. Sajjan Kumar, you work night shift today as well.'

They started up the stairs, Sajjan Kumar and Sinha unhappily lugging the lolling body of Ram Singh, who had started groaning softly.

'Take care of him tonight. If there is any chance of anything going wrong, then call me and the doctor, okay? I don't want any more journalist nonsense about police brutality!'

Sajjan Kumar nodded sagely. Custodial death was a necessary evil. Sajjan Kumar was its instrument. He spent his life on the brink of internal 'police brutality' enquiries. None had found him guilty because none had ever been conducted. Nonetheless, he could be suspended for a brief period. Without pay. This had happened once. Where the woman in question had been raped and still managed to escape. Thankfully she had died in hospital, before the police could get her statement. Which was a joke, because the statement was to have been taken by Sinha, who had been outside waiting patiently for her to die.

But Juneja didn't want anything to happen to Ram Singh or whatever the silly fellow's name was. He would have to do some more footwork and quite frankly a hell of a lot more brain work, to crack this case. But the weekend had begun well, he thought. Jospeh was out of the way and there was a 24-carat scapegoat available. There must be light at the end of the tunnel.

Early to bed, early to rise, makes a man healthy, wealthy and wise. Cleanliness is next to godliness. An apple a day keeps the doctor away. Give and thou shall receive.

All the little sayings he'd been brought up with, reflected Juneja on the way back home. None of them had proven to be true. Except the last with respect to oral sex, and that also only some of the time. So was it all rubbish? Was he to question his entire upbringing? He'd felt like that when he'd joined the police. The exam had been a breeze thanks to his good name. After that it had all been downhill. All the American detective serials had been little preparation for the job. None of the stupid detective novels he'd laboured his way through had either. He'd been stunned by the violence he was expected to deal with, on a daily basis. Again thanks to his good name, he got a permanent posting in Delhi. Other hapless souls got sent to places like Bihar. Which was great because you did no work and got a lot of money from the local ganglords. But they did occasionally have gang warfare and then you died. So maybe it wasn't so good. There were also all the places in between Delhi and Bihar. Who wanted to be a policeman in, say, Crappur somewhere?

Growing up had been hard. His mother had died in childbirth. A proclamation he made regularly and dolefully. Rajiv called it his favourite pickup line. It was. But that was today. His childhood, his puberty had been woefully mixed up. Sure there were people in Delhi who had been cool even then. Sunil must have been cool. Rajiv and he, Juneja, had been greasy, boring nerds. In Rajiv's case there were mitigating circumstances. Anyone with a grandmother like Rajiv's was blighted from birth. But what the hell had been wrong with him? Why had he given in to being a weirdo Hindu brat?

His aunt lived with them. His father's older sister. His father's much older sister. In fact she was his father's half-sister. The daughter of his grandfather's first wife, who had been largely infertile. She had yielded only one daughter over a period of twenty years of marriage. She also died in the process, paving the way for his grandmother. His grandmother had thus been three or four years older than her stepdaughter. His grandmother showed signs of rapid fecundity, yielding his father in the first year of marriage. His grandparents were on the way back home after she had had her second pregnancy confirmed, when a car hit their rickshaw. No one survived.

His father was thus brought up by his half-sister. Who was very much in residence, when Nikhil's mother decided to succumb to her delivery. His aunt, whom he called Mataji, never married. She was a tiny wizened old lady, with infinite patience and tenderness. Sure, she was conservative. Religion was a part and parcel of her life. Like Rajiv's grandmother, she too got up at four in the morning. But her prayers were conducted with dignity and a sense of privacy, in her own bedroom. Neither servants nor any one else were inconvenienced. His father worshipped her. She was the ultimate arbitrator in the Juneja household. She fasted when tenders were submitted, she fasted when he had English tests, but she'd never asked them to fast. She woke him up in the morning for school. Before exams, she gave him a handful of almonds, which were to make his brains work extra fast. And she smiled when he failed.

But she hadn't answered the questions he'd never been able to ask her. Like, why aren't I cool or will I ever have sex. Or would he loose his eyesight due to excessive masturbation. The last had been a chronic worry. Especially since he'd figured at that stage that no one, no girl would be willing to have sex with him. Ergo, was it better to become blind jerking off or should he preserve a little sight and/or sperm in the hope that he would find a willing victim?

Other people seemed to be oblivious to such problems. Had girlfriends, went to see films, heard strange music like Jimmy Hendrix, and had long hair. Once he'd tried to start a conversation with a cool gang. But the casualness, the unbearable lightness of their being, left him more depressed than ever. The way he was feeling today. Joseph out, the culprit in, so what was the problem? He pulled over on the side and thought about where he could go. Home is the place where, when you knock at the door, they have to let you in. Why not find out? He wasn't even in uniform!

The Jor Bagh house looked bereft, or was it his imagination? It was huge. It had recently been renovated. He'd read about the renovation in a magazine. The article hadn't mentioned him. His father would have ensured it. It was an open secret in Delhi but had never been printed. Out of the closet and yet in the dark. There were four cars lined in front of the house. Juneja wondered whose they were. Maybe visitors? His nerves almost gave way then. But he crept up to the house surreptitiously. There were no drivers that he could see. The watchman saw the shadow and called out. He swallowed, 'It's me, Juneja, Nikhil, I mean. Is anyone home?' The watchman was new. Charan Singh had obviously been retired.

'Who are you?' The question was polite but the watchman was obviously bewildered. Although Juneja was decently dressed, long live chic cool, he had been lurking suspiciously in the shadows.

'I am a friend.' What kind of answer was that?

'I'll tell them. Please wait here.'

Juneja swallowed. Run away? Wait? Before the questions could really formulate themselves, another male voice asked querulously about his dubious identity.

'Whose friend? Business?' It was Saraswat, Diwan Singh's father, his grandaunt's personal servant and as such an extension of her. God, he looked old.

Juneja swallowed. 'It's me!'

The watchman intervened, 'He said he's a friend!'

Saraswat came out to the gate. 'Nikhil....' He looked like he would faint. 'A friend? Nikhil?'

Juneja moved forward to help him before the man fell over. Saraswat's voice gave way, but his eyes were full. Clutching his arm he pulled him to the main entrance.

The watchman looked at them, obviously stupefied by this reaction to a 'friend'.

Inside the house, god, how it had changed, Saraswat tried to speak normally but the tears wouldn't stop flowing and Juneja found he couldn't tear his eyes away and couldn't speak very clearly either.

'Will you eat, I mean what will you have? You must be hungry. I'll go and arrange it. Your father is not in Delhi. I'll call your grandmother. You wait here.' He tried to leave without taking his eyes off Juneja and then realized his hand was still holding Juneja's arm. He tried to let go and then clutched it again and then as if not trusting Juneja to wait, looked blindly at him and pulled him along. The house was cool and utterly silent. Cold almost. ACs running full blast, or was it central air conditioning? His father would have moved heaven and earth to make sure that Mataji was comfortable. The white marble floor was new and gleamed its mocking welcome. But Juneja knew where they were going. And then they were there. At the back of the house. And suddenly things were the same. The open courtyard with its basil plant. Basil? He shook his head at his own Westernness. It was tulsi. Something no non-Indian understood. He saw the door at the end of the corridor. Obviously the interior decorator had been told where to draw the line. It was an old-fashioned wooden door with a brass bolt on the outside. Where had all the bolts gone? Gone to graveyards every one. He pulled himself together. Painted, the door had been painted. The paint scratched and the wood nicked was the way he remembered it. It was always kept open. With one exception – when she was saying her prayers. Then, not even on pain of death did you go in. You did not even knock. Juneja had seen his father wait a full hour in front of that shut door. And it wasn't even locked. Just shut. But now Saraswat just kept on pulling him. Juneja tried to pull away but Saraswat couldn't hold the sob. 'What else has she been praying for?'

As the door opened, Juneja's head reeled back to hold the smell, consume it and preserve it for a future hour of need. This smell. Worn, warm, nurturing. It enveloped him as it always had. Here, if nowhere else, at least, here, there was solace, the truth of love. She was sitting crosslegged on a chair. Since when? She had always sat on the ground. She looked up, 'What is it, Saraswat?' Her voice. Juneja felt his eyes film over. Her voice, had he done this, this exhaustion? He pulled away from Saraswat. It was time to run away.

Saraswat blocked the door as if he had read his thoughts. 'Look who has come? I told you, you don't need to pray, I told you, didn't I?'

She fumbled for her glasses and Nikhil smiled to see them. Designer Christian Dior. And then he knelt down before her, pressing his head into her lap, hoping desperately for acceptance before she could see his face.

His father was in Europe and called everyday. Twice a day. He would call again at 10 o'clock in the evening but Juneja didn't stay. She didn't try to dissuade him. It had been horrifying to see her. Like a cherished toy suddenly exposed to the harsh light of adulthood, cheap, tawdry and sullied. She was none of these things, but the shadows were lengthening. The old authority, the power, the invincibility and the safety were shreds left in his memory. Was it the same with his father? He didn't want to know.

He'd been unable to talk to her. Not really. Saraswat had run around like a headless chicken and alternately wept and cried, or was that the same? She had been almost mute at the beginning and just when he'd thought he'd killed her, she had given him a huge grin and wept at the same time. He told her all about the Talwar case. She knew them. All the old families knew each other. At least in Delhi. Well, he didn't tell her everything, like about her being raped or whatever the wretched female had been, or about her being pregnant. But he told her about being overworked and tired and being harassed by Gupta. He'd then had to stop her physically from calling up Gupta. She'd said something about having babysat him and his dirty diapers and what she would do to him. Juneja smiled. It was good to have someone who cared. To know the power still held. Yes, it still held. If she'd called up Gupta, it would have been embarrassing, but Gupta would have had to listen. Because she was old, because she was rich, because the Juneja name stood behind her, because his father would bamboo anyone who didn't listen to her and because he was the biggest kid in the playground.

It had been almost ten years. It seemed so ridiculous, so pathetic to him. How could he have done this to her? To Saraswat, to himself? Okay he still wanted to do it to his father. It was difficult to give up being independent.

But it's not like he'd ever been. Who was he kidding? If it wasn't for his father he wouldn't be able to afford his lifestyle, would probably not have made it to the police, and certainly wouldn't be in Delhi right now.

The city had become quieter. He was opposite the old Safdarjung Airport, where the lights still burnt a reminiscent orange. He couldn't remember when it had been functional. Today it was all Terminal-2. He wondered if there was a Terminal-1. He had no idea where it was. Certainly no one had any plans of making Terminal-3. He'd heard that the Delhi Airport was a disaster because the architect had forgotten to make provisions for a control tower. The story was so stunningly daft, it could only be true.

Juneja decided he wasn't ready to go home quite yet. A drive would do him good. He turned left and drove past the Lodhi Gardens, looming dark and menacing as all parks do at night. The Jawaharlal Nehru Stadium squatted like an evil silvery toad and the flyover was deserted. On the Ring Road he turned left past Defence Colony and kept going. Ahead lay LSR, the ultimate prepubescent wet dream. A girls' college. At one point men weren't even allowed to stand in front of it to pick up their girlfriends. It was only 'brothers' who were allowed.

He'd almost reached GK and on a whim, he drove into the market. In any case, he needed to buy cigarettes. Prince Paanwala was the stall to be seen at. Juneja found himself finally relaxing at this absurd thought. All fag shops were filthy, small hell-holes besmirched with red betel saliva. It was the nature of things. Although a Hindi proverb sniffed at biting the hand that fed it, no one had said anything about spitting at the paanwala. The paanwala sold the paan and the customers spat it back at him. Okay not at him but next to him, around him, close to him. Hell, close enough for him to smell it, to walk and to revel in it. Prince Paanwala, although a prince among pan vendors, was a paanwala and therefore to be spat at. Perhaps the amount of red spittle in the vicinity of the shop was a paean to the quality of betel that they sold. Maybe one paid taxes dependent on the amount of spittle the income-tax dudes found. It was true! Or it could be true. Juneja found himself pondering the complexities of the problem. Apparently they had caught some fellow who sold food in plastic plates by counting the plates in the trash can and thereby discovering he was a millionaire. How did one count spittle? Litres? Or bestrewn area, i.e. radius? Maybe there was a complicated formula, or maybe paanwalas like so many of their Indian brethren like ministers and politicians just didn't pay taxes.

In the days of yore, when Juneja bought only Marlboro, especially before going to the disco with a cool chick, Prince Paanwala was the only place you got Marlboro 100%. The only place where there was certitude of no pain or rejection. What rubbish he was spouting suddenly! This is what came of visiting relatives. Today, of course thanks to liberalization, every idiot sold Marlboro. The bigger problem was that every bloody fool also smoked the stuff. He, Juneja, had long switched to Gold Flake. Although his exclusivity was shot to hell, at least one could get the stuff everywhere and scoff at pretentious Marlboro smokers.

Being Friday night, the place was full of families out to dinner. The women and children, that is. The men were all sitting in cars getting drunk since restaurants with liquor licenses were rarer than hens' teeth. This was the kind of duty all policemen revelled in. Easy pickings. Either from the restaurant which paid in advance or from the customer, who paid on the spot. GK offered a choice of Punjabi, Punjabi Chinese and only for the well-heeled, strong hearted and turmeric coated, Punjabi Japanese. Juneja was sure that for an extra tip, you could get sushi pakoras.

He was sauntering over to Prince when he saw a familiar car. It was Rajiv's. It was empty. His first reaction was to march into the nearest restaurant, but he stopped himself. It *was* a Friday night, a night for families. Prince was crowded and this time another familiar face greeted him.

'Hey buddy!' It was Sunil.

'What's up, man?' answered Juneja, bracing himself for the ubiquitous male embrace. They touched, thumped and pulled apart in flowing practised moves.

'I called you at home but your fellow said you were out.'

'I'm here now, man! Any problem? The police can fix anything!'

'Don't need the police – just a cool dude! Sonia's cousin sister's here. In fact the two of them are sitting in the car. They both smoke Benson & Hedges so I figured our Prince won't disappoint us! I didn't realize the real Prince Charming would also be here!'

'I don't get you. What's the problem?'

Sunil smiled. 'Chill, man. I, or rather we, need another man for the evening. As her date, man. I thought you'd fit the bill.'

'Cool!' Chatting they walked towards the parking, where their respective cars were. Juneja's mind was only half on the conversation. Clothes, check, aftershave, check, shoes, shit, sandals, shit, shit, shit.

'Hi, I'm Sanju. Sanjana I mean!' She was tall, dark and thin. Really thin. Maybe it was the cigarettes. Juneja lunged forward to grab her hand and mouth inanities. Sonia was gabbing on about fate and how they had given up on him. He found himself lisping silently, her breaths were huge. Glory be! Thank God for fate, for grandmothers and for Prince. And she smoked. That meant she'd probably put out. On one occasion, when he'd offered this theory to a smoking woman, she'd been enraged and said that then the same should apply to him as a smoking man. Juneja had been happy to point out that it did. Now he just had to get rid of the shoes.

'So what's the plan, guys?' enquired Juneja in the silence that ensued at the simultaneous lighting of cigarettes.

'Nikhil, Sanju's here just for the weekend. She's leaving late Saturday night, or Sunday morning to be more precisely, for the US,' explained Sonia, 'so we thought we'll give her a rocking time before she becomes a foreigner!'

Juneja smiled, nodding his head in agreement. Rock, sure he could rock as well as the other guy.

'Have you people already eaten?'

'Not yet, man.'

'Then as a true Delhiwala, let me suggest Karim's in the Old City.'

'Nikki! But that's like so far away!' God, Geetu had infected Sonia.

'Who's in a hurry?' pointed out Juneja. 'Besides, after that we can go to the disco or a club, and before that if the ladies will allow me a trip to my flat, where I'll have to ask you to stand but to make up there is some very fine wine.'

'I don't drink any Merlot,' challenged booby Sanjana.

'I have a bottle of Shiraz open, but for you I'll open the Rothschild,' offered Juneja, hoping he was pronouncing it properly. Maybe Shiraz was 'z' silent, or was the stuff Arabic?

Sunil looked at them. 'I guess you've convinced us, Nikhil, but if you don't mind I'll stick to the Finlandia! Why don't Sanju and you go in your car and the two of us will follow you?'

Juneja ensured he was a step ahead of her as they approached the car. He'd had an automatic device installed so that on the press of a button the door lock would release. It meant he could suavely proceed to his own door without having to open the door for her like a bloody chauffeur. In the car he learnt she was going to New York to a fashion-design school. He automatically translated this to mean, that she was too dumb to do anything in Delhi or India, that her parents were rich and that she would be back in six months because although money can buy you a place in the US, you still have to clean your own bathroom and cook.

The girls squealed at the Chor Minar, Juneja kicked Diwan Singh and told him to produce some kebabs and get the booze out and threw himself in the bedroom. The entire thing had been a ruse to change his shoes but then he'd realized that he needed to warn Diwan Singh about fresh sheets and a possible guest in the morning. High time he got himself a cellphone. Every bloody punk on the streets in Hong Kong had had one, he reflected, tearing off his clothes and running to the bathroom for a quick shower.

No time to be careful with clothes. It was time for the emergency kit. It consisted of a brand new pair of trousers and shirt, socks, decent leather shoes. *Azzaro* or *Fahrenheit*? Doesn't pay to be obvious, take *Fahrenheit*. Why buy *Azzaro* then? Shit, take the first bottle on the left. *Fahrenheit*, okay. He was ready to kick ass.

The party was congregated on the balcony. 'One for the road or shall we leave?'

They shifted to Juneja's car because it was bigger and had a better AC. Sunil could either pick up his dinky car on the following day or spend the night in the guest bedroom. With or without accompaniment? Sunil's call, the bed was big enough, as Juneja pointed out to him discreetly.

In the car Juneja went for the usual opening. 'So Sanju, did you do your schooling in Delhi?' In Delhi everyone knew everyone. Linked as we were through binding chains of family, religion and society.

'No, I was in boarding school, St. Andrew's.'

Juneja congratulated himself on his guess: her parents must be rich, it was a hugely expensive school.

'Those were the days, man. The best days. None of this nonsense about job, relationships, children, children's school!'

Sunil laughed. 'You seem to be avoiding it just fine, Nikhil, but you're right, those days were good. You and Rajiv were together, right?

'Yeah, had our first drink together, first fag together, and threw up together!'

'I hated school. I'm so glad it's over. In fact, I think I'm an idiot to go to school again. But New York can't be that bad. Nothing can be that bad!'

Juneja followed the conversation with half an ear as he negotiated the traffic. School, college, latest trip abroad were staple ice-breakers. Now he could safely sit back and let the conversation flow.

It had been a good evening. Juneja heaved himself out of bed. It was 4.30 a.m. Great food at Karim's, mediocre jigging in some silly disco and then getting home at one in the morning for some fabulous sex. Dawn was just breaking, but since Sanju had to be at her aunt's at ten o'clock, he figured he might as well not sleep at all. Sanju was still sleeping. He'd wake her up in a couple of hours along with Sunil and Sonia, who were curled up in the other bedroom. The joys of a bachelor pad, thought Juneja as he fixed himself a tea-bag tea.

He stepped onto the balcony to enjoy the first cigarette of the day. The Chor Minar looked clean and fresh. He himself wasn't looking half as wasted as he should have. Nor did he feel terribly exhausted. Truth be told, he was feeling remarkably fit. It must be the sex. He should have it more often.

The evening had gone incredibly well from his point of view. There had been a little hitch when they'd parked the car near the mosque. Some junkie type of beggar had tried to paw Sanju. Not surprising, really. She was wearing a blouse that lacked a front. And of course, neither Sonia nor Sanju could be bothered to put their cigarettes out. Juneja and Sunil had had to grab the fellow and had then kicked his balls to bits in the side-lane, leaving the girls squealing with delight and admiration. All these modern emancipated women were actually quite thrilled when their lord and master protected them. In fact, they demanded it by wearing clothes that would create such a situation, where he would be forced to fight for them. So maybe it hadn't been such a hitch, smirked Juneja.

At 30 plus, Sanju was no virgin and more than willing to jump on board. It made it a whole lot easier that she was going tomorrow, or tonight as the case was. No silly love story and therefore no need to feign modesty. In fact, she'd been the one to suggest anal sex. He hadn't really understood what she was talking about, when she said something about taking the subway. He'd been quite surprised that she should want to discuss public transport in bed and had been about to embark on the advantages of taxis, when she'd turned on her stomach.

Hmm, had been better than he'd thought. But still, he preferred going straight down the street, he told her afterwards. Okay, she said, then let's go straight down the street. And they did.

Then she'd started about the whole school thing again. She'd really been serious about hating school.

'I don't know how you could've liked it, Nikhil. It was awful. All those silly people sitting in judgement of you, dumb teachers telling you what to do, threatening you all the bloody time. If those were the best days of your life, then you'd have been better off committing suicide at age 13!'

'C'mon Sanju, how can you take it so seriously? Think

of the friends, your buddies, the fun, sleeping late, parties all of that stuff, man. Being free of stress and tension. Not like today, man.'

'Free of stress and tension? Nikhil, if you believe that, you're deluding yourself. Peer pressure, crap from parents. Teachers, the endless hassles with boyfriends and girlfriends. If anything, I have less tension today than I did then! Never mind, let's just agree to disagree, okay?'

Okay, they found other things they agreed about. But right now, he found himself agreeing with what she'd said. It hadn't been all that free of stress and tension.

But this very stress is what had united him and Rajiv. A union borne of angst and unhappiness. And today Rajiv had found a way out. A way without him, Nikhil Juneja. He had been left alone.

The Chor Minar seemed to look shorter than usual. Maybe it wasn't just a Tower of Thieves. Perhaps it was a stolen tower. Just like happiness needs to be stolen from the endless hours of sorrow and loneliness. And that was what he was so afraid of. Being left alone to cope with it. Was all this just postcoital stress? Sanju would be gone today. Rajiv had already gone. Sunil had Sonia. That left Sajjan Kumar. And Joseph. And the dead Talwar chick.

And him pondering over this rubbish.

Sonia was the one who finally dropped Sanju. She said it would be better if Sunil didn't not appear so often at her place till things were cleared up. Sunil looked a bit sour at that and Juneja resolved to ask him as soon as the girls left. The farewell scene with Sanju was as discreet and civilized as Juneja had hoped it would be. Besides, she looked like she couldn't wait to get into the car to find out what the hell Sonia had meant. They went off together to the car. It turned out it wasn't Sunil's car at all, which didn't surprise Juneja – it was a little Maruti 800. He'd been surprised to see Sunil driving it yesterday. If he wasn't wrong, Sunil had been nipping around in a Honda City, the last time they'd met up for a drink.

Sitting on the balcony after a massive breakfast of scrambled eggs Indian style, spiked with green chillies, onions and coriander, they settled down with Indian style tea. Cooked with milk, sugar and cardamom till it was thick. It was the only kind of tea that Diwan Singh knew and was willing to make. It was also probably the only known beverage to man that could stand up to those Indian scrambled eggs, said Sunil, when Juneja apologized for the shortcomings in his cook's repertoire.

They decided to go to Sunil's health club at the Hyatt for a swim in the afternoon and maybe do a film after that.

'I'll get the newspaper. Yesterday was Friday, the flicks must have changed,' offered Juneja. When he returned Sunil had lit up and was pensively contemplating the Chor Minar.

'Hey buddy, you cool?' queried the host.

'No, man, don't ask. Bloody hell! Women are the pits!'

'I was wondering about that one,' interrupted Juneja, rustling the newspaper into shape. 'Things between you and Sonia didn't seem all too smooth after your illicit night of passion!'

'Screw you! Illicit! Were you eavesdropping?'

Juneja nearly dropped the newspaper in shock. 'What the hell is that supposed to mean? Why should I have been eavesdropping?'

'Because that's what she said, man! Shit, Nikhil, I'm sorry, look why did you say that?'

'Illicit?' He continued at Sunil's curt nod. 'Because that's what...' Juneja was completely nonplussed. Yes, why?

'Because it's what they say. You know, in newspapers and all.'

'Man, Nikhil, this entire thing is getting bizarre. I told you about my cousin, Vineet.'

'No,' retorted Juneja immediately. Was more gossip coming his way?

Sunil lit up the next cigarette with the butt of the last. 'Can your Jeeves make us some more coffee or anything?'

'Sure, but he only makes this tea, okay?'

'Yeah, okay. I guess it's too early to hit the bottle!'

Juneja was feeling increasingly alarmed. Sunil was a great guy. Was he serious about alcohol at this time? Diwan Singh graced the request with his usual sullen acquiescence.

'So, the tea's arriving. What's the problem?'

'Man, Nikhil,' answered Sunil, chain-smoking some more, 'Vineet is my cousin. He's getting married to this Talwar chick. I thought I had told you about it. Any way, it's no big deal either way. There was some bloody hassle that the aunt or some wretched relative had been pregnant and then committed suicide or something.' Sunil paused to hunt for some more cigarettes.

Juneja told him to sit and went into his bedroom to pull out a new carton. So the news was out. The point was, who had leaked it?

He returned to see Diwan Singh with the tea tray and some dry fruit. Typical Diwan Singh, bad-tempered and generous at the same time.

'So your cousin's going to marry the chick, pregnant aunt and all?'

'Well, I think he'd have been forced out of the entire thing. I mean he's pretty obsessive about the woman – his girlfriend I mean. But the point is not my cousin, it's Sonia. Now the police have arrested the servant and my aunt called me yesterday and said that this is just some usual type of domestic crime, so they'll have to say yes to the marriage because although the girl is ghastly the family is quite decent. And this is where my goose gets cooked.

'Sonia says if your cousin can marry this trash woman, why can't we get married?'

'What the hell does that mean? Usual type of domestic crime?'

'You know what I mean, Nikhil. Wake up in the morning with your throat slit!'

'A bit tough to wake up then but I get what you mean! But what about the aunt being pregnant? I mean, the woman can't help having her throat slit by the servant but she can help being knocked up, can't she?'

Sunil smiled. It was strained but he didn't seem to have lost his sense of humour completely. 'Man, Nikhil, you sound like my aunt. She's been trying every excuse in the book. But quite frankly, Vineet is so hot about Bahar that I don't think my aunt will have a choice. And now that the Talwar aunt is dead, who cares about her being knocked up or knocked out.' He took a sip of the tepid tea and manfully tried to suppress a shudder as Juneja laughed.

'God, Nikhil, I like Sonia and she's hot in bed but I'm not made for this marriage bit, man. I mean, in the beginning all women say they're not into relationships and they can take it as hard as a man but then after three months – *three months*, Nikhil, that's really the crucial period. In three months she's screwing your happiness instead of your dick!'

Juneja imbibed this knowledge hungrily. In his experience it was hard enough to get a woman for three days, much less be worried about her wanting to hang on after three months. But now was probably not the time to get into the subject. He'd better try and do something for his career.

'The Talwar family is decent?'

'I don't know, man. Rumour has it that their finances are a bit shaky. That's what my aunt wants me to find out. You know, my uncle, Vineet's dad, has been diagnosed with Parkinson's. Vineet and I will share the business together in the near future. He's a really nice guy. A bit immature, but otherwise really decent. He's only 24. But I'm seriously not looking forward to this Bahar woman on his arm. She's really cheap.'

Juneja nodded. Family business was sacred. Everything and nothing made a difference. If Sunil didn't get along with his cousin or the cousin's wife, it meant slaughtering the cash cow. 'How do you know that the Talwars are in financial trouble?'

'Man, Nikhil, I don't! I'm asking you!'

'Me? How the hell should I know?'

Sunil had the grace to look embarrassed. 'No, but your father would know.'

It hurt. It really hurt. Was this what the entire newfound closeness had been about? Later, Nikhil, later. You need to focus right now. He wants something from you, get something in return. It would do the gossip rounds immediately but what the hell, it was true and it would keep the mills grinding.

He tried for a relaxed tone. 'My dad's not in Delhi right now. In fact I was in Jor Bagh yesterday. To see my grandmother. Because Dad's not in town I popped in to have a look. You know, see if everything is okay, if she's taking her medicines and stuff.'

Sunil tried to nod encouragingly but Juneja could see the difficulty he was having. What was going on? Did Juneja now have contact with his family? If that was the case, then it was no big favour to ask him to ask his not so estranged father for some inside information, was it?

Juneja continued, 'So you want me to ask my father about the Talwars?'

'Nikhil, I'll be straight with you. After my parents died, my aunt and uncle took care of me. Vineet is like my own kid brother. The problem with Bahar isn't her aunt or the money. It's that, that...' Sunil faltered and looked at the overflowing ashtray for inspiration.

'Nikhil, I, we, all of us, my aunt, my uncle, we love Vineet. We care about him and we want him to be happy. And we don't think Bahar is the right girl for him. I'd really appreciate it if we could just stall the marriage a little. Please, we're really worried. Please. We really care about him.'

Juneja nodded.

The health club was great. The swim, the only way to beat the heat. In the evening they tottered off to see a film. They'd been unable to decide which would be the better time-pass, *Ace Ventura: Pet Detective* or *Timecop*. Sunil had his way and they went off to *Timecop*. More suitable, he said, since Juneja was a cop.

'C'mon, Nikhil, you'll learn how to do your job better!'

The special effects were good but the film was lousy, plus there was way too little sex. By the time the film ended Juneja could feel the the absence of sleep making its presence felt. His head hurt everytime he moved it and his eyes hurt all the time. He didn't feel sleepy, he felt knocked out. Sunil looked quite grungy as well.

'Sunil, sorry, man. But I have to quit the scene now.'

Sunil smiled back. 'What's happened to us? Suddenly we're old! I'll give you a buzz tommorrow. Maybe we can go for another swim?'

Juneja nodded and after a final thump left for his car.

He had a hard time keeping his eyes open and for once was glad to see Diwan Singh's grumpy face.

Diwan Singh looked at him with disgust and pushed him into a chair. He was told to take his shoes off and have a quick shower during which time a glass of milk would be warmed for him. Juneja did exactly that. He didn't think he'd be able to keep his eyes open for the milk but Diwan Singh looked so stern that he dared not sleep without draining the glass and then it was oblivion, blessed oblivion.

The morning brought Diwan Singh and, for a change, black tea. Cooked to a fine twist in the usual way but even Diwan Singh couldn't thicken water with sugar although from the taste of it, he'd been trying. Juneja's questioning grunt brought a single-word answer? 'Curdled.' From the looks of it Diwan Singh was too. Juneja would have given his left arm to see what Diwan Singh would do to the milkman on Monday.

Diwan Singh moved around the room picking up clothes, which surprised Juneja. Usually all this clearing up stuff happened in his absence. But maybe Diwan Singh was in a hurry, which meant Juneja should get the hell out of the bedroom. He picked up his cigarettes from the bedside table and juggling the cup of tea, made his way towards the balcony. Dumping the stuff on the table, he turned to go back into the house to pick up the newspaper, only to see Diwan Singh standing there.

'Is everything all right?'

'You went to Jor Bagh?'

So Saraswat had been talking.

Juneja didn't answer. Picking up the newspaper he made his way back to the balcony but Diwan Singh was never one to be perturbed by slights.

'You told them about Joseph?'

Juneja sank back into his chair. So that was what this was all about.

He tried for taciturn authority. 'That is a police matter. I can't discuss it.'

Diwan Singh looked at him and Juneja had the feeling that the gaze was hard.

'Your colleague is in trouble. You should help him.'

After this pronouncement Diwan Singh finally left him in peace to peruse the papers at leisure. This bloody OJ Simpson case was going to go on forever at the rate these fools were going on. Murdered his wife, silly bugger! The Talwar case had shifted to the third page. With a little luck, he'd be back on the front page come Monday. Okay, Tuesday. Monday, that fool would talk to Gupta, afternoon or evening press announcement, Tuesday headlines. Surely the Talwars could be persuaded to take care of his family. After all, the chap was going to jail without any details about alleged pregnancies being leaked to the press. In about ten years the idiot would be out, richer than he could ever hope to be.

Maybe all servants should quit working. Just walk into people's houses, slit their throats, go to jail and let their erstwhile employers take care of their families. Okay, there were little things like getting the odd spinster pregnant but after all, all jobs require some amount of ingenuity. And to earn that amount of money, one had to be prepared to do a little work...

Juneja leaned back. It was hot. So what else was new? The Chor Minar glowered at him. It looked particularly malevolent. Saudamini Talwar, OJ Simpson, Joseph. The list seemed endless. People just didn't seem to be able to have normal sex lives. In any case, by tomorrow the case would be wrapped up. He was wondering whether he should call up the station to check on the condition of Ram Singh or whatever his name was, when the telephone rang. Startled, he spilled tea on himself. Thank god it was tepid, but there would be hell to pay with Diwan Singh. He was still shaking his dripping hands when Diwan Singh called for him. 'Rajiv!'

This was another problem with Diwan Singh. He never called anyone, including his lord and master, sahib or sir or anything. Insolent fellow! Maybe he should tick him off?

'Hi, man, what's up?'

'Hey, Nikhil, bastard, I saw you on Friday in GK and even came out to look for you. Where'd you go?'

Juneja felt himself cringe. It was true. He'd violated the sacrosanct rules of friendship. If you meet someone else, had sex or a fight, or the promise of the aforementioned, you must asap call up the best friend for a gossip session, also called tell-or spill-all. Rajiv, of course, always got mixed up.

Rajiv continued, 'I thought I saw Sunil there. Were you with him? C'mon man, spell-all!'

Juneja decided to make up. He made a peace offering, 'Nothing man, just some sex on the side!'

'Bastard, you had a piece?'

'C'mon Rajiv,' Juneja laughed. 'You don't want to know about the horny details, do you?'

'Bastard, what are you doing?'

'Now?'

'Right bloody now!'

'Nothing.'

'I'm coming over right now.'

'To hear the horny details?'

'No. To whip your ass! See you in ten minutes. Keep the whip handy!'

'Rajiv, hang on a sec!'

'What is it, you donkey? Feeling scared already?'

'No, bastard, horny! Can you do me a favour?'

'Man, Nikhil, my life is getting spent doing you favours. Shoot!'

'Just ask Geetu if you can get me a packet of milk. Only if she has one spare. Our milk got curdled this morning.'

'I get it. Haven't had your tea, so you're sitting around feeling constipated, huh? Okay, okay, I'll get the milk. See you and don't forget the whip!'

Rajiv ended up taking almost half an hour but Juneja was feeling much better about himself. He hadn't told Diwan Singh that Rajiv would be bringing the milk. That would really piss Diwan Singh off. He hated any kind of perceived condescension regarding his way of running the household. Rajiv would in all innocence give him the milk at the door. He, Juneja, would only have to ensure that he happened to be there at the same time. Then he would graciously thank Rajiv, abuse the milkman and make out how it wasn't Diwan Singh's fault at all. Perfect!

He managed to pull it off, too. Only, just as he was airily saying that they could now, at long last, drink some tea, Diwan Singh gave him a sardonic grin. Juneja felt himself redden. Was he that transparent?

He ushered Rajiv into the drawing room, where he'd pulled in the chairs from the balcony. The AC was on full blast. For 11 a.m. it was much too hot.

'So, man, you really want to drink tea? Or a chilled gin and lime?'

'Nikhil, I don't know! I'm too hot to decide. My parents are out with my car because their car's gone for servicing. Geetu's out shopping with a friend and she took the small car because her bloody friend's car conked out and I thought it doesn't make sense to pull out the Mercedes for the three minutes. Biggest bloody mistake of my life! Man, I need water. Cold water. And I need to clean my feet. In this weather I thought slippers would be okay but the streets are so bloody filthy!'

'Okay, relax, it's clean here. I'll get the water and stuff organized. Will you stay for lunch? I'll tell Diwan Singh, okay? You go into the bathroom.'

Leaving Rajiv mumbling to himself, Juneja called for Diwan Singh. He managed to give him directions for lunch without looking directly at him. He also told him to take all calls and not put any through to him. He'd had enough of being harassed. Having done so, he collapsed in a chair to light a much needed cigarette.

Rajiv and his cars. It was so typically Delhi. Rajiv's dad would have the big car, his mom, if she chose to drive, a smaller car, but they could share a uniformed driver. The driver would wear his cap only in front of dad and be bareheaded in front of mom. Rajiv's grandmother was, however, the oldest and therefore there had to be a car for her as well. And her car had to be the biggest. In this case it was the Mercedes. Since she hardly ever went out, the car, a vast behemoth, stayed in the garage most of the time. Rajiv had tried taking it to the factory a couple of times but the roads were so pot-holed that the car had to be repaired after almost every drive. Rajiv's family was big on small cars currently. What with the Mercedes, there wasn't much space to park the rest in any case.

He sat up with a jerk. If Rajiv had a five-car household, was it not possible that the cars parked outside the Jor Bagh house all belonged to his father?

He was still pondering this manifest injustice when Rajiv came back looking distinctly better.

'Man, I feel like, like reborn!'

'Water for you?'

'Perfect.'

They sat down for a chat. Juneja felt the tension draining away from him. How could he ever have doubted Rajiv? A relationship like their was made of steel. They knew and liked each other inside out. It was this stupid case that had been screwing his happiness and thankfully, that too was getting over on Monday.

'So,' concluded Juneja, 'the night was really hot but poor Sunil got it in the backside from Sonia in the morning! Apparently, she's wanting to settle down and get married and have kids and all that conventional I-love-mummy stuff, man.'

Rajiv looked down and shrugged. 'Man, Nikhil, you can't really blame her. The woman must be over thirty and she's been dating Sunil for ages, man. I mean, if nothing else, her parents must be wanting her to settle down.'

Diwan Singh came in and announced lunch, looking more dolorous than ever.

'No, Diwan Singh, you bring the food in here on a trolley. It's too hot, please?' That was Rajiv. Juneja had already started getting up.

Diwan Singh gave Rajiv a warm smile. 'I have already brought it on a trolley. Just hold the door open and I'll wheel it in!' He shot Juneja a triumphant glance and left looking distinctly cocky.

'You okay, Nikhil?'

'Sure, I'm fine, just fine.'

Lunch was good. In Rajiv's honour, Diwan Singh had made special chicken and there were leftovers from the past five days, so there was plenty of variety, as Rajiv pointed out.

'Besides, Nikhil, I haven't eaten this stuff, so what're you getting worked up for? Also, you don't seem to have been eating much at home either. Look at the amount, man, we'll never finish it!'

That was just Rajiv being nice and underestimating his appetite. They polished off the lot and then lolled around like indolent lords.

'Man, Rajiv, this is a perfect Sunday afternoon. No wonder Sunil doesn't want to mess it up with bloody Sonia!'

Rajiv had pulled over another chair and was busy with the act of getting horizontal. Juneja already was.

'No, Nikhil, Sunil's only making excuses. Because he's not in love with her or whatever. If he was, he'd want to settle down as well and have kids and all.'

'Rajiv, you make it sound like every man's dream! And if that's the way you feel, where are your chubby cherubs after five years, no, it's more than that, isn't it? How many years have you been married, man?'

'Almost ten.'

'So where are your dream kids?'

'I can't have any.'

'Be serious, Rajiv.'

'I am, Nikhil. My sperm count is too low. We've had endless tests but there's nothing to be done. Geetu tried IVF several times but she miscarried and so we're giving it a break. It's very traumatic for her.'

Juneja tried to say something but somehow the words seemed to be frozen in his throat. The bloody AC had choked his throat.

Rajiv wasn't expecting an answer in any case. Not that a question had been posed.

'We found out almost immediately after marriage. In the first year. It's genetic or genital or genetical or something. I can't understand these weird medical words, in any case.

'Geetu's parents even asked for a divorce but she didn't agree. She said God will take care of us and give us a baby when he sees fit.'

Rajiv left at tea time. He said Geetu would be back soon and would want to show him all the shopping. Some cousin of his was getting married and Geetu was organizing the gift shopping for the family. That was nice of her, Juneja was able to offer at this stage of the farewell proceedings.

Monday morning dawned as mornings tend to do. Promising the crackling heat of the late afternoon, but at this time still soft and caressing.

It had drizzled a little last night. Juneja sat on the balcony, drinking in the smell of the parched earth consuming water at long last. The dust had settled down and the leaves glistened in the light of the silvery streetlamps. The street had been silent barring a few stray dogs, who'd grumbled a bit before finding shelter in the Chor Minar. He sat there for a long time. He felt overheated and incapable of coherent thought. The Chor Minar seemed to be enjoying the small shower. It looked unconcerned with the world's problems.

He'd not known, what to say. How could Rajiv be, you know, the I-word? Nobody he knew was. Nobody anyone could know, could be. He had let Rajiv talk and he had been quite matter of fact about the entire thing. Bloody hell! He'd had ten years to become matter of fact about it. Apparently everyone knew. Okay, not everyone, but certainly his parents and her parents and the yowly grandmother and Rajiv's sister, because her husband was a doctor, and all the doctors and their assistants and nurses and stuff.

In fact, Rajiv said, he'd had hundreds of appointments. In the beginning he'd had to jerk off in glasses, which in itself had been quite ghastly but the discovery of the certainty that it was his fault, that he wasn't manly enough, had been a lot worse. Then, they had had marriage counselling and psychological support, both alone and with the familly. Juneja paused mid-cigarette. That meant that all the bloody shrinks knew now. No, no, no. The shrinks had known as well. He'd tried, no, he was still trying to come to terms with it. That Rajiv was, you know what he was. Hell, half the bloody world seemed to know, what he was. As well as the fact that Rajiv hadn't, you know. Hell, this was no time to be thinking of that. But what was he supposed to think? He could hardly have spent the last ten years thinking of Rajiv's potency or lack of it! Now, that would have been really weird. So, he could only have thought about it or cared about it, if he had been told. Which he hadn't. So how was he supposed to care about it?

Basically this meant that Rajiv had been lying to him all these years. Yes, lying. He'd been hanging around some corny fertility clinics and he'd not told him, Juneja. His best friend. Who shared the details of his dirty rogering. No, called him for lunch, yes, organized lunch, so that Rajiv could be titillated by the details of the newest Juneja conquest. And why had Juneja done this? Had he called up Rajiv to ask him to come over? Had he felt the need to brag about his rogering experience? No. That was the answer, no. No, he hadn't. Rajiv had wanted to know.

He'd wanted the horny details. And Juneja had done it. He'd told him. Because he'd thought Rajiv led an unhappy life, a frustrated life. A sad life. But that this was the cause of his frustration, this was just lying. Here Juneja had been, complaining about children, about the neighbour's son, about all and sundry and their malevolent desire to procreate and Rajiv had listened to him and nodded and the truth was this. This was the bloody hypocritical truth.

Rajiv had said that he intended to start talking about it now. He'd said it was nothing to be ashamed about. And that his family and Geetu had really helped him. And, and this was the straw that had crippled Juneja, Geetu had told him that he should tell Juneja.

'Nikki loves you so much,' she had told Rajiv. 'You must share your sorrows with him. He'll be hurt otherwise.'

Juneja had woken up no wiser for the the counsel of the night. His head was heavy and he felt the weight of the world on his shoulders. Diwan Singh seemed to sense it and was particularly friendly. He didn't mention the tea, cooked as usual, nor did he underline things with meaningful grunts. In fact, Juneja caught a stray hum every now and then.

The drive to work was relatively easy. It also just happened to be 7.30 in the morning. Perhaps other Delhites had better things to do at this hour. Juneja didn't. Sinha was sitting around. He jumped at the sight of Juneja, which in itself was a sight worth seeing.

Juneja looked at him glumly 'Has Sajjan Kumar come in?'

'Sir, he had night shift yesterday, so he is, maybe, sleeping.'

That meant Sajjan Kumar had been drunk as a lord and was now sleeping it off.

'Where is this fellow?'

Sir, Sajjan Kumar?'

'No. Sinha, what is wrong with you?' Juneja could feel the explosion coming. This was not going well. But maybe if he vented steam with Sinha, he would feel better later?

He inhaled, ready to lampoon, when he got a glimpse of Sinha's face, grinning ingratiatingly at the back.

He whirled around to behold Jt. CP Gupta. 'Sir, what a surprise!'

'Arre, Juneja, that Talwar boy, I keep forgetting these people's names, called me yesterday. He said that you have been very efficient. That they had never thought that the servant would touch a hair on that girl's head. But you know servants today. In any case, they are very happy with you. But I thought, such a big case, Nikhil will want me to be there. So, I came this morning, hmm? So, where is this fellow?'

Sinha had been grinning throughout this speech.

'Gupta, sir, our Juneja sir, is one in a million, sir.'

'Better than me even, Sinha?'

'Sir, what are you saying? Juneja sir is always saying how much he is learning from you!'

You couldn't top Sinha. Juneja refused to try.

'Sinha, Gupta sir has very little time to waste. Where is the servant of the Talwars? Bring him to my office. And send Sajjan Kumar in as soon as he gets here, all right?

Sinha translated that into *sober*, nodded and went off to get the servant.

Since Gupta was going to be in attendance, Sinha would ensure, that the fellow was cleaned up and all overt signs of his fall down the stairs were patched up.

Juneja called Gupta's PA to say that Gupta was in his room, in case of an emergency, and that the PA should send some tea or coffee in. Juneja would have killed for a cigarette but he didn't want to give Gupta the satisfaction of holding forth on nicotine addiction.

They had barely sat down when Sinha made his entrance. Ram Singh followed. He was pale but otherwise calm, and given the condition of the police station, remarkably clean.

'So, Ram Singh,' started Juneja, 'you have had enough...'

'No, Juneja. Let me chat with him. After all, I am an old man, indulge me a little. My life is full of administration and forms and reports. Let me have a small share of your inquiry. Just a little fun?' He gave Juneja a smile that would have put a shark to shame and Ram Singh a coy, paternal laugh. 'So, Ram Singh, you have been working for the Talwars for how long now?'

'Sir, more than twenty years. I came as a fifteen-year-old boy. My father was a worker in the Talwar factory. But then there was an accident. And he was killed. He got stuck in a machine.'

And to make sure there was no fuss with the newspapers or some silly NGO types, they gave you a job, thought Juneja, exasperated with the proceedings.

Impervious to Juneja's take on employment law, Ram Singh continued, 'So, since there was no one to support my mother and my three sisters, the Talwars very kindly gave me a job. They are my all in all, sir. My parents, my god, sir.'

Juneja got up as the PA came in with the tray. This entire life story business bored him to tears. At some stage Ram Singh would go into denial. Hopefully Sajjan Kumar would be awake by then and they could continue with getting a confession out of the fellow.

In the meantime Gupta seemed intent on playing the benevolent grandfather. He barely bothered to look up at

Juneja or at the proffered cup. Ram Singh was blathering on about his loyalty, his love, his service, his devotion to the Talwars.

Gupta interrupted the paean. 'So, why should they say you got Saudamini, Pinky Baby, pregnant?'

Ram Singh looked back at Gupta. He seemed horrified. His eyes were full. His mouth worked convulsively.

'You know she was pregnant?'

Gupta nodded. 'They say you raped her, you know. Then she was pregnant. That you killed her. To hide that she was pregnant. Then the secret would have been out. And then you faked the suicide. But I want to hear the truth from you.'

Juneja was gaping at Gupta. Was the man mad? It had been bad enough to give the game away to bloody N.K. Talwar. Gupta himself had said that this could become a political case. The moment this bastard got a lawyer, their collective goose would be skinned, stuffed and cooked. He paused. Should that be geese then?

Meanwhile Ram Singh was still playing the sobbing widow. Juneja felt a reluctant admiration for the man. What drama, what expression, what tragedy! A knock on the door made him look up. It was Sajjan Kumar. Sinha must have warned him about Gupta. Other than the red eyes, there was no sign of his binge. Juneja's troop was unswervingly loyal.

Sajjan Kumar summed up the situation immediately. He went behind Ram Singh to be in position for the *look*. Just then Ram Singh spoke. 'Yes, sir, I have betrayed Talwar sahib. I killed her. I got her pregnant. I killed her. I broke my word to Talwar sahib.'

It all happened at once, thought Juneja in retrospect. Gupta looked flabbergasted, Sajjan Kumar impressed, Sinha complacent. Gupta had refused to believe it could be over that fast. He'd tried to sway Ram Singh, told him to take his time, to think it over, how dire the consequences would be. But good old Ram Singh would have none of it. After Gupta told him that he would have to sign a confession, he demanded to do it then and there. That the confession would first have to be written hadn't occurred to the illiterate bastard.

Juneja, as usual, had to do all the work. He kicked Sinha and told him to get on with writing the confession. Gupta wanted to approve it but it didn't matter. They had a confession. And if Juneja could actually believe the evidence of his ears, a voluntary one.

Gupta went off to his office. His PA would call up the Talwars to give them the news. The news would be given to the press in the evening after all the formalities, the confession, arrest and so on had been completed.

Gupta assured Juneja of a special mention. Juneja himself knew that Gupta would have to do it. The Talwars would ensure it.

He sat back for an overdue congratulatory smoke as Sinha came in with the confession. Juneja stubbed out the cigarette with a sigh. Off to Gupta's office for the bloody approval.

Gupta was looking pensive when Juneja entered. Juneja answered his inquiring glance with a single, laconic word, 'Confession.'

'Yes, Nikhil, you read it out. I want to compare it with the postmortem details. My PA has taken out the report, wait a minute, where is it? Ah, here...'

Juneja started off in a drone. 'I, Ram Singh, do confess, blah, blah...'

Juneja left Gupta to concentrate on the trash. He was wondering if he should mention his trip to Jor Bagh. Maybe that would increase the pressure on Gupta.

'Stop, Nikhil. This is the problem!' Gupta looked exultant, thought Juneja distrustingly.

'Is there a problem, sir?' And if there is, Sajjan Kumar will fix it in the basement, he added silently.

'Yes, Nikhil, look. No, no, you get that fellow, what is his name, Ram Singh in here. Just a minor detail.'

Juneja stalked out. He would get in touch with his father. On bended knee. Just so he didn't have to put up with Gupta's pathetic idiosyncrasies any more.

'Sinha, bring that Ram Singh here!'

Sajjan Kumar rose instead to the occasion. 'Sir, I'll take care of it.'

'No,' declined Juneja regretfully. 'Gupta wants to see him.'

The men exchanged meaningful glances and Juneja walked back into Gupta's office, followed by a sad looking Ram Singh and a waddling Sinha.

'Ah, Ram Singh,' beamed Gupta. 'You said you did it. Tell me, my boy, what about the sleeping pills? When did you give them to her?'

Gupta looked triumphant. When Ram Singh denied all knowledge, he, Juneja, would have a big bamboo up the wrong end.

'I gave them to her in the evening. They are from Dr Sahni. He is the family doctor. I gave her a double dose.'

Juneja felt faint. Was Ram Singh really the murderer? Was God so merciful? He vowed to go to the temple. Some day. Tomorrow. Next year. Maybe.

Gupta looked bitter. 'Sinha, take him out.' He waited for Sinha to close the door before turning to Juneja. 'Look, Nikhil, I want this case to be closed. Without any loose ends. You go to this Dr Sahni. The Talwars will give you the details. I don't want the case to fall through because of any loopholes.' He turned away. It was a clear dismissal.

Not that Juneja minded. He could be magnanimous in victory. He left quietly.

Outside, he told the PA to call up the Talwars, to give them the news and to get the contact details of the family doctor. It was sad to see Gupta clutching at straws, but what the hell? Juneja shrugged. It wasn't any skin off his bloody nose. He'd barely made it to his office when Sinha appeared with a slip of paper.

'Sir, the address.'

'Thank you, Sinha. Tell Sajjan Kumar we'll leave in twenty minutes. Send me some coffee.'

He sat down and lit up. Sinha was still standing there.

'Yes?'

'Sir, Joseph? Is everything all right?' Nosy bastard.

'Get the coffee and tell Sajjan Kumar.' Sinha knew how hard he could push it. He left without a struggle.

Juneja looked at the slip. Defence Colony. D-Block. Hmm, decent address. No more Pratap Singh nonsense. It was the right address.

Life felt good. Sod bloody Rajiv. He, Nikhil Juneja, had cracked an important case, maybe things were going to improve with his father, maybe the next promotion would come faster. He didn't need a friend like Rajiv. Or Sunil. Life was good. God loved him. He looked at the slip of paper again. It reminded him of Joseph and his silly prayer slip.

Juneja heaved himself to his feet. Sanju hadn't said anything but he'd felt quite, well, weighty was the word, compared to her. A gym was probably the answer. Meet some cool chicks as well.

Sinha was standing outside.

'No, Sinha, I will go alone with Sajjan Kumar. I am expecting important calls. You take them, okay?'

Sinha nodded his sad acquiescence. He was in disfavour.

Outside, Juneja felt his muscles relax despite the crackling heat.

'C'mon. Sajjan Kumar, Defence Colony.'

Sajjan Kumar grinned adoringly back at him. His boss had done wonders. Everyone was talking about it in the police station.

Juneja smiled back benevolently.

Traffic was going to be bad. The office rush had started. But Sajjan Kumar was a tank. He'd get them through.

'Shall I put on the beacon, sir?'

'No, Sajjan Kumar, we are in no hurry. Just relax.'

'Yes, sir. Congratulations, sir.'

'Thank you. Have a cigarette?'

This was the height of camaraderie and Sajjan Kumar looked gratified. They smoked in silent contentment, when Juneja felt his conscience nag him. It's a small thing, Nikhil, do it.

'Sajjan Kumar?'

'Sir?'

'Something bad has happened to Joseph. To his daughter, you understand?'

'Yes, sir.' Sajjan Kumar had done so many bad things to so many people, Juneja wondered how he could understand anything else.

'I want you to go there in the evening. You are not to tell any one at the station, all right?'

'Yes, sir.'

'You find out and solve the matter, okay?'

'Okay, sir, no problem, sir.'

Juneja knew this to be true. This was a Sajjan Kumar crime. He'd know what to do. Juneja was made for sophisticated crime. Bastard, Ram Singh! He'd known the fellow was up to no good. Hadn't even wanted to give them cold water. Bastard murderer.

Dr Sahni's clinic in Defence Colony turned out to be exactly what Juneja had expected. A huge complex of builder's flats. The clinic was on the ground floor, the good doctor probably lived upstairs and by the looks of it, he had two sons, who also lived with him. They were also doctors, he ascertained from the signboards. Juneja always felt somewhat suspiscious of such doctor families. Medicine was a business like any other. And weren't the best businesses family run? Yes. But not in the Juneja family. So? Never mind, Nikhil, never mind.

Sajjan Kumar knew that there was no need for him here. He settled down for a comfortable snooze as Juneja marched in. It was like a hotel. White, clean flowers, pretty girl behind the counter. Only the slightly overpowering smell of detergent gave the show away. Perhaps it was deliberate. Might be a bit embarrasing if a patient got taken in and demanded a whisky.

'My name is Juneja. Addl CP Nikhil Juneja. I want to see Dr Sahni.'

'Good morning, sir. Would that be Dr P.K. Sahni or Dr C.K. Sahni?'

'Who is the doctor of the Talwars?'

'Sir, I am not allowed to discuss other patients, sir.'

Nonplussed, Juneja didn't know what to say. Besides, all the initials were bothering him.

The girl tried again, all the while smiling toothily, which only served to distract Juneja. 'Sir, Dr P.K. Sahni is the urologist and Dr C.K. Sahni is the fertility expert. We offer a variety of fertility treatments, sir. Have you already...'

Juneja cut her short before this went any further. 'No. No, I am not a patient. I am here as a police officer. I am conducting an inquiry. Do I look like a patient to you? Do I look impotent or what?' He was shouting, he discovered from the petrified look on her face. Behind him a door opened and a young man in a white doctor's coat came out.

'What has happened? Vasudha, are you all right? Who is shouting? This is a respectable clinic!' This last was directed at Juneja.

Juneja found himself spluttering. 'This chit, this girl, your receptionist asked me if I was impotent!'

'No, sir.'

'She is my wife!'

'Who are you?'

'Dr C.K. Sahni.'

'Urologist or fertility?'

'Fertility.'

'I am looking for another Dr Sahni. He is the family doctor of the Talwars. This is regarding our inquiries in an investigation. Criminal investigation,' he added. Die in hell, bastard!

'That would be my father, Dr S.K. Sahni. He is not in Delhi right now.'

'Then you please have a look at his records. It is a simple matter but unfortunately quite urgent.'

Dr C.K. Sahni didn't look happy. His wife was still looking scared.

'I can have a look. But I am not sure, if I can help you.'

If you want to, you mean, translated Juneja modally, furious with himself. He swallowed hard and turned to the pretty wife. 'I am sorry for the...you know.'

'No, sir, it's fine, sir.'

Somewhat mollified, Dr C.K. Sahni ushered Juneja into a doctor's room. It smelled slightly musty, the detergent no longer so sharp.

Dr C.K. Sahni settled down behind the desk, opened a few drawers. 'My father rarely sees patients any more. He is 76. Now, who do you want?'

'Talwar, Saudamini Talwar.'

'Hmm, P, Q, R, S, T....Here we have it. Talwar. Saudamini, you said.'

'Yes, your father had prescribed her sleeping pills.'

'Well, not really sleeping pills. Just mild tranquilizers. Together with anticonvulsants.'

'Anticonvulsant? Does that make you sleep?'

'Well, Inspector, umm?'

'Addl. CP Nikhil Juneja.'

Dr C.K. Sahni held on to the last bit, just as Juneja had hoped.

'Comm. Juneja, she was being slightly sedated in keeping with her condition. Anticonvulsants are given to prevent, well, convulsions, you know, fits.'

Her condition? How could this guy know about her pregnancy? Had the Talwars brought the girl here?

'Her condition? What was her condition? How bad was it?'

'Comm. Juneja, I told you, I am not her doctor. Saudamini Talwar.' He consulted the folder. 'Yes, she has been my father's patient for the last twenty-odd years. Not that there is much to be done in these cases but the patient needs regular supervision and medical check-ups.'

Last twenty years? She couldn't have been pregnant, thought Juneja, relieved.

'So what was her condition?'

Dr C.K. Sahni looked mildly surprised, 'She is retarded. Severely retarded. That is why the sedatives and the anticonvulsants. I think, Down's Syndrome.' He looked sheepish. 'My father's handwriting is not so easy for me to read! Today we use computers for our records. So much better,' he grumbled in an undertone.

'Retarded? You mean, mentally retarded?'

'Yes, Inspec– I mean Comm. Juneja. I am afraid I can't tell you any thing more just like this. I would have to look at the case in more detail. Or I can ask my father, if you like?'

Juneja wasn't quite sure of what he liked.

'I, no, not really. I need a confirmation from you regarding the medical prescription. And I'll let you know about the rest.'

'Okay. If you'll wait I'll get my stationary.'

Juneja sat back, inhaling musty detergent. Retarded, what did that mean? Why hadn't Khurana told him? Or was it in the medical report bloody Gupta had been perusing? Had he, Juneja, missed this detail? What did it mean?

Dr C.K. Sahni returned holding his letter pad. 'So, you want me to confirm the prescription?'

'Yes, with the date, dosage etc. You know, she has been killed.'

'Killed? Oh my God! This is the Talwar case!'

'Yes,' anwered Juneja, flattered by the interest.

'So have you apprehended the killer?'

'Domestic crime. It was the servant.'

'That is terrible. Terrible. My wife is very scared of being left alone. My father is visiting relatives. In the evening, she doesn't like to be alone with the servants. My brother, Dr P.K. Sahni, has just got married. They are on their honeymoon. In Disneyland. Paris. Euro-Disney, you know?'

Juneja nodded to show that indeed, he knew.

'This retardation,'

'Yes?'

'Means she was like?' Juneja's imagination faltered. How was she? How had she been?

'Like a child. That is how I would explain it. Like a child who can't, who doesn't grow up. Slow, you know?' added Dr C.K. Sahni chattily.

Juneja nodded to show that indeed, this too he knew.

Dr C.K. Sahni held forth on domestic violence for some time and accompanied Juneja to the door. The toothy wife wasn't there. Maybe she'd gone to keep an eye on the servants. Juneja felt constrained to offer another apology.

'You know, your wife, that impotent. Actually my friend is impotent. He has a problem. Low sperm count. That is why my reaction.' There, it was out.

'No problem, Comm. Juneja. Whenever you want, you can consult me. You don't have to feel shy. We can do a lot these days.'

Dr C.K. Sahni shook him firmly by the hand at the gate and left him alone.

Joseph hoped his mind would go blank, the way it so often did these days. Sajjan Kumar had discovered him in a state of complete bewilderment on the street yesterday. He was on his way home from CMI and didn't know how to go home any more. In his misery Joseph had started stammering and then weeping. He found Sajjan Kumar surprisingly easy to talk to. Although he must have been tired after a long day's work, he listened patiently to Joseph's account.

It had been hell. Recapitulating that horrible day, the search, the insecurity and the hideous finality at the end of it. The brief joy, they had felt when they had found Glorious, only to be hurtled down a one-way street of never-ending nightmares.

It was only Tuesday. How should he spend the rest of his life? Get rid of time, this thing that meant he had to keep obsessively thinking about what had happened. What should he do? They had taken Glorious to a doctor, who had confirmed the rape. There was considerable damage, but the doctor said it would have to wait. He didn't want to do anything much right now. The child was traumatized enough, he said. Joseph had had to leave the room at that point. He'd have started weeping in front of Glorious otherwise.

Jamuna Elizabeth and Kamla Doris hadn't been told. Or not in any detail. They were both too young to know about such things, Mary had said. They spoke to the nuns and the nuns said that the children should be protected. Protected. The very word made Joseph feel sick. Protected. He'd betrayed Glorious. He had betrayed her. Talking about naked women and their small clothes with Mary. They had been laughing, drinking tea, having a good time. And all the while, his Glorious, his child, his baby had been crying out for him.

He leaned back, hoping for the blankness, the emptiness to consume him. Anything that would bring relief from pain, from this pain that had no future but itself. Its infinite realms containing its past, enlightened to perceive new periods of pain. Words they had learned in school. He'd never understood them.

'Joseph?'

It was Sister Felicity. He pulled himself to his feet and managed a grimace of a smile.

'Joseph, it is wrong, it is sinful to despair. We are all his children. He loves us all equally. He will provide. You must not give up. Mary, Gloria Godaveri, they all need you.'

Joseph let the words wash over him. After some time Sister patted his hand and left him to slump into the chair again.

Since it had happened, Joseph had spent as many hours as possible at the CMI, helping out with the other children. He couldn't bear to sit at home. He couldn't bear to see the girls. Two whole and one so damaged. Soiled goods, people would call her. Like her mother. Her real mother, Mary had wept.

'They will say we did not take care of her. That because she is not ours, we let this happen.' The words had cut open Joseph's heart. Was this the reason? Was this why he hadn't heard Glorious cry out that day? Didn't they say it was instinct? The instinct between mother and child. And what about the father? Was he only a provider? And even as a provider he had failed. He couldn't even get Jamuna Elizabeth a bicycle. Not that he would let her cycle on her own now, he thought feverishly.

Why wasn't his brain blanking out? Why was he thinking about this all the time? How could he go on like this? What should he do? Who should he turn to?

'Joseph?'

Joseph looked up, aching to be distracted. The man looked familiar but Joseph couldn't place him.

'Om Prakash, I am the watchman from the Talwar house.'

Joseph pulled himself together with a visible effort.

'Loss in the family?'

'Yes, there was a, a loss. Yes. How are you?'

'So sorry.'

'Yes. Thank you. How come you are here?'

'My daughter you know...'

'Yes, of course. She was having dowry problems!' Other people's daughters also had problems. Thank the Lord! He loved them all equally.

'Yes, of course. I am so sorry. I have not been able to do anything about it. We, Juneja sir and Sajjan Kumar, have been very busy. You see, the Talwar case has been taking up all our time...'

It was Om Prakash's turn to interrupt. 'Yes, that was very sad. Nobody could have known that it was Ram Singh.'

'What do you mean, Ram Singh?'

'Ram Singh has been arrested for the murder of Pinky Baby.'

Joseph looked at him. He was astounded. The weeping servant? How could this be possible?

'I am very sorry. You know the loss, the tragedy in our family,' he started stammering.

Then collecting himself he asked, 'If you have time, can you tell me about it? I had to leave work in a hurry because, you know.'

Om Prakash nodded understandingly. 'Let's go outside. There is a roadside tea stall. We can have a cup. Here I cannot smoke,' he added, a trifle abashed.

It was dusk. Joseph turned his eyes away from the setting sun. Tomorrow it, too, would be whole again.

'How is your daughter?' he inquired politely.

'Well, that entire marriage affair with that fellow has not worked out. Now the nuns have suggested one fellow from the CMI. But my wife does not want it. She says he is a lower-caste convert. All our community will reject it. Women, caste, all this is very difficult for a simple man like me!'

Joseph smiled, although his heart wasn't in it. He didn't care about caste and he loved his women. They waited for a charging bus to drive past, before they crossed the road. Joseph cringed. Everything reminded him. His mad search. How could he ever forget?

At the tea stall Joseph decided to treat Om Prakash. After all, he hadn't done anything for his daughter.

Om Prakash was only too happy to accept. They settled down on the edge of the pavement. Om Prakash lit up a beedi, exhaling with a happy sigh.

'You don't smoke?'

'No, I never touch tobacco.'

'Maybe it is good. Maybe it is bad. Bad, because you never enjoy it, good because you will go to heaven!'

Joseph smiled. He wasn't going to heaven. Apparently, neither was Ram Singh.

'What about Ram Singh? I thought he loved Pinky Baby?'

Om Prakash guffawed. 'Yes, he definitely loved her. He loved her a lot. There can be no doubt about this. I, myself, have seen him screwing her!'

Joseph was thunderstruck.

'What do you mean? Ram Singh was having relations with the daughter of the house? Why did she not tell her family?'

Om Prakash shrugged and took a deep drag of the noxious beedi. 'I asked him. He had been doing it for quite some time, you know. I told him, she will get pregnant and then what will you do? But he said...' Om Prakash's voice dropped for fear of being overheard. 'He said that Talwar sahib had told him it is okay. Talwar sahib gave Pinky Baby some medicine. Then no babies will be made.'

Joseph could hardly understand, what Om Prakash was saying. His already awry world was reeling.

'Her brothers said that she should have relations with Ram...'

'Not her brothers, silly. Her father. Talwar sahib, who is in hospital. Ram Singh said he told him to give her love because nobody else loves her.'

'But, but...'

'Arre, Joseph, what but, but? These are big people. They have big problems. If Pinky Baby was my daughter, I would have made her marry Ram Singh. But they did not want this. And now look the poor fellow panicked killed her.'

Juneja spent an industrious Tuesday morning. First off, he had called Khurana. The entire Dr Sahni bit needed reiteration. Not that it changed anything, but one must keep all ends covered. The news at that end had been disconcerting. Khurana had been suspended. Indefinitely. Now what? Juneja wasn't sure. But he couldn't ponder over Khurana indefinitely. At least not now.

The report on the Talwar case had to be completed and handed in, the press release, suitably laudatory, had to be worded and maybe a small private celebration could be planned. The prescription from Dr Sahni had been attached to the report. He had called the Talwars in the morning and spoken to N.K., who had been happy to laudate. Especially after Juneja told him about his visit to Dr Sahni. Juneja had added that he didn't think he needed to mention his findings to Gupta.

Gupta, in turn, had sadly admitted the possibility of an out-of-turn promotion. Juneja was thinking of taking off a bit early, when Sajjan Kumar popped his head in.

'Sir?'

'Sajjan Kumar, what is it, you bastard?'

The polite greeting made Sajjan Kumar feel immediately better and he allowed his body to ease its way into the room. 'Sir?'

'Sajjan Kumar, I asked you what you wanted. Stop saying Sir.' This nicety was bound to be lost on Sajjan Kumar, realized Juneja almost immediately but before he could explain, Sajjan Kumar asked if they could go out.

Juneja understood immediately. It was personal. Private business. It was 2.30 p.m.

'Lunch?'

'Yes, sir,' answered Sajjan Kumar, grateful to have been understood so easily.

The drive lasted fifteen minutes. It was a roadside café next to the Delhi-Haryana border. Dusty and filthy, but the food was divine. Cheap, fresh and piping hot, to say nothing of the enormous number of green chillies. Postpone the private celebration a bit, thought Juneja. Might be a bit embarassing to be farting at one's own party. Bad form and all that, old chap.

But Sajjan Kumar wanted something.

'So, Sajjan Kumar, what is the problem?'

'Sir, it is this matter you told me about yesterday.'

'The Talwar girl.'

'No, sir, Joseph.'

'Yes, of course. What did you find out?' Pray let this be short and sweet.

'Sir, I asked around in that neighbourhood, sir. There is a local pimp, that I know. He said there is a fellow over there, who has done this sort of thing in the past as well. But he usually takes street children. You know, sir, there is a large floating migrant labour force in the slum area. Their children. They don't complain.'

Juneja was about to give utterance to his disbelief, when Sajjan Kumar continued, 'Those children are used to it, sir. It is a matter of every day occurrence. And, sir, these people are in Delhi today, in Panipat tomorrow. They are usually construction workers. I tried to talk to them. One of them even offered me his daughter!' guffawed Sajjan Kumar.

'And did you take her?'

Sajjan Kumar paused. He wasn't very sure what the right answer was. Macho or conscientious? Juneja saw him struggle. He wasn't sure either, where the truth lay.

'No, sir,' answered Sajjan Kumar deciding piety couldn't be penalized even if it made him look less manly. 'I wanted to ask them questions about this fellow, sir.'

The possible danger over, he continued more freely, 'Sir, they all identified the same fellow. Joseph told me, that evening the girls, his daughters I mean, were playing hide-and-seek. I think this girl was hiding behind some rubbish and this fellow probably thought she was a ragpicker. Very unfortunate for him, sir.'

'Very unfortunate for him!', echoed Juneja, astonished.

'I mean, sir, he did not mean to, you know, sir, otherwise, sir, I mean.' Sajjan Kumar trailed off. Juneja was lighting a cigarette. This could be the calm before the storm.

'The girl was hiding behind some rubbish and so this bloody bastard thought she is a rag picker and he can rape her? Is he deaf, dumb, blind or retarded?'

'Retarded, sir.'

'What?'

'Sir, I don't know these big words, sir, but a local shopkeeper said he is a junkie. He smokes brown sugar.

And otherwise also he is slow. The local shopkeepers give him some food, otherwise he would die of starvation. He sleeps on the street.'

'And they also give him some brown sugar out of charity?'

'No, sir. He is also known, you know, sir.'

'He is also known? Not to me.' He drew in a deep breath. 'As what, Sajjan Kumar?'

'As a prostitute, sir.'

So what does one do now?

'And what have you done, Sajjan Kumar?'

'Sir, I have arranged for some relatives of mine who live close by to pick him up. They will give him the thrashing of his life and then drop him off at the Delhi border, 30 kilometres away. I don't think he will make it back. I mean, find his way back. Also, the police will not get a bad name.'

'Time we went back to the police station, Sajjan Kumar.'

The ride back was the usual oven journey. Juneja figured his acclimatization for the year was now underway. He no longer felt the heat that much.

At the police station, he found it in his heart to feel quite avuncular towards Sajjan Kumar.

'Well, Sajjan Kumar, I think your solution is the best. Tell Joseph about it in the evening and also tell him to see me tomorrow. Can't have these old bastards pawing our children, hmm?'

'No, sir. He is not old. About 14, maybe 15, I think. I saw him, sir. One of the shopkeepers showed him to me. I couldn't believe it, sir, barely shaving and already all this nonsense. But I will tell Joseph, sir and send him to you.'

Juneja wasn't sure if there was a trace of admiration, or was it envy, in Sajjan Kumar's vioice. Maybe it was time to call it a day. He made it home by five o'clock. The first thing he did after he told Diwan Singh he'd be home for dinner was to strip off and shower. The water was lukewarm. Diwan Singh had filled up the usual bucket but Juneja found it silly to heave pitchers of water over his head. In a couple of more weeks, even this would not be possible. Lukewarm was one thing, boiling another. Bloody stupid overhead tank. He pulled on his thinnest, softest, oldest T-shirt and a pair of shorts. Time for a gin.

He'd just about settled in, when the phone rang. Diwan Singh came in, proferring the telephone.

'Jor Bagh.'

'What do you mean Jor Bagh? Is it Mataji?'

'No, it's Jor Bagh.'

Before Juneja could ask any further Diwan Singh left the room.

He picked up the receiver gingerly. 'Hello?'

'Nikhil. This is – this is your father.'

Juneja swallowed and tried to continue the conversation manfully. 'Are you back in Delhi?'

'No, I'll be returning in another five days. It was good of you to visit your grandmother. She misses you.'

And you don't, you bastard?

'Saraswat will be bringing a mobile phone for you. Then Mataji can keep in touch with you more conveniently.'

Convenient for whom, bastard?

'Although obviously I too would be happy if you would drop in at the Jor Bagh house. At your own convenience, of course.'

Of course. What should he call his father? Juneja's mind was working feverishly, trying to think of a suitable moniker. He'd always called his father Papa. Obviously he couldn't now. So should it be Mr Juneja or was that totally brainless?

'Nikhil, are you there?'

'Yes, yes, I'm here.' His bloody father could just keep on calling him Nikhil! Bastard!

'How are you?'

'I'm fine. Umm, how are you?' Scintillating stuff, Nikhil.

'Khurana has been suspended,' he blurted out suddenly.

'In your case? Because of the Talwars?' His father's tone was razor sharp.

Juneja felt the alarm bells going off but he couldn't figure out why.

'No. At least, I don't think so.' He paused. Was this a favour he was asking for? Never mind, he'd ask and then figure out.

'Can you do anything for Khurana?'

His father sounded amused. 'If Peshi wants my help, he has only to say so. And since when do you call him Khurana? I thought it was Uncle Peshi!'

It was only the humour in the voice that kept him quiet. Otherwise he'd have shown him. Oh, yes, he'd definitely show him. Peshi, indeed! His father was one of the few, who knew that Khurana had a first name and he was probably the only one who called him by it.

'Nikhil? All right, call him Khurana. He probably likes it!' Juneja maintained a stoic silence. He called Peshi Khurana, he called his father – nothing. Which is what they were to him.

'Speaking of the Talwars, can I ask you something?' This *was* a favour but after all his father was also asking him for a favour, wasn't he? Stay in touch with Mataji, use a mobile phone, weren't those favours, huh?

'Go ahead.'

'What is their financial situation like?'

He heard his father smile. 'Not good. They have five properties on sale.'

'Won't they get a good price for them?'

'No. I'm buying them.'

Juneja tried to think of a cutting rejoinder. 'Congratulations.'

His father burst out laughing. 'Thank you, Nikhil. It was good talking to you. Maybe we can do this again. In the not too distant future?'

'Umm, umm, okay.'

It was a small okay. But it was an okay, isn't it? Wasn't it?

'Good bye, Nikhil. Take care of yourself. And I'll stay in touch.'

'Bye.'

Twenty minutes. The call had lasted twenty minutes. Twenty minutes from abroad. That which is called foreign. From him, who had become quite foreign. At least to him.

The early night helped. He'd had a hard time sleeping after the phone call. In the old days, he would have called up Rajiv, they would have had a drink or two and maybe discussed his father. They would have celebrated the completion of the Talwar case and maybe now, that Sajjan Kumar had done it, Juneja would have regaled Rajiv with stories of vigilante justice à la Sajjan Kumar. He would have been able to discuss his father with Rajiv. Not in some silly psychological, let me hold you and love you so that you feel protected sort of way but in the right way, the sensible way, the way they had always done these things. Not with conversations about impotence and wives and stuff.

Instead, he'd tossed about in bed, letting the conversation play through his head over and over again. Rajiv would have told him whether he should take the cellphone or not. Maybe he should have demanded a car instead. No way he could ask Sunil. That would mean letting Sunil know that the contact between him and his father was...

What was it? Sporadic. All right, he had sporadic contact with his father. Should that be to his father? Never mind. It was sporadic. It wasn't, it wasn't hostile. His father gave him money, presents, Diwan Singh. Maybe that was his biggest present, Diwan Singh. Juneja never gave him money. Other than for cigarettes and food. Presumably he drew a salary. Juneja had no idea how much and from where. Maybe he should ask him. This thought terrified him so much, he immediately went to sleep.

Despite the troubled sleep, he got up feeling calm. It had drizzled. The morning was clean and the air was sweet. He settled down with tea and a cigarette, having demanded a decent breakfast of Diwan Singh. Whatever his salary was, obviously he was happy with it. Diwan Singh was hardly shy. If he wanted more, he would have said so and besides, you don't just demand financial details of people.

He sighed deeply as the doorbell rang. At this hour, it could only be their arch enemy, the milkman. Juneja tottered out to support Diwan Singh in hurling choice abuse. They spent a satisfactory quarter of an hour haranguing and screaming in turns. It was like the Sajjan Kumar – Juneja act. Honed to perfection. I'll screw your nine sisters nine times with a nine-foot pole by nine o'clock tonight. Nice touch, or should that be a nine touch? They managed to get ten rupees off the monthly bill and went inside with the glow of a job well done. The appalling stench of burnt eggs dimmed the glow and Juneja retreated to the shower. Hopefully, Diwan Singh would get breakfast ready. He heard the doorbell ring again. Bastard milkman, may he have painful haemorrhoids ever after.

He came out to see Joseph standing in the corner. He was holding a bouquet.

'Joseph?'

'Good morning, sir, Sajjan Kumar gave me your message.'

'Oh, yes, I had forgotten. Tea?'

'No, thank you, sir. He told me about the Talwar case, Sir. Congratulations, sir.' He stepped forward with the bouquet.

Juneja was stunned. No one had ever given him flowers before. He wasn't sure if this was totally cool or completely gay. He took them and tried for a weak smile. But Joseph seemed to want to talk and didn't want any reaction.

'Sir, I must tell you something very truthfully, sir.'

Joseph was obviously having an equally hard time of it. He drew a deep breath before continuing, 'Sir, when Gupta sir gave me this assignment in the beginning, I was very apprehensive.'

Makes the bloody two of us, thought Juneja. Not that my apprehensions have stopped.

'Sir, I am sorry, sir, I am sorry.

Juneja spoke. He had to. 'For what, Joseph?'

'Sir!' The man was struggling to find the words, 'Sir, I thought you, I thought, I thought wrong of you, sir. And I have to say sorry for this. Sir, I thought you would not help me and sir yesterday I sinned again, sir. When Om Prakash told me you had arrested Ram Singh, sir, I thought you have done this, sir, I am sorry, sir, I thought you have done this for money.'

It was said. Juneja looked away. Was he just an asshole? Anyone who felt like it came and screwed him over.

But it was Joseph, who had tears running down his face. His voice was steady and his face composed. 'Sir, I am sorry. It was wrong of me, sir. I have sinned against you, sir. Om Prakash told me that Ram Singh had been having relations with Pinky, with the *deceased*, sir. He said her father had permitted it. That her father had provided her with contraception,' articulated Joseph carefully. 'Om Prakash said that Ram Singh panicked when she got pregnant because now everyone will know. So he killed her in this dastardly way.'

Juneja was looking at his feet. Joseph couldn't tell if he was listening or not. He was just standing there, the bouquet in one hand. Joseph knew he had to say more.

'Sir, what you have done, for my family, for my daughter, for us all, sir, I will never forget it, sir. My wife, my children, we are indebted to you, sir.'

Juneja looked up, 'Then you had better take the bicycle.' Joseph opened his mouth to refuse but Juneja raised a hand in admonition. He called out to Diwan Singh to put the flowers in water.

They went outside to the garage. It was just after eight o'clock. Children stood in front of the house, waiting for the school bus. They had a mathematics test, it seemed, from the way they were talking.

Juneja left Joseph to open the garage. Diwan Singh had already cleaned it on that fateful day. He wheeled it out. Joseph had evidently been talking to the children, among whom was also the neighbour's gaping son.

'Here, Joseph.'

'Sir? Is zero odd or even? I would have said even but that's odd, isn't it?'

Juneja shrugged. 'When both have nothing, it's even.'

'Sir, but then nothing has changed.'

'What did you think would change?'

Juneja looked away. It had ended. 'You had better come to office from tomorrow. I have told Sinha that there was a loss in the family and that you had gone to the village.'

Finally it was his turn to turn and leave the other guy standing.

He came up to see Diwan Singh holding a carton.

'This has just come from Jor Bagh.'

It was the cellphone. It was smaller than the cordless phone and looked not unlike a remote control. Juneja held it in his hand. It felt like a weapon of mass destruction. One you could aim and say, I have money and I am great. Why did he then feel so defenceless?

'Breakfast is ready.'

'I'm not hungry any more. I have to go to the office in any case.' It seemed to be the only thing that mattered. Talk to Ram Singh before he was carted off to a jail to await trial.

But he made a quick call to Sunil before he left.

'Hi, Sunil, just wanted to give you the info you wanted.'

'Hey, Nikhil! What's up, man?'

'Not much, Sunil. Sorry, I really have to make this short. I have some urgent work coming up and I'll be very busy during the next few weeks, so I thought I'll just let you know about the Talwars before I forget.'

'Thanks, Nikhil, I really do appreciate this.'

'Sunil, they seem to be doing damn well. They have some four-five property deals coming up, so they can't be having any problems.' Juneja hoped it was the right answer.

'Shit. That wasn't the news I was hoping for. Seems like we'll have to let this wedding happen. Nikhil, I owe you. Thanks a ton, man.'

'No sweat, Sunil, just invite me to the wedding!'

Sunil was clearly taken aback but it was too late to pull back.

'Hey Nikhil, you don't have to tell me that. That's understood. Both you and your dad are automatically on the guest list. Right on top!' It had been the right answer, you and your dad, indeed.

After some more small talk, Juneja managed to get away.

One last phone call would help, he decided. He called the station and got hold of Sinha.

'Good morning, sir!'

'Sinha, I'll be in office in twenty minutes. I want to see Ram Singh, the servant of the Talwars. Don't let him be shunted off to jail before I have spoken to him, okay?'

'I should keep him here, till you are here, sir?'

Juneja sighed. But at least the guy had understood the gist. 'Yes, Sinha, just keep him there, okay?'

'Okay, okay, bye bye, sir.'

Juneja dropped the phone, as if it burnt. Bye bye. Stupid bugger.

Joseph pushed the cycle along, feeling three parts euphoric, one part numb. The news, that Sajjan Kumar had given them, had left them dumbstruck. Never, he'd said to Mary, had he expected Juneja to fight for him like this. Mary had shaken her head. She, too, had been amazed.

'Joseph, he has made the entire neighbourhood better and safer. Not only for our children but also for the other children.' Now they could live safely again.

Mary had suggested the flowers. All rich people gave each other flowers, she'd said. Better than giving sweets or anything traditional. It showed good taste. So he'd bought the flowers. They hadn't been cheap. But Mary had said, at least hundred rupees. Even hundred and fifty. But what should he do now? He'd never thought that Juneja would give him the cycle. In fact, he had forgotten all about it. How should he take it home? A taxi would cost too much money. He looked around. Thank god these phone booths were now everywhere. How had people stayed in touch before? He would call up the station. Especially after Sajjan Kumar could pick him up. Now to find a phone booth....

The Talwar-Malhotra engagement was announced within days of the arrest. Something about this being the express wish of Saudamini Talwar. The *deceased*, as Joseph would have said. The wedding was planned for November. The death of Saudamini Talwar had been a huge trauma for Old Man Talwar. He wanted to be able to witness the wedding of his eldest grandchild. Then he would be able to tell Saudamini Talwar all about it in heaven.

Juneja couldn't believe the crap some people spouted. But Sunil had piously given him this nonsense. He'd also invited Juneja only to the reception. The affair was basically low-key and really family only, but Juneja was family, wasn't he? Juneja had refused to take the hint. Although he had had another brief conversation with his father in the past month, pride prevented him from asking a) Sunil, whether his father was invited and b) his father, whether he was going. Either way it didn't make any difference.

Tonight was the reception and he, Nikhil Juneja, would be there come hell or high water. To bless the newly weds as the card said, but also to congratulate the family and, be truthful, Nikhil, to pick up a piece of the possible action aka ass. He shrugged mentally. Beggars can't be choosers. And better beg a piece of the action rather than lose it.

Now, clothes. Traditional suit? No. Made him look like a penguin. He'd have to do something about the paunch. Indian ethnic? Boring. If he was wearing a suit, he'd look like a dick at a disco. And the thought of going to a night club in Indian ethnic made him shudder. Besides, it was much too hot to wear silk. The mercury didn't seem to have realized it was November and daytime temperatures were still well over thirty.

He opted for painfully correct beige trousers with a blue long-sleeved shirt. Made him look like an executive type. He'd stick out, but so what? If Sanju was there, he'd still be able to score. Aftershave? What the hell, he'd take *Old Spice* today. Maybe Sanju would get a kick out of screwing a guy who smelled like her father. Oedipus complex and all that.

He left home thinking Oedipus was strange name for a woman, who liked to have it off with her father. Or was it the name of the father? Maybe he'd got it wrong, but he was quite sure it was Oedipus. That's what everyone said. A past girlfriend had even suggested to him that he had one. But then, that would mean that he wanted to screw his dad, or did that mean that Oedipus was a man? Maybe the entire thing had to do with some place or with the inventor of the complex. Calm down, Nikhil, this is really unnecessary. It'll be a breeze. Like he'd said to Ram Singh during the course of their last meeting. Life will be a breeze now, won't it?

'The Talwars will take care of your sisters. How many do you have? Ten? And then there's your mother and of course your wife and all your brats? Made a nifty killing, haven't you?'

'I have three sisters. I have no wife. I have no children.'

'Oooh! Faithful to Miss Pinky, hmm? Pity she was whoring around!'

How could he have said that? He shrugged. He'd said a lot of things. Good, bad and mostly meaningless. That's life.

No tacky five-star hotels for the Malhotras. The reception was at home. Home being a sprawling farm house in South Delhi. The neighbouring piece of farm land was being used as a parking lot. Naturally, with valet parking for donkeys like him, who were the chaufferless exception. The festivities were to be sombre, Sunil had said, as a mark of respect. That meant diamonds rather than gold, if Juneja understood the code correctly. He sauntered down the sombre white carpet, having been asked discretely for his invitation card in the parking area. The entire place was festooned with flowers. Jasmine, lily of the valley, white oleander were everywhere. Must be the Devi or the Malhotra touch, thought Juneja appreciatively. The oniony Talwars were quite incapable of this kind of subdued brilliance.

Sunil, dressed in magnificent Indian ethnic, including a matching turban and a rope of dull, antique gold around his neck appeared to greet him. Juneja smiled. They hadn't met since the forced invitation. Sunil hadn't called and neither had Juneja. But he had thought often enough about Sunil.

'Hey, Nikhil, good to see you, man!' They didn't do the manly thump. Juneja had stuck his hand out.

'Sunil, the place looks great. Really tasteful!'

'My aunt got some interior chick to do it. Apparently Bahar's aunt swears by her.'

'The dead aunt?'

'No, man. Another aunt. Really hot looking babe!' Ah, Devi! Difficult to think of her as anyone's aunt...

'You must introduce me. I like all hot looking babes, aunts or otherwise!'

'You're out of luck, man! She couldn't attend. She's in the family way. Health problems. But Nikhil, just don't mention the aunt, okay?'

'Because she's pregnant?' asked Juneja in well simulated surprise.

'No, no, I mean Saudamini, not Devyani. I mean, the dead aunt. It's all very sad and the family react very touchily. The bastard servant was a family retainer, you know, and they're very cut up about it.'

Juneja nodded understandingly but Sunil was already looking over his shoulder.

'Nikhil, you're going to have to excuse me. Get yourself a drink. Just chill, man.' He grimaced self-effacingly. 'I have to play host.'

Juneja tried for an understanding smile this time and moved away. Sunil was marching with a grin on his face towards a family of four who had just arrived.

Juneja looked around. The place was huge and provided ample space for the four hundred-odd people who had already arrived. He could see a small stage set up at one end, where some woman was singing. The newly wed couple were thankfully not set up on a stage with thrones but seemed to be mingling with the guests and receiving their presents among the crowd. Juneja shrugged – he hadn't brought a present. Nor did he wish to bless the newly wed couple. A voice from the future seemed to speak: No more games. No more walking. No more fun. Boring. No fun – for anybody. Act your old age. Relax – this won't hurt. Sooner or later, this entire thing will come to an end. Why throw good money after bad?

A waiter proffered a tray with drinks. He answered Juneja's raised brow with a bow and said, 'Johnny Walker Black, sir. But I can also bring you gin, vodka or wine, sir.'

Juneja declined the offer and helped himself to a glass.

No, no water or soda or ice. Just neat. Holding the amber whisky, he walked on. Sanju anywhere? Pity, there was no hope of a bitchy chin wag with Devi. Silly girl, to get pregnant. Maybe that would be the ice breaker with Rajiv? A crumb of gossip? Maybe not. Flaunting Rags' potency in his face wasn't perhaps the most diplomatic thing to do. He'd have to think of something there. He hadn't spoken to Rajiv in ages. If he remembered right, since the impotency heart-to-heart.

So where was the action? He saw a familiar face and swore. He ducked out of sight and tried for the other side. God knows there was enough space to escape unnoticed. He walked straight into N.K. Talwar, who gave him a vague smile before his brows came together in a flash of recognition. 'Aren't you that policeman?'

At Juneja's swift nod, his mouth tightened. 'What the hell are you doing here?'

The answer came from an unexpected quarter. 'Ah, Narendra, have you met my son Nikhil?'

Juneja refused to turn around. Talwar exchanged niceties with his father and told both of them through not very clenched teeth, how welcome they were, but Juneja refused to turn around. Ultimately N.K. left, using the same line as Sunil: he needed to attend to the other guests. Juneja refused to turn around. He'd have to. He took a deep breath and turned. His father smiled at him. Or an old man, who looked like his father used to.

'Thank you for the cell phone.'

'It was a present for your promotion. Are you using it?'

'I have to learn to use it properly.'

His father nodded. 'Keep in touch. I, your grandmother, none of us have much time.'

Juneja nodded and looked away. By the time he could bring himself to look again, his father was walking away. Slowly.

Get on with it Juneja, get on with it. And then he saw Raghav.

'Hey Nikhil, man, I've been meaning to get in touch with you!'

'No problem, here I am.'

'Devi told me you'd handle it, man, thanks a bunch.'

'Why thank me, Mr Talwar? Thank Ram Singh. He's taken the rap for you, hasn't he?'

Raghav looked at him in silence before looking away at the house. He knew there wasn't much to say.

The questions could only come from Juneja.

'Why?'

Raghav answered the house. 'I tried to stop them, man, but they said she didn't deserve to get married. That she had to know her place. Besides, the kid could have been retarded. Or whatever.' Whatever.

'Whose kid was it?'

'Whose? Ram Singh's obviously.' It hadn't been obvious to Ram Singh.

'And you told him it wasn't. You told him she'd been unfaithful. How could you?'

Raghav was evidently impervious to him. He continued to speak to the house. 'I tried to stop them, man...'

Juneja asked before he could stop himself, 'Why did you eat chicken?'

Rags looked dumbfounded. 'Why? Because I like it, I suppose. What do you mean?'

Juneja was about to answer when he heard it for the third time. 'Do make yourself comfortable, I'm afraid I have to attend to some...'Raghav broke off. It was unnecessary. They both had others to attend to. The chicken and what his share of it was going to be could wait.

In the parking lot Juneja rummaged about in the dashboard. It had occurred to him on the way out. Where was the wretched cell phone? If these things got much smaller, he'd never be able to find them. There it was. It had fallen under the passenger seat. He tapped in the number. He'd start using the adress book after he'd read the manual, which looked like a door stopper.

'Hi Rajiv? Man, you've got to hear this. Dumb sardar introduces his girlfriend to his friend macho sardar. Jaspinder, he says. Just done that, the macho sardar answers!'

It was weak, he knew. But Rajiv's laugh would be strong. He hoped.